THE ART OF SACRIFICE

THOUGH WE BLEED

PRAISE FOR THOUGH WE BLEED

"Filled with beautiful stories and poems, *Though We Bleed* forces readers to feel a multitude of emotions. This collection perfectly captures the essence of what it means to be alive."

—Moriah Chavis, Author of *Heart of the Sea*

"The thread of Jesus' sacrifice is stitched through every text, continually assuring readers that, while sacrifices must be made to achieve freedom, those sacrifices always make a difference. In general, I so appreciated hearing a range of commentaries through stories and poems on the current age of self-discovery and customization, some lighthearted, some dark, some fantastical and imaginative, some contemporary and deeply realistic. *Though We Bleed* truly does have something for everyone. This anthology is smart, bold, tender, and brave."

—Stephanie Pineda, Freelance Editor

THOUGH WE BLEED

Anne J. Hill • Lara E. Madden
Yakira Goldsberry • Beka Gremikova • Maseeha Seedat
AudraKate Gonzalez • Vanessa E. Howard • Ali Noël
Kelly Hellmuth • Elaine Wells • Miriam Stuart
Natalie Noel Truitt • Crystal Bailey • Liz Koetsier
Cassandra Hamm • Emily Barnett • Hannah Carter
Denica McCall • Mary E. Dipple • B.R.R. Cannon
Claire Tucker • Brooke J. Katz • Andrea Renae
Rachel Lawrence • Jess Brady • Morgan J. Manns
Hailey Huntington

THOUGH WE BLEED

Printed in the United States of America

Paperback ISBN: 978-1-956499-25-4
Hardback ISBN: 978-1-956499-26-1

Originally published in July 2024
Published by Twenty Hills Publishing

Cover Art by JV Arts
Interior formatting by Dragonpen Designs

Edited by Anne J. Hill, Lara E. Madden, Ellaina Ruse, Sarah Harmon, Ali Noël
with help from Andrew Winch, Beka Gremikova,
with beta reading from AudraKate Gonzalez, Rynn Ely, Brooke J. Katz, Aisling Revell, Natalie Noel Truitt, and Caitlin Sayers

Book created by Anne J. Hill, head of Twenty Hills Publishing, with the help of Lara E. Madden.

Poems chosen by Elaine Wells

CONTENT WARNING:
Difficult Childbirth
Violence
Minimal Swearing

Anne J. Hill:

To my younger self, and everyone who fought for me when I wouldn't fight for myself

Lara E. Madden:

To all who fight for freedom, and to those who will fight once they have learned its worth

TABLE OF CONTENTS

Introduction 13

PART ONE: THE SURRENDER

Forgiveness Sings 19
Anne J. Hill

I Could Go Back *25*
Ali Noël

Works In Progress *27*
Lara E. Madden

Flailing *37*
Anne J. Hill

Tethered *39*
Rachel Lawrence

Beast *41*
Cassandra Hamm

Ink and Seawater *45*
Vanessa E. Howard

The Bell and the Hammer 47
Ali Noël

Blades for a Cloth 49
Anne J. Hill

The Breaking *53*
Ali Noël

Into the Light *55*
Natalie Noel Truitt

Fight 61
Denica McCall

Shrouded.. *63*
Anne J. Hill

Liberated From Darkness.. *67*
Miriam Stuart

Little Rock.. *69*
Liz Koetsier

Surrender *79*
Denica McCall

Wither's Reckonging *81*
Hannah Carter

A Prize Worth Seeking.. *85*
Ali Noël

Day In and Day Out *87*
Anne J. Hill

Unmarked Graves *91*
Kelly Hellmuth

PART TWO: THE SACRIFICE

The Mermaid in the Library *95*
Andrea Renae

Sleep, Oh Captain *107*
Anne J. Hill

A Sprinkle of Pixie Dust.. *111*
Hannah Carter

Unky.. *119*
Anne J. Hill

Motherhood.. *123*
Ali Noël

4,380 Days ... 125
Andrea Renae

Breaking Protocol ... 127
Crystal Bailey

For Babi ... 133
Beka Gremikova

Not Enough ... 137
Jess Brady

The Price of Going ... 143
B.R.R. Cannon

My Old Kentucky Derby ... 147
Hannah Carter

Kingdom ... 151
Denica McCall

Who I Die Beside ... 153
Anne J. Hill

Rydinger and the Wolf ... 157
Anne J. Hill

Underground ... 161
Kelly Hellmuth

A Moment to Remember ... 165
Elaine Wells

Ember ... 169
Yakira Goldsberry

Eleanora and the Dream Collector ... 173
Ali Noël

A Light in the Dark ... 181
Hailey Huntington

Rope ... 185
Vanessa E. Howard

For Ellie ... 187
Lara E. Madden

PART THREE: THE STAND

Secret Beautiful Things *195*
Lara E. Madden

Would You? *211*
Anne J. Hill

The Weight of Floating *213*
Emily Barnett

Free as a Bird *221*
Ali Noël

Crimson Offering *223*
Brooke J. Katz

Unravel *227*
Morgan J. Manns

Stains of Red *233*
Anne J. Hill

Hope *235*
AudraKate Gonzalez

The Wrong Monster *237*
Mary E. Dipple

Child Unborn *239*
Anne J. Hill

Exoskin *241*
Vanessa E. Howard

Eucalyptus & Pomegranates *245*
Anne J. Hill

The Fifth Prisoner *249*
Claire Tucker

The Book of Jude *255*
AudraKate Gonzalez

Hail Mother Earth 257
Lara E. Madden and Anne J. Hill

Eye to Eye 263
Maseeha Seedat
The Bird of the Night 275
Anne J. Hill

Acknowledgments 279
About the Authors 281

Our shout into the void:

To speak, though we're small

To stand, though we fall

To rise, though we're scared

To fight, though we bleed

INTRODUCTION

Freedom is worth sacrificing for. Whether we struggle for our own freedom from trauma or addiction, for the freedom and security of our families and loved ones, or for society's freedom from tyranny and lies, the fight for true, selfless freedom is always worth the sacrifices it demands.

Throughout the process of writing and editing this book, we have often referred to it as our "shout into the void." It will not be heard far off, we know, and it may fall on deaf ears. And yet, it's worth doing, because the message is true. To take a stand, though small, to say what must be said, to do what we believe must be done, is our goal. We aim to say, with entertainment and beauty, that all humanity is made in the image of the Creator God, and that we cry out for freedom because it is the human birthright. Not the freedom to cause harm, to do evil, or to destroy, but to think, create, build, and express.

This kind of freedom is of utmost importance to the human soul, and we must protect it no matter the cost. We must speak, write, heal, laugh, weep, live vibrantly. We must do good in a dark world, rebelling against hatred, tyranny, and hopelessness.

We must shout, even if we may not be heard.

We must stand, even if the fight seems fated against us.

Though We Bleed is a very small contribution to a battle that has been raging since humanity's origin and will continue until our end.

We sincerely hope you enjoy it.

—Lara E. Madden and Anne J. Hill

PART ONE: THE SURRENDER

FORGIVENESS SINGS

After the Events in *The Wolfman's Heart*, in *Wither and Bloom*

ANNE J. HILL

I *STILL LOVE you, son.*" Father's words are a war between haunting and comfort.

I pace my room on all fours. It's safer, locked away from the human world, when I'm able to hide behind my wolf fur. And right now, all I want is to be invisible. To sweep away the memories of the past weeks and seep into the floorboards of my father's house.

So much has happened.

Several weeks have passed since I made plans to court Lily, and the war still rages on. I doubt it will end anytime soon. The people are too furious about having a blood-born on the throne for them to back down.

Nothing at home has been the same since Father . . .

Mother didn't kick me out of the house, but we don't talk. Cali doesn't even pester me anymore. And all I want is to flee.

Perhaps I can find my birth family, if they're still alive. Or stay at Brimwood with Lily . . . No, I won't risk her reputation.

There's thick mumbling by my door, something about singing. But my head feels like it's underwater, and my thoughts are too heavy to pull free.

I can't get most of that dreadful night out of my head. Worst of all: Father's cries as he tells me he still loves me. The images race in my head like a steam engine on a looping track.

Footsteps trail away from my door.

Tears fill my eyes and stick to my fur. I shake my head to fling them off. Whining, I sink down on my stomach and place my chin between my front paws.

Lily's red ribbon catches my eye. I never take it off my wrist.

Remember, I forgive you. You need to forgive yourself.

Lily's words crash around in my head. I can't leave without her. But staying in my father's house is choking me to death.

Heaving a sigh, I will my wolf form—my comfort—away. A flash of pain travels down my limbs, and then I'm back in human flesh.

It's time to go.

I toss several trousers and shirts into my suitcase, and then my watch, flintlock, tricorne, and topper. Father always said a smart man owns both a tricorne and a top hat for different occasions. I happen to dislike all hats, but both of these belonged to my father, and I can't bear to leave them behind.

I click the suitcase shut and sit on my bed, waiting for the sun to set. Once I hear Mother and Cali drift off to bed, I slip out of the house through the creaky front door. Though I'm not sure yet where I'm even headed.

"Vivace?" a soft voice says behind me as I step off the porch. I turn to see Cali sitting on a step. "Where are you going?"

I frown. "You're supposed to be in bed."

She shrugs and rubs her eyes, and I realize she's been crying.

Because of me.

Wincing, I crouch down beside her. "What's wrong?" *I know the answer . . .*

Cali sniffs and pushes her straight black hair behind her ear. She looks so much like our father. "I miss you."

My head jerks, and I blink rapidly. She's meant to be crying for Father, not me. "I'm right here."

She shakes her head. "You just hide in your room all day. You never talk to me anymore. Or sing to me. Momma says to give you space, but I don't want space. I want my daddy, and I want you." She wipes at her eyes.

I clench my teeth down on the inside of my cheek. Have *I* been the one avoiding them, not the other way around?

I taste blood on my tongue and realize I've been biting my cheek too hard. "I'm sorry, Cali. I know you hate me—"

"No." Her face scrunches. "My tummy is grumpy and all icky, but I don't hate you." She plays with her tiny fingers on her lap. "I kinda wanna slap you, though."

I lean my head back a little out of instinct. "Would it make you feel better?"

Cali rubs her eye with the back of her hand. "I dunno."

I brace myself. "Go ahead." *How much can a nine-year-old slap hurt anyway?*

She glances at my face, then at her hand, and then back again. Her brow furrows and I'm not sure if it's in confusion or anger.

I nod and close my eyes. "Do it."

The wait is agonizing. But if slapping me is all it takes to get my sister back, I'd rather be slapped daily than have to leave.

The air is still for several moments until I hear her start to move. I pinch my eyes shut more, forcing myself to stay still.

I feel her hand rest down on my knee to balance herself and—

She crawls onto my lap and throws her arms around my neck. The movement makes me fall back against the railing. My arms dangle, and I want to hug her back. But I can't bring myself to—until I catch sight of the red ribbon on my wrist.

Remember, I forgive you.

I take a deep breath and wrap her up in my arms. She grips me tighter. "I'm sorry," I whisper in her ear. Her hair tickles my lips.

She sniffs, and her little body shakes, sobbing against me. I took this little girl's father away, and yet I'm the one comforting her. Nothing makes sense anymore. Father should be here, not me. And he would have been if it weren't for me. He was the Pirate King and spent his days at sea and would only come home every few months. The times he was gone, we all would miss him so much. I used to sing Cali to sleep and promise her that her daddy would be home soon to sing to her himself. But now he never will . . .

I open my eyes and blink back tears.

The front door creaks open, and Mother steps out. Her nightgown flutters in the breeze. We look at each other. Silent.

She turns and goes back inside. I see the flicker of a candle in the kitchen. She shuffles around for a bit, pots clanking about, and after a few moments, comes back carrying three tea cups. Mother sits on the step, sets the cups beside us, and whispers, "Your father was very proud of you. Both of you."

I bury my face into Cali's hair so Mother can't see me cry. Swallowing lumps of guilt and sorrow, I let them burrow in my stomach. I haven't told anyone this, but I manage to mutter, "He . . . he told me he still loves me . . . At the end . . ."

The world grows quiet except for the rhythmic song of the crickets surrounding our little home.

Cali coughs, and I run my fingers through her hair. She's stopped crying, still cocooned against me.

"If I just leave, you two can be happy again," I whisper.

Mother squeezes my shoulder a little too hard. "We're your family, Vivace. You're not going anywhere. *You* make us happy."

I wince a little. "But how?"

She cups my chin and looks me dead in the eye. "Because you're my son, blood or not."

Tears drip down my cheeks.

Mother pulls us both against her. "Are you ready to finally talk to me?" Her eyes fall on Lily's ribbon. Mother touches it and lifts her eyebrows in question. "You haven't taken this off since that night." Her face pinches in concern, and then softens. Her lips curl upward and her eyes squint in that *oh, I see* look she does. "Where have you been sneaking off to so often?"

I feel a small smile creep up. "A new friend gave it to me. Um, Lily, the duke's ward. She said it's to remember . . . remember she forgave me." It feels stupid saying it out loud, and I sink back, embarrassed.

But Mother truly smiles for the first time in weeks. "She forgave you, too?"

The "too" warms in my chest. Mother knows who Lily is. She knows how I'd almost killed the duke, too, if it hadn't been for the Emperor's healing magic. I hadn't told her how the whole experience *somehow* bonded Lily and me. It shouldn't have. Lily should hate me, but she claims she knows it was an accident and I was trying to protect my own kind. Which is true, but if I'd only had the foresight to ask questions instead of reacting, Father would be the one holding Cali right now.

Mother takes a deep breath and speaks through what sounds like a thick fog. "I'm sorry, Vivace. I know this isn't your fault. I've been mad with your father and taking it out on you."

This, I didn't expect. "Mad at *him*?"

She nods. "If he hadn't lied to us, if he'd just told us that he was a spy for the Loyals, none of this would have happened. You wouldn't have felt the need to chase him, to defend your kind." She shakes her head. "But I know he was protecting us. You *both* were trying to protect us, and what happened was an accident. It's not his fault, and it's not yours."

I shake my head. "No. It's my fault. I react too fast without thinking. I always have. He told me so often . . ."

Mother cups the back of my head and kisses my temple. "You can't dwell on that, sweetheart. Go see Lily more." She pats my cheek. "You're fond of her."

Cali giggles a little, and the sound warms me, or maybe it's my intense embarrassment. "Vivace is in *love* with a *girl*!"

I clear my throat. "I never said that." But the heat rising on my cheeks is surely giving me away. "I barely know her."

Mother smiles and sips her tea. "Well, get to know her." She stands. "Drink your tea, and it's back to bed for both of you."

I nod and squeeze Cali before letting her go. She climbs off my lap, grabs her mug, and heads inside.

Mother pauses at the front door, looks over her shoulder at me, and says, "Never forget, I still love you too. No matter what."

I give her a smile and nod. She slips inside, and I lean back on the railing, finishing my tea. The urge to flee is gone.

That night, I sing Cali to sleep.

I COULD GO BACK

ALI NOËL

The scars of freedom
are thick on me
Angry, red reminders
of the battles won, at a cost
The world is more comfortable
with contoured perfection, curated lines
Than a face marked by life
a limping heart, an honest tongue
I could go back
to a life of bondage-living
the world's idea of free
But I've crawled through the trenches of sacrifice
climbed out marred, but clean
And I am free
Free indeed

WORKS IN PROGRESS

People Watchers Part Three

LARA E. MADDEN

SUNLIGHT STRETCHES ITSELF against the yellow walls of my living room. The prim throw pillows, each in warm blue hues that coordinate with the carpet, are tossed haphazardly to one side of the couch. In the kitchen, dishes overflow the sink, and disposable plates rise high over the top of the garbage can. Laundry is piled in strange places in my usually spotless apartment, and there's a week-old wine spill in the hallway. I've discovered what happens to me after a mental break, and have become what I never thought I would be: a *mess.*

To add insult, the person who caused it all is sitting on my couch, uninvited.

She shouldn't be real. I try to think her away, but every time I open my eyes, she's still there. I have considered every possible solution. At first, I was certain that I was schizophrenic, but I have no other symptoms. I want so badly for her appearances to just be hallucinations. That's all they can be, right? Because it's absolutely impossible that this barefoot-twenty-something, with an ill-advised pixie haircut, sitting cross-legged on my favorite pillow is—

"Your creator." She finishes my thought aloud. "Hey, is there any more coffee in the kitchen? I could use a top-up." She indicates her half-empty mug and I try not to grumble. I snatch the mug from her hands and walk out to retrieve the coffee press that I rarely use.

"I know you're more of a tea girl," she calls from the living room. "Thanks for pulling out the French press for me."

Do I have a choice? I'm tempted to snap back, but I'm more composed than that. I'm not the sort of person who makes snarky comments, even when I'd like to.

"Well, *choice* is a funny word," she replies nonchalantly, as if we are having a casual philosophical chat.

I haven't gotten used to being in conversation with someone who can read all of my thoughts—more disturbing yet, a person who is capable of *composing* my thoughts as I think them—and I despise it.

"Look, Catalina," she says as I hand her the steaming mug. She gives an apologetic smile before continuing her thought. "I'm only here right now because I need you to start writing again."

"Make me."

"The story will feel more organic if you choose it yourself."

I fold my arms tightly, lifting my chin to look down on her. "And why exactly would I do that?" The words come out more bluntly than I would normally allow, but it's been a long week. "If you control everything I say, do, or think, then why should I try to do anything at all? Why should I even get out of bed?" I run my fingers through my unbrushed hair and try to remember when I last washed it. Or cleaned my apartment, walked out the front door, wore makeup, ran a load of laundry—anything, really.

For the first days after my author initially appeared to me, I floated around in a state of shock. I wandered through my routine on autopilot. I nearly convinced myself that it had all been my imagination, except that these strange things kept happening. Coincidences. Signs—as a more superstitious person might suggest. Tools would appear just as I needed them. A neighbor would say something offhandedly that would relate to a situation in my private life. Then, the strangest sign of all, writing time would magically appear in my schedule.

As I allowed myself to begin entertaining the idea that Lara's visitation might have been real—that, consequently, I might *not* be real—thinking back over my life, I realized how plotted and intentional my life story was. Every moment, every detail set up perfectly for the whole piece to culminate in this present reality, the *great* right here and now.

That's when everything stopped.

"I've taken up meditation," I tell Lara in a defiant tone.

"*Mmhmm*, I know," she says. She blows across the steaming mug and sips her coffee. "You think that if you do nothing, say nothing, and think nothing then you can have control over your life."

I roll my eyes, trying to draw my temper back in. All of the frustration and confusion of the past weeks is simmering to a boil, and my tight composure is hanging on by a very thin thread.

"Why did you come here?" I ask. "Why did you speak to me at all? Is this some sort of karma or just your sick idea of a joke?"

"You wouldn't like me very much if I told you."

"I don't like you now!"

We have a stare-down, and I am certain that I'm going to win before I remember that she's writing everything I'm doing right now and can make my expression whatever she likes.

"It doesn't exactly work like that," she says, responding to my thoughts again.

"Answer the question."

"Ahh, okay." She shifts in her seat, throws back the last half of her coffee in one long gulp, and gestures with her hands as if she's trying to explain but the right words won't quite come. "I . . . um. Hmm. How should I put this? Okay, well, you're a writer, you'll probably get it—"

"Just *answer the question*, Lara."

"I needed a twist ending for a short story."

I stare at her for a long time. I'm sure this exhausted, irritated, deadpan expression is permanently engraved in my features by now. I must be a terror with the dark circles under my eyes, the frown lines carved between my brows, and my hair a dark, stringy, tangled mess.

"You ruined my life for a gimmick?" I ask very slowly.

She does a half-shrug and opens her mouth, but hesitates too long.

"You *ruined* my *life* for a *gimmick*?!"

"I . . . Yes, I guess I did."

"You guess?! I have been losing every last string of sanity over these past few weeks. You're the one with the keyboard! Just delete the scene and change my life back to normal!"

"I can't do that; the story is already published."

The news comes like a punch in the stomach, knocking the air out of my lungs and all the fight from my body.

"Well then . . . can't you just . . . give me amnesia? Or something?" Anything. Please.

"I need you to start writing again. And *you* need it, too. Amnesia wouldn't take your problems away; it would just give you new ones to hate me for."

"Yeah. . . ." My voice is so quiet and far away that I'm not sure I even spoke aloud.

Lara gets up from the couch and reaches out to touch my arm. "You're going to be alright, Catalina. You just need to take the next step forward now. You have to write. It's who you are." She smiles softly, and for a moment it feels possible that things could be all right again one day. A corner of my mouth flicks up in a half-smile. "Also," she says, "My publisher needs a new story ASAP. So I need you to get on top of that. We're past our deadline."

My smile drops back into an angry frown. "Excuse me?"

She slips past me into the kitchen and picks up a bowl of oranges, tosses them all at once into the air, and begins to juggle them. I watch with my arms crossed. The gall of this woman. The utter disrespect. The complete and utter idiocy. Appearing unwelcomed, disassembling my life, juggling my oranges. How dare she.

"Ha! I wish I could do this in the real world!"

Then, before I can blink, Lara is gone, my kitchen is empty, and the oranges are back in their bowl.

"Wait, what? Now you're just going to leave?" I shout at the ceiling. But there's no reply. I am once again alone with my thoughts.

It's three days after the Visitation. I'm sitting on the floor in my office, staring across the room at the laptop. I am at a standoff with my author. A battle of the wills. And the thing is, I *want* to write, more than I have ever wanted to before. But I know that it's because *she* is making me want to write. So here I sit. And I will stay here until—

"Hell with it all." I shake my head and get up off my butt. As I open my laptop for the first time in months, my mind is swimming with everything I want to put on the blank page. But I have to put up some sort of a fight, so instead of writing, I walk away. I clean my apartment, take a shower, and comb my hair. I run a load of laundry and pay some bills. I have a terrifically frustrating moment of realization that, although these chores have taken all day for me to accomplish, they probably took Lara no more than forty-five seconds to write into existence. I scream at the walls. I pour a very large, very strong vodka tonic. And then, finally, I sit down at my computer to write.

"Are you satisfied now?" I say aloud. The computer switches on before I can touch the power button, the password fills itself in, and a new document opens. I roll my eyes. She must be very satisfied, indeed.

I type the line: *Jefferey has been handling things relatively well, considering the circumstances.*

Well, at least one of us is. I sigh and continue.

He has returned to his routine, and has strongly considered psychiatric help in the wake of the strange night when he encountered his stalker. A stalker who revealed to him that he was a character in a book and did not exist. Lately, he avoids being home alone so he won't have to think about what took place a few weeks ago. But he's home tonight. I can see him in his kitchen through one of his apartment's big windows.

I decide the most courteous way to reintroduce myself is to send him a text message rather than showing up on his living room sofa, like some *people might.*

My message says, "This is Catalina. everything that happened a few weeks ago was real. I want to apologize for that and see how we can both move forward with our lives."

I watch as he picks up his cellphone. His chest rises and falls quickly as he reads the message and he glances around as if he's looking for an escape. I hate that I have to do this to him. I wish I could turn back time for both of us. But Lara already published that damn story, and now those scenes are locked into place with no hope of changing them. I send another message.

"If you want to talk, I'm at your front door."

He opens the door five minutes later. I understand his hesitation. I wouldn't want to see me either.

Jefferey looks me in the eye for a full minute before he says, "You aren't real."

I look down at the ground, trying to think of how to respond, and then meet his gaze again with what I'm sure is a sad, tired expression. "I know," I say quietly. "Can I come in?"

He hesitates, then steps back and swings his arm toward the living room. "Yeah, um . . . you can sit if you want . . . can I get you tea? Or something?"

"I like Oolong," I say. I shuffle past him into the living room and sit awkwardly on the couch.

"Just ran out." He sets the kettle to boil on the stove.

"Check again, middle drawer on the right."

Jefferey pulls open the drawer. I know a new box of tea is in the right-hand corner, and that he's staring at it wide-eyed. I can't see him from my perch on the couch, but I hear a nervous chuckle and the sound of the cardboard opening and two mugs being taken down from the cabinet.

"Can a hallucination do that?" I call out from the living room, trying to break the tension. He doesn't respond.

I glance around the living room, trying to get familiar with the details again. I study furniture. I make rustling sounds until the cat comes out from under the sofa I'm sitting on. I even glance into his garbage can, where I see the crumpled invitation to his ten-year high school reunion.

Now there's an idea!

Jefferey sets a steaming mug in front of me, interrupting my thoughts.

"Thanks." I take a sip and then ask, too abruptly, "You aren't going to your high school reunion?"

"No, uh-uh. I wasn't planning to," He chuckles. His demeanor has relaxed slightly as if he's slipped into happy denial and is pretending we're old friends. "I don't do that kind of thing."

"Is there any way I could convince you to go?"

"I haven't seen any of those people since I was eighteen, and I'd rather keep it that way. Why?" He takes a sip of his tea.

"Well, you know. I'd learn a lot about you. For the book."

He almost chokes on his tea. "Oh. Yeah."

A tension enters the room. We take small sips of our drinks in silence.

"I'm sorry," I tell him. "For all of this. I was so flippant with your life. To you, this is all real, and I didn't . . ." I don't know how to finish the sentence, so I try again. "I wish I hadn't written that scene that way. I should have hit delete, started over. I don't know. It shouldn't have gone like that."

"Can't you . . ."

"No, I can't delete it now. The scene has been published already. Not . . . not by me. But it was published."

"So that's that."

"Yes."

"I thought it was all a dream."

I shake my head and drain my cup, then set it down gently on the side table. Jefferey looks like he's running through all the possible implications, trying to come up with a solution. As if his problems were numbers that wouldn't add up right, and all he had to do was run through them again to solve them.

I know the feeling.

"Wouldn't it mess things up for me to do something out of character? Like going to an event I wouldn't normally attend?"

I shake my head. "I'm not sure, actually." I stop to think for a minute, tilt my head, and scrunch my eyebrows together. "I can't force you to do anything, really, because I only ever write you to do things that are consistent with your character. So . . . I think I'll leave it up to you."

I sit back from my computer as I realize that I have no idea what he's going to choose. This is a strange concept. I've always thought of myself as being in control, but maybe the story of Jefferey's life is one that we've always been writing together.

Jefferey gets up to add more hot water to his cup.

"What am I going to do next?" he asks.

"You tell me."

He chuckles dryly and shakes his head, then takes a sip from his mug. He pulls it away when it burns his mouth, then shoots me an annoyed grimace. After a pause, he puts the mug down on the table with a loud clink.

"I'll go," he says.

My eyes widen. "Oh," I say. "Wow, okay. Great."

"Wait, you actually didn't see that coming?" he asks.

"No. You're actually going to attend the reunion?"

"I'll do it. If you can make Sara Harrington fall in love with me."

"Sara, whom you tried to ask to prom?" I laugh. "No promises."

"What? Why? You could write the scene however you want, just have her say yes if I ask her out. You could make me better looking too. And more interesting. Maybe you could add some cool experiences to my backstory too—like swimming with sharks, or skydiving. Oh, or maybe I fought off a pack of lions on a safari once."

"That's not how this works. You go to the reunion, you act like yourself, and I'll let the scene unfold naturally. I don't take requests. And I'm not changing your memories."

One of Jeffrey's cats jumps up on the couch's side table and rubs its head against his hand.

"Where'd the dog go?" I ask.

"I gave him to a friend. I only got him to guard the house when I thought you were stalking me. Turns out I'm not much of a dog person."

I smirk. I could have told him that.

"You know," he says, "this whole thing is very, very weird."

I nod. He has no idea how deep the rabbit hole goes.

"But I'm sort of getting used to the idea of having an author. Of being a character. It's not so bad. My life is still my life. It's not any different than it was before. It . . . took me a while to wrap my head around it, but I think it's going to be okay."

He takes my empty mug and carries it to the sink with his.

I leave the scene, letting the cursor blink in the open document, and go to my kitchen.

"Lara!" I call out, looking at the ceiling. My neighbors probably think I'm insane by now, but I hardly care anymore.

I jump when she appears, sitting on my countertop with her feet swinging.

"The moral of the story could have been a little more veiled, you know," I tell her, rolling my eyes.

"Yeah, well, you could have written more of a plot. But we have what we have."

"More of a—" I pick up a shoe and throw it at her head. She reaches up and catches it easily.

"Ha!" she laughs. "I would never have caught that in real life. This is fun; we should do this more often."

"I get it now. Are you happy? Jeffrey is my character, but I don't control him. I'm your character but you don't control me—"

"Exactly. And I have an Author, but I also have free will." She shrugs. "We're all characters in stories. None of us exists in a vacuum. And we all have to come to terms with our authors at some point."

"I still don't like you," I tell her, even though she knows already that it isn't entirely true.

"That's okay." She grins. "How you feel about me is entirely up to you."

I stare at her for a time and realize that I believe her. I let out a long, frustrated sigh and look away. "Where do I go from here, then? How do I live my life now?"

"Well, you've gotten through the hard part, which is realizing that you can't be so fantastically *controlling* of everything."

I glare at her. "I am *not* controlling!"

She holds up her hands in mock surrender.

"The next step," she continues, "is to take responsibility for the things you *can* control. For what's in front of you, and the things you were made to do. If you want to live free, you have to give up both the idea that you're supposed to control everything and the idea that you can affect nothing."

I glance at my computer through the open office door, and when I look back at the counter, Lara is gone.

"You know your little Sunday School lesson was *very* on the nose." I roll my eyes again and smirk, knowing she can see me. "You should work on your subtlety."

I walk back to my computer, back to Jeffrey. Closing the door to push away the distractions, I pull my hair into a ponytail and crack my fingers over the keyboard.

It's time to write a story.

FLAILING

ANNE J. HILL

When
memory is
all you have

Sorrow shipwrecks
ripping families
apart

When the one lost
bound everyone
together

Now we
flail for
a lifeboat
in the sea

Fighting our own
battles against
the same enemy

Grief

Extending a hand
through our own pain

Built from
the wreckage
still a family
just...different

A new normal
that's not
normal
at all

TETHERED

RACHEL LAWRENCE

ARE YOU FREE tonight?

Taylor remembers the day three years ago when Ethan's text flickered onto her phone screen like a warning light.

Yes, I am free, she'd wanted to respond. *Free and unattached. And I'd like to stay that way.*

But how do you tell someone, without sounding like a jerk, that you can't imagine a life where you don't get to do what you want—when you want—and answer to no one but yourself?

Maybe she would have been tempted to consider his offer if she hadn't just talked to her sister Hattie, who'd had to cancel her girls' trip to New York because her baby was sick, again.

Or if she hadn't watched her friend Vanessa give up a career she loved to move across the country with her new husband.

Or perhaps even if her coworker Sam hadn't turned down her invitation to get their nails done together because she needed to "take care of some things at home." And besides, Sam had explained, they were watching their budget now that another little one was on the way. She'd bristled at the time, but beneath her irritation, she'd felt the same emotion for them all.

Pity.

She couldn't wrap her mind around the idea of feeling so tied to anyone else. So dependent. So *trapped.*

So she'd tossed her phone onto her floral bedspread and pretended she'd never received the message.

But, over the following months, Ethan had offered Taylor something much better than a dinner date.

Friendship.

The kind that made no demands. The kind that came with genuine conversations at her desk between meetings, a ride home when her tire was flat, thoughtful questions, silly memes exchanged on stressful days, modeled selflessness and grace.

The kind that expected nothing in return but left her wanting to reciprocate. The kind that eventually found her calling her sister with an offer to babysit her nephew. And purchasing a plane ticket to visit Vanessa when she needed a familiar face. And showing up at Sam's door with a box full of nail polish that would be smeared over the tiny fingers of giggling little girls.

The kind that slowly linked her heart to his one day at a time until she realized that it wasn't forming a chain at all, but a tapestry. One that came with a safety and warmth she'd never felt before.

His patient love had gently untangled all of her loose ends and helped her imagine the possibility of a bigger picture, showed her the beauty of connection.

She still often thinks about that first text, saved in her phone all these years later. "If it wasn't for you," she whispers as she snuggles beside him on the porch swing one late summer evening, "I'd still have no idea what I was missing." Her eyes water as he kisses the top of her head and she looks out over their backyard. It's filled with neighbors, friends and family, talking, laughing, living life together. She is tethered to each one, hemmed in by all the ways they've stitched themselves together, a truer version of herself because of them.

She rests a hand on the belly she's sharing with a new life and smiles.

Tonight, she thinks, *I am more free than ever.*

BEAST

CASSANDRA HAMM

There is a beast inside him.

Sometimes he is a fairy tale prince,
sweeping her off her feet,
leaving her breathless
with declarations of obsession.

Then he shifts.

His humanity cracks, revealing
wildness she has to tame.
His lips are brands
searing her skin,
the muscles she admired
now her chains.
He lashes out, drawing blood,
staining her scarlet,
that savage smile telling her
This is what you want.
This is what you deserve.

She should have tried harder
to please him,
should have watched her words
for possible offense.
Apologies spill from her lips
as she gives him what he wants
to make him happy again.

Long-forgotten words whisper,
Love is not easily angered—
But the old tales know nothing of
managing moods and soothing tempers and
placating beasts.

Usually the beast is dormant,
waiting just beneath his perfect skin--
waiting for her best attempts at perfection
to inevitably fall short.
Love is patient, the old tales say,
but the tales know not
the strain she puts him through
with disobedience and perceived unfaithfulness.
She is lucky
to have a prince like him,
who loves the unlovable—
who loves *her.*

His words, vacillating sweet and savage,
draw her back time and time again.
She is fire when he touches her,
each piece of her melting away
until all that is left is
what he wants.

Love is not selfish, the old tales say,
and she feels it deep in her bones.

She has denied herself ever since
she chained herself to a beast.

But when has he ever
denied himself for her?
When have her needs ever
come before his own?
I need you, he says.
But she feels herself slowly cracking
under the pressure of his expectations,
and when she pulls against the chains,
smiles turn to snarls.

Love is kind, the old tales say.
When has he ever been kind?

In the tales, princes retain their humanity.
Maybe hers is no prince after all.

Now, when he tells her to bend,
she stands tall.
The change starts--
hands twist into claws
and teeth sharpen into points.
They sink into her flesh,
and he waits for the groveling,
knowing that pain is power.

This is what you want.
This is what you deserve.

But she has never deserved this.

She tears herself free
of both claws and chains,
the fire he tried to snuff out

blazing in her eyes.
He snarls and screeches,
but she does not yield.
The power he wielded is no more,
stolen back by
the girl who no longer needs him.

She flees, that simple act
a feat of courage.
He roars after her,
lies spilling from perfect lips.
She does not turn around.
His cries fade into distant echoes.

She is reforming, relearning
who she is without the beast.
Her heart is a charred ruin of
cracks and scars and memories,
sometimes traitorous, wishing for chains
because at least they came with love.
No, not love—what she thought was love.

Love is kind, the old tales say.
And maybe that means
kindness for herself, too.

INK AND SEAWATER

VANESSA E. HOWARD

I CLUTCH THE small notebook in my hands as I watch the waves roll onto the beach at Mustang Island. A brown pelican, a gracefully ugly beast of a bird, soars past me on the whipping wind.

My therapist told me to start an anger journal. I hadn't allowed myself to rage, she said. So I bought a dollar store notepad to be angry in. Decorated with hearts on the cover. My upbringing and my faith emphasized forgiveness, and I worked hard at it. But in our fourth session, she said I had skipped over the anger and it was getting in the way of my healing.

In the little heart-covered notebook, I dove into my past and wrote out the hurt. I named names. I wrote my fury at my molester, his family, the trial, and the cops. I scribbled it all down. How he stole from me. How he changed my thirteenth year from possibilities to nightmares. How he skewed the lens I saw men through.

His mom reached out to me years later, wanting to set up a meeting to make amends or something. I refused. I don't hate him. Dislike, anger, disgust—sure. But hate? No. I don't hope the other inmates beat him to a pulp. On the contrary, I hope he gets counseling and treatment. I just don't want to expend brain power on him again. Ever.

I'm done. I'm done with it all.

The waves crash in front of me. My toes sink into the sand as the ocean washes over my feet in a gritty cleansing. A little way down the beach, my husband hunts for unique shells. Bless that man. He reversed my mixed-up lens. Before he wandered off to give me some space, he squeezed my hand and asked me if I was sure about this.

I'm sure.

The pelican lands on a nearby piling. It folds its great wings and settles its bill against its chest, watching me, waiting for my next move.

I rub the notebook between my palms. All those words. All those words gripping on to me. The words hold me hostage. Maybe they did help me, heal me, move me forward. But now they're holding on too hard. And I don't need them anymore.

I want to let go of all the emotions—the anger, the bitterness, the confusion, all of it. Just release it into the ocean and move forward with life.

The pelican pumps its wings and lifts into the air, awkward and ungainly one moment, powerful and soaring the next.

I take a salt-scented breath.

Flinging it like a frisbee, I hurl the notebook into the Gulf of Mexico. The water will wilt the pages, leach the ink out, and swallow the words all the way down to the bottom of the sea.

THE BELL AND THE HAMMER

ALI NOËL

Sometimes
Beautiful things are best left alone

Sometimes
The gentle toll of a bell is all that stands
Between the Great Before and After

It's a moment that passes
And with each aching chime
You feel what was
Ebbing, ringing, spreading
Into the air, forever out of reach

But, sometimes
To bring the hammer down
To strike and break
Is exactly what you need

Sometimes
You can only learn, or change
Or fit into what is meant for you

After you've given yourself permission
To swing

BLADES FOR A CLOTH

ANNE J. HILL

WALDREN IMAGINED THAWING by a fire and dying there peacefully. The empty fantasy mocked him as he shuffled to Linitor's Temple, his tattered clothes still wet and dirty and his hair turned to icicles from his accidental dip in the river. And he'd lost track of his cloak five years prior, give or take a few months. Hard to keep track of such things these days . . .

Snow coated the steps leading up to the temple doorways, and shards of ice hung precariously from the window ledges. One shove, and they could pierce a man to death. *That might be a mercy.*

A warm flicker of light emanated from the windows. So close he could almost feel it. He had only to make it up these mountainous stairs and through the doors, and then his fireplace fantasy would become reality. But even after days trudging through the most treacherous landscape this kingdom had to offer, he doubted the elvish monks would grant him entrance, even if he shared their blood. Waldren's breed of chaos should never have been allowed within a mile of this place of worship. Not someone who'd done and endured such horrors in only twenty short years.

He'd given up everything to free himself from the slave trade. And now he might still die for it.

Snow crunched under his boots. *Thank Linitor above for these boots!* He could barely feel his toes, but he knew firsthand that it could be worse. Like his pointed ears which he was certain were purple. Not to mention the frozen blood on his stomach. He'd wrapped a stiff arm around his torso, holding himself together. Each step he took seemed to bring him no closer to the stairs.

If he had stayed home five years ago, none of this would have happened. But there was no way in Linitor's Hell that he could show his face back there now. Not after he'd gotten his mother killed. Not after running away. Not after going through the worst years anyone could imagine under the thumb of slave traders. He shuddered, and not wholly from the winter cold.

He'd changed his name. It was Waldren now. His true name bled of his half-elvish lineage, and things like that got him five years in hell. No, he would never speak *that* name again. It was tainted by *his* voice.

As he let out a long, frosty sigh and collected himself once more, Waldren's boot thudded against the bottom step. He looked up at the mountain before him. Climbing those stairs might be the death of him, but so might the snow.

Waldren picked his foot up, but he never did recall what happened next.

Heat danced across his cheek. A muffled voice spoke over him and something nudged his shoulder. Waldren groaned and rubbed his face. *Am I in heaven?* No, too sore for that. *Hell?* No, too quiet for that. Whatever the case, he was exposed. He wished he still had his dagger, or any weapon really, but the traders had taken that from him too.

"Hello?" The voice was gentle.

Waldren blinked rapidly until he could make out a blazing fire a few feet from his face. He jerked his head back, which only shot pain down his spine. "What the f—"

"You fell," the voice said.

He ignored the pain—something he'd mastered in years of late—and pushed himself into a sitting position. Kneeling beside him was a wrinkled man. He wore a red hooded cloak with an even darker red sash around his waist. A golden dragon medallion hung from his neck.

"You're a monk?" Waldren asked.

"Yes." The man bowed his head. "I do hope you don't mind. I found you bleeding on our steps and brought you in for the night. You'll find your wound is healed."

Waldren frowned, lifted his stitched shirt, and looked down at his stomach. His skin showed no sign of being torn. Waldren eyed the monk. "What do I owe you?"

The monk smiled. "Nothing. Come." He offered Waldren a hand up.

"No one helps without wanting something in return. Name your price." He didn't take the hand as he pushed himself to his feet.

The monk tilted his head. "Actually, I have something for you, Tepharē."

Waldren's breath caught at his birth name, and he stumbled back from the man. "How do you—"

The monk held up his hand. "I knew your father. You're safe here."

Waldren's chest ached. He'd never met his human father. Nor did he know much about him. "Is he still . . ."

The fire crackled and popped. Outside, the wind howled in the darkness.

With a furrowed brow, the monk shook his head. "I'm sorry. He passed many years ago. But I have something of his that I think he would want you to have."

He watched the old elf carefully. "What is it?"

The man directed Waldren to an dilapidated chest and lifted the lid. He pulled out two short swords, the blades flashing in the firelight. Their grips were black and laced with silver, and the pommels were in the shape of dragon heads. "Your father was a warrior from Conwell before he laid down his blades and took up the cloth."

Waldren studied the swords and carefully took them from the monk. A gentle scrape of his thumb revealed a remarkably sharp edge. "You allowed a human into an elvish temple?"

The monk smiled and dipped his head. "Linitor is a dragon-god to all souls. Though this temple was built and run by elves for centuries, who are we to deny a human? Your father asked me to hold onto his swords, lest he be tempted to return to bloodshed. But now, they are no longer mine to bear."

Waldren had shed enough blood himself just escaping the slave trade. He could do so much more damage with the likes of these two blades. Linitor above knew he had the skill for it after years of fighting to survive on the streets. The thought sent a shiver down his spine. He both feared and relished the power coursing through his veins and how much stronger that might be with the aid of these blades. He slowly looked up at the monk. "And my father . . . he was happy here?"

"He was joyful but troubled. He found some semblance of peace among the books in the library." The monk studied Waldren. "You look just like him, except for the elf blood that runs through your veins."

Waldren's chest thudded. The blades clanked together in his unsteady hands. Perhaps he, too, could find peace in this temple. He ran his finger along the spine of the blade, watching his own eyes in the folded steel's reflection. He didn't know for how long, but something told him he needed to stay at this temple.

Waldren swallowed and handed the short swords back. "Keep them just a bit longer."

Maybe someday, when he was ready, he would reclaim his father's blades and set out a stronger man in both mind and body.

Waldren traded his father's blades for the red cloth of Linitor, the dragon-god of the southern lands. He would forever bear the marks of a slave, but in due time, he would be ready to move out into the world a free man.

Waldren is a character from Anne J. Hill's upcoming debut novel, Thorn Tower

THE BREAKING

ALI NOËL

She's always preferred the confinement of the tree line
Blurred into the shadows, safe from the reaches
of the exposing golden air

She's avoided the meadow for so long, now a creature of the woods
Accustomed to dangers lurking beneath the trees
snapping of branches, cries in the night

She takes in the open space, what if something should come?
Being hurt in the light would leave a greater mark
than any wound in the woods, pain is expected there

She steps out into the warm grass, dizzy from fragrant flowers
Tilting her face towards the warm, quiet sun
and something within her breaks

Her heart? No, she's been there before
A sparrow calls from above, she watches the little wonder
swooping, singing, free

Free, she smiles
the breaking
free

INTO THE LIGHT

NATALIE NOEL TRUITT

CAMPBELL LEAH BARNES was the biggest fake she knew.

She got ready at five o'clock in her campus bathroom. She wore mom jeans and a bright colored t-shirt, and tied her blonde hair up in a bandana. She put on makeup, but not too much, because being a youth group leader was a delicate balance between being cool and being a good example. She was lucky though, because she had thirteen-year-olds, and she was in college—college stories automatically made her cool.

She stepped out of the bathroom to see her roommate lying on the floor, playing a video game instead of doing homework. "Leaving soon?"

"Yeah." Campbell smiled brightly, the blanket of shame that she wore everywhere tightened around her. *No one can know. No one can know. If anyone knows, they will never look at you the same way again.*

The youth pastor had warned the youth group leaders of what tonight would be about, and ever since he had told them, Campbell's stomach had felt upset. They were going to talk to the youth about the dangers of porn and sexual sin. Campbell was all for this, because it was something that was destroying their society. But her firsthand experience made the rope of shame she wore around her neck continue to tighten.

Her roommate didn't glance up from her game. "See ya later."

Campbell refused to let the smile leave her face. "Have a good night!" She left the dorm building and went out to the campus parking lot. She drove the fifteen minutes to church, blasting Christian music and refusing to talk to God. She swallowed past the lump in her throat, her chest constricting. She knew that the God that she had found as a child was still out there and full of mercy, but she was messing up nearly every day, and it was so hard to approach Him when the shame threatened to squeeze the life out of her. Especially, when every time she did approach Him, the same verse rang true. She had heard it in chapel one day at school, and it had been stuck in her head ever since.

James 5:16. Confess your faults one to another, and pray one for another, that ye may be healed.

The thing was, Campbell *had* told someone before. But they told her it was disgusting, and only a guy problem, not offering her any of the answers she so desperately sought. Whenever the thought of telling someone popped into her mind, she briefly considered telling the youth pastor's wife, Brianna. Brianna was never scared to tackle tough topics at church. But the thing was . . . people could surprise you. Campbell's friend certainly did. So every time the thought nagged at her mind, she shoved it aside and hoped that the guilt would go away and that, one day, she would be able to defeat this all on her own.

Campbell pulled into the church parking lot. She couldn't imagine anyone here knowing her secret. The thought made her dizzy with fear. Especially because this was a *boy* problem. She didn't know a single girl that struggled with porn. She pushed the thoughts out of her mind. When she walked into youth group, she wore a mask. She had to be someone that these young girls could look up to, and that certainly wasn't someone deep in sin.

She walked through the parking lot, past the group of middle school boys that were playing basketball until fellowship time started.

"Hey, guys!"

"Hey, Campbell!" one of them called. A couple of them echoed 'hey's' and 'hi's.'

Campbell walked into the building and to the office where Pastor Henry, his wife Brianna, and the rest of the youth group leaders met to pray before the real chaos started. Sunday nights were always a lot, but they were also Campbell's favorite night of the week. They were fun, and they left her feeling like she was doing something good in this world. But tonight, as she walked into the room, her hands were sweating and she felt sick.

"Hey, Campbell," Henry called from the front of the room. "Glad you're here."

She waved in greeting, then sat down next to a girl she had known from church since going to college.

"Anyone have any prayer requests?" Henry asked, looking around the room.

They prayed, and then hurried out to supervise the first hour of youth group. This time was set aside for games and fellowship. It allowed the kids to interact and to build a community. When Campbell had become a youth group leader at the beginning of the semester, she remembered how awkward this hour felt,like it just dragged on. She would have to either slip into a game with some junior high students or try to make conversation with people that she didn't really know.

But now this was her community too.

Soon they went into the sanctuary, and the worship music began. Campbell sat with another youth group leader and some of the teens in the youth group. Campbell loved this part. She loved putting her hands in the air and praising her God with fifty other people, but tonight something was tugging at her heart. Something that had tried to get her attention for nearly two years now. She tried to push the thoughts away and ignore the gnawing in her stomach and the guilt that clawed at her chest.

How great is our God . . . Sing with me, how great is our God . . .

The words echoed through her and she chanced a silent prayer. *I can't tell anyone. I just can't. But can you help me defeat this another way? Because I want to be free from this, but no one can know. I want to finally move forward. Please.*

Once worship ended, they sat.

Two seventh grade girls talked and giggled in the row in front of Campbell. Campbell whispered, "Go ahead and quiet down. The sermon's going to start."

She pulled her Bible out of her bag and leaned back in her seat, tapping her leg. Campbell dreaded hearing the words that Pastor Henry would preach tonight, knowing that they might bring up the familiar conviction. *Tell someone. Bring your sin to the light.*

Henry started a video. It was full of statistics of teens and young adults using porn. It told the story of a man in his twenties who had been addicted for ten years and now had found freedom. But what stuck out for Campbell was that it talked about how everyone used to think it was only a guys' issue, but that it wasn't true. Statistics for men and women were nearly the same.

When the video ended, Pastor Henry started his sermon. There were people surrounding Campbell, but she knew that she was still the odd one out. Even with the percentages of women exposed to porn going up, she knew that there was no way anyone else in this church was struggling with this. The shame threatened to squeeze the life out of her. If they found out about her, they would think that she was messed up. Disgusting. Broken.

Her heart was racing as she looked around the sanctuary. She had isolated many times since she had started watching porn, but she had never felt so alone in a room full of people before. Her eyes welled with tears, and she swallowed hard. A wave of dizziness swept over her, accompanied by the horrible feeling that she might be sick to her stomach. She jumped to her feet and rushed out of the room, hurrying to the bathroom.

Campbell hoped for an empty bathroom, because right now the careful mask that she always wore was nowhere to be found. She opened the bathroom door and didn't see anyone, but then she noticed that the big stall door was locked.

Not alone. I need to get out of here.

She turned to go, but she heard the door open, a baby coo, and then Brianna say, "Oh, hey, Campbell."

Campbell didn't turn around to face her. Her shame felt palpable in her sweating palms, flushed face, and too-fast heart. She knew that if she looked at her, Brianna would know her secret.

For a moment, the only sound in the bathroom was the baby's soft murmurs. Brianna then said, "Are you okay?"

Canpbell's heart pounded, and she knew that she had to get out of there. "Yeah." *You sound terrible. Try again.* "I mean . . . I don't feel very good."

"I'm sorry to hear that. Are you sick?"

I'm the biggest fake I know.

Campbell turned around, but she still couldn't look at her. She focused on the baby that Brianna cradled instead. Campbell knew that she needed to tell someone—to tell anyone—to find freedom. She wanted to scream. She took a deep breath to steady herself, but then her voice broke. "I just . . . have a lot going on."

Brianna took a step towards Campbell and squeezed her arm. The baby flailed her arms and reached for Brianna's necklace. "Do you want to talk about it?"

"It's . . . it's bad." Campbell began to sob, her shoulders shaking, and her chest heaving. "I never thought I could hate myself this much.

"What's going on, honey?" Brianna asked.

Campbell squeezed her eyes shut tightly and shook her head. The words that her friend said a year ago rang through her head. *That's disgusting, Campbell.* But another voice was stronger. *Bring your sin to the light.* She continued to cry, unsure if she would be able to even get the words out.

"Campbell, look at me," Brianna said.

Campbell forced herself to open her eyes and look at Brianna's face, but she still couldn't meet her eyes.

"What's going on?"

"The last time I said it, my friend was so terrible." The words came out in a hiccuped rush. She wasn't sure if they made any sense. "I told myself I would never tell anyone again."

She nodded, rocking the baby. "I'm sorry they made you feel that way. But whatever is going on, I promise you, God has more than enough grace and love for you. And *I* love you too."

Campbell nodded, but the words were still trapped by a lump in her throat.

"Does it have something to do with the service tonight?" Brianna's voice was soft.

Her lungs threatened to suffocate her, but she nodded.

Brianna took her hand with her free one and squeezed it. "Honey, this isn't the first time I've had this conversation with someone at church. It's okay. What's going on?"

"I've been watching porn," she sobbed. As soon as she said it, she wished that she could take the words back. Her throat constricted, making it nearly impossible to breathe. Campbell wished that she could disappear. A wave of dizziness overtook her, and she closed her eyes.

"I think sometimes telling someone is the hardest part," Brianna said. Campbell opened her eyes, but she didn't look up at her. "But you did it. There are practical resources that can help you. You're not alone in this, Campbell. God sees you, and He loves you, even when you sin. He has more grace for you than you have for yourself. There's so much hope here, and I'd like to help however I can. For now, can I pray with you?"

Campbell nodded. Her next breath came easier. Her hands were shaking, and she still felt dizzy, but she felt a little bit lighter too.

As Brianna prayed over her, Campbell felt the knot in her stomach begin to unravel. She knew this would be a tough battle, but she'd finally started to put on armor. One step at a time.

FIGHT

DENICA MCCALL

Wishes under moonbeams
And wounds in shadows
Secrets fly like dandelion offspring
The wind takes its victims
The sun bleeds you raw
Until your wishes turn to ashes
And your childhood is shrouded
Fear holds you hostage like bats in their caves
Safety clinging to you but you're barely beating to
The rhythm of what you once knew
Stars open you
Night sings to you
Chanting in the silence that there must be more to you
Tell terror it has no claim
Tell pain it has no stake
You can give and you can take
But those bedtime hopes are like ropes hanging from the sky
Grab a hold, start with one
Until you find you're swinging from one to the other
Lost in the wonder
A strength not your own

Shout the fairy tales until they become more than fantasy
Recite the truth
Over and over and over again
Fight through the fog
And let life win

SHROUDED

Based On True events

ANNE J. HILL

A A CLOCK TICKED in the corner of the shadowy room as the sun descended. Pink, orange, and purple rays decorated the darkening blue sky. But Pearl hardly noticed the beauty. Instead, lying in her bed, her eyes gazed at the screen in her hands as she sent messages to the person her heart longed to be with, but her soul revolted against. Someone who had offered to defile her bed, and Pearl had slowly but gladly accepted. Soon, defiling even her love for the God who created her. But to her, this person was her desired setting sun—who had sweetly isolated Pearl from everyone who *knew* her.

If Pearl lingered here, would she lose everything she had once held dear? Her family, friendships, integrity . . . her God?

She ignored such sorrowful thoughts and focused on the spike of dopamine this person gave her. With hearts and "I love yous" texted back and forth, Pearl set her phone aside and settled in for the night. Alone, upstairs in a room that had once brought joy to her childhood, but now felt like a prison cell.

A weight pressed on Pearl's chest. She knew. Pearl *knew* in the innermost parts of her being that nothing was right. Not anymore. She'd traded her God for a blasphemous mockery. But it would be all right, somehow. If she merely kept moving, kept her head down and plunged deeper into the darkness, the guilt in her stomach would someday go away. The rules need not apply to her, not for now.

With an inward middle finger to her Savior, Pearl shoved the twisting in her gut away.

Sleep evaded her. Tossing and turning, unable to find comfort in the sheets. So, as had become a custom as of late, Pearl pulled out her phone and opened up hypnotic recordings meant to help her sleep. To make her feel weightless and . . . empty. The first few times she'd done this, she'd gotten an eerie sense about it all, but that was back when she was more attuned with the God of her childhood. Now, it only served to calm her body, mentally obeying whatever the foreign voice told her to do, what things to picture, what things to give of herself. Opening herself up to be filled with nothing. Harmless enough, she thought.

Sleep soon came, though not before Pearl whispered sweet violence to herself. Into the darkness, she drifted. And it happily accepted her with open arms and a demon in the corner of its smile.

Pearl was not prone to nightmares. At worst, they were mere annoyances, or thrilling adventures as if she were thrown into an action movie. But not tonight.

In dreamland, a doll sat in the corner of her room. Watching. Shrouded in shadow. Eyes black with murderous thoughts. *Evil.* Dolls had always made Pearl uneasy, but nothing like this one. She was sure she was asleep, somewhere in her consciousness telling her that this wasn't real.

Only, it felt entirely real, and the lines between awake and asleep blurred. The room seemed to close in on her. Shaded figures circled above her head, pulling the walls in closer. Closer. The doll now rocked on an unfamiliar creaking chair. Somehow, Pearl knew this doll had come from the attic, the door in the other corner of her room. From the dark recesses of isolation. Except that there was no such doll in the attic, or in all of the house.

The weight on her chest caved in. Paralyzing fear like she'd never felt before clawed at her throat. The master of her soul was calling for her through fangs. Pleased by her terror. By her indulgence.

The doll's face plastered itself to the forefront of her vision. Searing black eyes. A smile that felt on the verge of human but fell categorically short.

Pearl flashed her eyes open, hoping to see the light of day. But night still weighed heavy, and the room felt thick, localized on her chest, in her throat. Cautiously, she glanced to the corner of the room where the doll had been. Empty. The weight did not leave. Even with the doll gone—Pearl was now undoubtedly awake—the sense of pure evil still hung in the air.

She didn't see it with her eyes, but darkness swirled around her, through her. A sight she could not place. She gripped her bedsheets, unsure if this was only a nightmare, a childish fear of the dark, or if it was something much, much deeper.

Either way, her lips that had forgotten how to pray, whispered, "God, make it go away." Let her drift from the terrors of her reality and blissfully slip away. To be free.

Her heart sank. She wasn't free . . . not anymore. She'd walked back to her chains and locked them on her own ankles. Phantom chains pinned her down. She squeezed her eyes shut. She couldn't go on like this. Battling against the God that had bled for her.

"Help me," she whispered.

Slowly, the thickness dissipated. The darkness shriveled, obedient to the God who cared for the soul who'd run far—even knowing what catastrophic choices she would make next, knowing this night would not be her victory. Instead, it'd be a memory she would later return to and remember the battle He'd fought for her that night. That the terrors weren't merely dreams, but evil forces clutching for the isolated soul that had willingly made itself an easy target.

Knowing that so many redeemed-years-later, she would shed tears thinking of how He had been watching over her even as she clung to everything He despised.

What a good, good Father.

LIBERATED FROM DARKNESS

MIRIAM STUART

"These are not chains," he said,
As he shackled my wrists.
"You are not a slave," he reassured,
As he dragged me away.
"This is not a prison," he persuaded,
As he locked the cell door.

I waited for his promises.
I watched for his reward.
But time revealed his trickery,
And uncovered his devious guile.
I looked for an escape,
But did not find a way.

I should have seen the irony.
I should have perceived his lies.
Now he tells me
With a sneer,

That I am his captive forever,
There is no help for me.

Down in the pit,
When all seemed lost
And I was forgotten,
I saw a light,
A flicker of hope,
A whisper of deliverance.

"I have redeemed you," my Savior comforted,
As He unlocked my cell door.
"You are free," He assured,
As He unshackled my wrists.
"You are my daughter," He said,
As He brought me home.

I see truth in His eyes
And love in His words.
I understand His grace.
I am free from deceit
And from bondage.
I am liberated from the darkness.

LITTLE ROCK

LIZ KOETSIER

THE CAVE ECHOES with the rhythmic drip of water and distant voices. Soft, glowing mushrooms along the cool walls barely light my path to a door made of stiff animal skins sewn roughly together. I anxiously breathe in the deep, clay-scented air.

"Should I do this Sylvie?" I ask, lifting my rat up to eye-level.

She licks my nose. I tuck her gently back into my patched leather coat where she settles down amidst a few useless trinkets and a three-pronged fork I used to untangle my hair this morning.

Rocking back and forth from boot toe to heel, I raise my hand and ring the rusted bell over Munya's door. The bell's warbling ring is tinny and crusty in the hollow cavern space. It grates on my nerves.

"Enter." Like wind through the tunnels, a deep feminine voice invites me in, and Sylvie wriggles in my pocket at the unfamiliar voice. I reach deep into my pocket, resting two fingertips on top of her smooth little face. She pushes her tiny nose against my hand and tastes the damp, nervous sweat on my fingertips.

"Well?" The voice from the cavern draws the word out deliberately.

Gathering all my courage and a breath of ancient air, I push the animal skin flap aside and step into the chamber. Inside, the walls are dotted with large yellow and tiny violet mushrooms which provide the only light. A woman, whose hair has gone white except for a streak of darkness over her left eye, sits behind a carved, stone desk. She looks up from whatever she is reading. Its pages are the same yellow as the mushrooms on the walls. Her lips, an unusually bright shade of red, lift into a smile.

"What is your name, and your age?" There is a huskiness in her voice. I shiver. The elders tell me Munya knows many, many things.

"Eva Moon. I will be twenty in one month."

One manicured eyebrow rises. "You are Yuri's charge. The little orphaned rock he found abandoned at the mouth of the cave sixteen years ago."

Rock. She called me a rock. I refuse to react to this unforgiving nickname for those of us left behind from Above. *Just nod, Eva.*

"What have you come for then?"

Inhale. "I want to go back." Exhale. The cave smells of strange spices I am not familiar with, and something bright, tingly, and nice. Is it the scent of the sun? If so, how did she get it? They say that sunlight warms you from the inside out like rare spices, that once it kisses your face, you will crave it again and again.

I try to imagine crawling up a thick, wide stalagmite, breaking the surface of the ground, and lifting myself up into bright light. But I can't. I barely remember the sun. I don't know if anything I see in my mind is a memory or made-up dream. I stopped asking Yuri what the sun is like long ago, but I still think about it every day.

He can't remember at all. He's been underground for so long, that his eyes no longer see. Will I grow blind, too, if I stay forever? I look up, and repeat, "I want to go back to Above."

Her eyes widen. "Many little rocks say that they want to leave, and yet they never do." She drums her fingers on the opened book. "I will tell you what I always tell the little rocks who come to me. If you do this, it will cost you. You can never return. Yuri must disown you. You will lose your home, your only family, your security and protection. Everything."

"I know." I have thought this through. I hate to hurt Yuri, but he doesn't understand how the cold and dark weaken my heart, dampen my soul. *Eva, these walls protect you*, he would remind me, telling me again how the sun's light stains and poisons your skin. How the cool, wet darkness of the caves keeps us safe.

Munya chuckles. "I require a sacrifice if you want to see the light, Eva."

Not unexpected. I wet my lips. "I'm willing to pay it." Even if the sun poisons me, a short life in its fierce radiance is better than this cold, stifling one. I take one step forward. "I have treasures, antiques, novelty items from Above.

I have the best rats in Underground. They are very good at finding the leftovers from before the war."

"I don't want rats or gems or antiques, Eva." Munya flicks her wrist and leans in, her eyes darkening. "I need your voice."

My voice? Subconsciously, my hands reach for my neck, touching my throat. I never considered my voice to be an item to barter. Would I need my voice Above? Were there many people left in that world to even talk to? If not, perhaps I wouldn't need it anyway. "Why?" I ask and swallow. A lump travels down my throat.

"Yuri has a key to a secret lair, does he not?"

"Yes, he does," I reply cautiously.

"And you know what is in that lair."

Every week, Yuri asks me to drink from the Life well. I remember the first time he found it. The way was long and winding. He made me build a door with a lock so that no one else could go in. After he drank, the scrapes and cuts from mining were gone. He stood taller.

"What does my voice have to do with the Life waters?"

"He lets you into the lair."

I close my eyes, a silent acknowledgement. How many times has he begged me to drink it? *I'll take care of you as long as you live. You'll live a long, long life.* But I don't want a long and dark life, so I have always refused.

"With your voice, I can convince him to let me in." She stands, and I can see that her legs are misshapen, crooked. "I need it," she whispers.

Her admission sends chills down my spine. Perhaps it is true that it would ease her pain, but my gut tells me her intentions may not be completely pure.

Sylvie wiggles in my pocket again, and I look down to see her poke her small brown face out, twitch her nose, and dip back in just as quick. How could I give up my voice? I push my hand down into the pocket with Sylvie and wrap it around her small body, hoping her warmth will give me courage.

"Won't he notice I am gone?"

She shrugs. "I only need your voice to get in once."

I rock back and forth again. "Is there nothing else I could give you?" my voice croaks.

Munya stands and tilts her round face. "My dear, if I asked you for something that you cared so little about, wouldn't that defeat the purpose of a true sacrifice?"

The cost is high. Clearly, this dark life has twisted her heart, and I refuse to become bitter or blind from years underground. All we do is trade meaningless, rusted, broken things for food, a bigger cave, and a fork—instead of a brush—to comb our hair. We scrape stones for every inch of survival.

Sometimes I sneak into the forbidden Story Cavern and listen to the elders who lived Above before the war. They talk of the sun as if it is precious gold. Rare, desirable, warm, and lovely. I ache to bask in it, to breathe the free atmosphere. I want that. I want to be free.

"I will give you my voice," I say, trembling, but resolved.

She stiffens. Her gaze locks onto mine, a warning. "There is no going back, Eva."

"Will it hurt?"

"Losing something always hurts," she says, then turns and hobbles to a shelf on the back wall, filled with dented, tin boxes. She peeks inside several and shoves them back. It does not take her long to find what she wants. One item, a necklace with a curled snail's shell, she holds up to a mushroom's light to inspect for a moment.

Then she hands me a wooden box, and a pair of glasses with shaded lenses. Why anyone would make glasses like these, I cannot fathom. *Aren't glasses meant to help you see better, not worse?* I frown at Munya.

"When you first see the light, it will be too bright. Wear these."

"How do you know this?"

She shakes her head. "Not everything you've been told is true. When you get there, don't think, just run."

I turn the oval box this way and that, and open the lid. There is nothing inside except a mirror on the lid.

"I hear things, sometimes, behind this wall. If it is the monster that I think it is, do not look at it. It could turn you to stone. But if it sees itself, it will turn itself to stone."

I shudder, and my heart beats like the dinner drums, one beat for each last second I own my voice. Maybe even my last moments of life. I think of turning back, of giving up. But when I look into the small mirror and see my own gray eyes blinking back at me, I think of Yuri's dead gaze and broken soul. I could die every day, over and over, or I can die trying to live.

I close the box with a snap and shove it into my pocket, resolved. Perhaps I should think of what my last words could be, or give Munya a message for Yuri. Nothing profound comes to mind. Nerves hollow me out like an echoing cave. Leaning across the cold, stone desk, I say, "Please tell Yuri that I love him. For all his rules—he has been like a father to me."

Her eyes flit upwards from the shell to my gaze. She blinks dark lashes. "He knows."

"But you will tell him for me," I insist.

"You are sure you don't want to tell him yourself?"

Heart twisting, mind racing. But no, this is right. "If I tell him, he'll try to stop me. Yuri did what he thought was best for me. But I can't live in this dungeon anymore. I'm suffocating here."

"Are you ready, then?"

"I'm ready." Freedom, just one sacrifice away. Sweat coats my palms.

Munya holds the shell up before my face. "Then sing," she commands in a soft voice.

I close my eyes and begin a gentle lullaby. I think of how Yuri rocked me and sang to comfort me when I struggled to accept the always-night of the dark caves. My voice falters as I begin, but grows stronger. It is a song about promises, about the Creator's care, the one who is our fortress. The notes become effortless. I cannot even feel them, and then I realize that it *isn't* me. I open my eyes. The shell glows with an inner light, which dims as the song fades from it. When I open my mouth to speak to Munya, no sound comes out. I am mute.

Tears break from my eyes at the loss, but I can't dwell on it. I must go. I mouth, *Where do I go?* to Munya, hoping she can read my lips. She points to the shelf.

How? I don't understand.

"Listen," she says, and she leans close to the bookcase and sings. Lilting and haunting, it rises and falls like the dripping water in the southern caves. At the last note, the softest *click* can be heard from inside the shelf.

She leans back, and gently caresses the stone wall, a nail scratching the stone. "This cavern knows my voice."

I marvel as the shelf swings open wide, surprised that I never knew such magic even existed. But I begin to tremble as the mouth of a deep, dark tunnel yawns just seven steps away from me.

I may have spent the majority of my life in dimness and dullness, but rarely this kind of true, thick, lonely dark. Even during Sleep Hours, the mushrooms continue to glow with a humble light.

Yuri made me promise to never walk into any fully dark cavern. Living things lurk around unlit corners and wait in the depths for a snack. I do not wish to be a snack. Sometimes, while treasure hunting with the rats, I hear snarls in the distance. Other times, the acrid stench of blood wafts through air pockets. I have seen brown, broken claws in low-traffic alleyways.

Cold, cold air steals the breath from my lungs as I back away. My voice was one thing, but this is entirely another. I fear true darkness.

I can't. There is no light to show me the way, I try to say.

She sighs, but turns and plucks a mushroom from the wall with a small *pop*. No sooner has she removed it and holds it out to me than a breeze washes over us, and the glow begins to fade. Trembling, I back further and further from the entrance. Perhaps I have made a mistake. I came to Munya to find a way to the light, and she shows me into a tunnel of death. Have I traded my voice for death?

Is there no other way?

"No. I'm sorry."

Sylvie shifts suddenly in my pocket and attempts to climb out. I reach for her, stroking her back to calm her, although my hand shakes. But she insists. She doesn't need words to tell me when she senses something. Her nose twitches, sniffing the air. Can she smell our escape? Biting back tears of fear, I hold her up to my face where she affectionately licks my cheek. I understand now.

How far? I ask Munya, cradling Sylvie beneath my chin.

"The tunnel is straight. Your rat is clever. She will smell the way out. Put the glasses on. You won't see in the dark anyway."

It takes me only a few moments to find Sylvie's harness in my pocket and fit her in it. Then I wrap the thin leash in my left hand. When I look into the tunnel again, my heart falls to the stoney ground, but I take one brave step forward.

I am all too aware of the chill whispering through the tunnel mouth, waiting to swallow me. Sylvie wiggles again, ready. It is now or never. I shove the glasses onto my face.

The second I set her down on the ground, Sylvie scampers forward, and the string in my hands becomes taut.

The further we walk, the thicker the darkness grows. I am hyper aware of my hollow breathing, clomping steps, and Sylvie's skittering claws. Is this what it is like for Yuri every day? No wonder he was afraid of being alone.

The journey does not get any easier the further we go. Time seems immaterial. Without a light, there is no way to see ahead and my feet catch against jutting stones and debris. I pitch forward with a loud gasp and pain explodes in my knee. When I reach to touch the sore place, my hand comes away wet and sticky. The second time that I walk into a cavern wall, I bang my knuckles up pretty good, and hear Sylvie cry out with a startled, painful squeak. Did I nick her tail? As I grope for the way forward and hold my breath, praying she's not crushed, I feel the leash in my left hand tugging me onward. I sigh in relief and my breathing echoes, echoes, echoes, and water drips.

We continue for the longest time, and then a pinprick of light dawns ahead, like the golden light-mushrooms in the caves, but even brighter.

I gasp in startled awe, and something shifts nearby. The sound repeats, and then I hear measured, thumping steps, and a scraping sound like claws dragging across the ground every third thud. Sylvie lets out a piercing shriek and dashes forward. The tunnel reverberates with a heavy, throaty rumble. If I had a voice, I would scream like Sylvie, too, but all I can think to do now is *run*.

She has done her best, but her tiny legs won't be fast enough to outpace a monster. It's my turn to lead now.

I scoop her up and start running towards the light while pushing Sylvie safely into my pocket. My right knee aches with every step. The terrain softens beneath my feet, stone giving way to dirt. A stitch in my side pinches the moment the rumble becomes a rasping growl. Claws grate behind me. Gritting my teeth, I give it all I have. I need to use the mirror, but I am afraid that if I stop and turn, I might accidentally make eye contact. No, I need something to hide behind. A wall? A barrier? The cave mouth!

The further I sprint, the more clearly a light comes into view. My eyes begin to sting from its brilliance. Perhaps the sayings were true, that it may kill me in moments. But now it is death by monster or death by light, and the light seems less painful. It is more pure than any fire or shining gem. I ache to touch it, and yet I am physically unable to look. How will I run if I cannot see?

The monster is breathing and growling at my heels. I must do something.

Claws scramble and scrape behind me as the tunnel mouth widens, but I keep my eyes on the ground, nearly blind with tears as the light douses me in warmth. The dirt terrain changes to the strangest patched emerald, like a weird coat or shaggy moleskin that grows and crawls across the ground wherever the sun's fingers reach.

A guttural growl.

Searing pain across the back of my leg.

If I could scream, I would.

In mad haste, I dash out of the opening and around the mouth of the cave, trying to ignore the sharp pain in my calf. With one hand I clutch the mirror in my pocket, draw it out, and pop the lid. I have one chance. Pinching my eyes shut, I lean around the rugged edge of the cave, aiming the mirror at the beast. I'm praying, hoping, crying with all my heart this is not my last glimpse of the sun.

Suddenly, the roars cease, and I collapse to all fours, gasping for air while my eyes remain closed. I lay there until I feel the pain in my knee pulsing again, and a sharp ache in my calf.

The softest breath of sweet and pleasant air washes over me and I bask in it, memorizing this first taste. My ears are filled with a million tinkling melodies.

Slowly, I open my eyes, and am immediately entranced by the dancing sunlight whispering over my skin. It doesn't burn as I imagined. It is gentle and nice, and I marvel that it doesn't stain me the way Yuri said it would. Will that take time? If it does, perhaps I have more than I thought. This is nothing like I remembered, and yet, I feel a sense of *home*. It's as if I have been here before, but cannot place when.

Still blinking and squinting, I begin to assemble this world together in glimpses, like puzzle pieces, as I wait for my eyes to adjust. There is so *much* color, but varying shades of emerald dominate across this cavernous—or whatever this place is called—space surrounded by the tallest, thickest mushrooms I have ever seen.

Small, brown bat-like creatures with sharp, pointed noses swoop and dive in the air, disappearing into the green mushroom tops and flitting out again. They are the source of the intricate melodies surrounding me, making me ache for my lost voice. If I sang, would they sing back? What is this place? Am I truly alone? I suppose I mistakenly thought that I would leave the caves, and there would be people here, but I see no one. *What good is freedom if you've no one to share it with?*

When I shift my body to look around, the movement causes my calf to sting and bleed again onto the emerald ground-rug. The pain, fatigue, and worry make me cry like a baby. I sob in deep gasps, and tear pieces of my coat away to wrap around it.

I'm wrung out from survival, and utterly lost. This is all beautiful, but I don't know where to go, or how to live here. I take off the shaded glasses to wipe my eyes, and remember the peculiar thing that Munya said to me before I left.

Not everything you've been told is true. When you get there, don't think, just run.

She never said where to. *Don't think.* I am thinking this was a stupid mistake. *Just run.* I could run back or I could run forwards. To go back would be worse off than I am now, returning to the caves with no voice and no future. Or I could risk going forward, finish what I started. Maybe it could be better. *Don't think, just run.*

I push myself up, and run awkwardly through the giant clusters of mushrooms. I want desperately to capture more of this world with its colors and hues, but every time I look up, my eyes sting and tear anew. My foot catches on a hard mushroom's foot sticking out of the ground, sending me falling towards the soft surface. I manage to twist and land on one side of my hip while my hand cradles Sylvie safely against the other. Pain radiates from my elbow and shoots down my hip and already-injured leg.

"You there. Are you alright?"

I open my mouth to scream for the second or third time today—I've lost count—but no sound comes out.

A tall man with cave-dark hair and aquamarine eyes stands over me.

A person. A real living person from Above, and he spoke to me. His skin doesn't look badly stained at all. *He's not dead. Could I live under this sapphire sky forever?* Relief and hope overwhelms me and I cry again, quaking and chattering.

He holds out his hand. "Is something the matter? Let me help you."

He is so kind. I take his hand in both of mine and let him pull me up, but I don't let go. This is real. This is already more than I hoped for.

"What can I do?" he asks.

I point to my throat, and shake my head. Will he understand?

"You can't speak."

I nod, and sigh. Yes, he understands.

"Are you alone?"

Nod again.

"What happened to your leg?"

I am like a cave fish, opening and closing my mouth with no sound coming out. Finally, I make claws of my hands and bare my teeth.

"A beast?"

Nod again.

"Come with me, and I'll get you cleaned up." He puts his arm around my back and at my waist to help me balance, but it is awkward for me to hold onto him with the strange narrow case along his back.

"Oh, sorry, those are my hunting arrows. Maybe this will be better." He brings his arm back, offering me his forearm, palm up. I lay mine parallel to his, and that works better. I smile up at him and lace our fingers together.

Squeezing his hand, I smile through the fountain of tears pouring down my face. My lips form the words *thank you* but it seems insufficient for the moment. He only nods. There are no words for this, even if I could speak. He seems to understand enough. I am finally free, and there is light ahead.

"What is it?" He asks, seeing my tears again.

Sunlight. I form the words with my lips, blinking up to the light, and looking away when it stings. I also point to a soft patch of moleskin on my coat. Will he know what this means, and who I am? *I am from Below.*

He gasps, and looks back towards the cave. "You're from Underground?" He tilts his head in the direction I came from. "No one has come from there in years."

Yes. Sighing in relief, I mouth my affirmation. Then I step away, trying to make him understand that I'm never going back.

"No, you don't have to go back. Come with me."

Where?

"To my home. And I will take you anywhere you want to go."

I can't help the wide smile that lights my face, pulling tight on my cheeks. In a happy, relieved moment, I sigh and close my eyes, letting the sun warm my nose and kiss my eyelashes. *Sun at last.*

SURRENDER

DENICA MCCALL

Surrender
I've heard the voice in my head tell me over
And over again
Discharge your disappointments
And dance on them like they didn't exist
Liberate your expectations so you won't be shattered in the end
Because you've broken too many times
Bonded together after,
Yet brittle now,
As if every moment is precarious

I've projected disappointment in recent times
Attached it to my hopes and my fears
Acted like things will happen
So I don't fall into tears
But
Courage has been my motto,
The rope I cling to after slipping
What is it then? What does it mean
To wield this thing we liken to bravery?
Is it to expect the good and forge forward accordingly,

Or
Is it anticipating the bad, bracing my heart for impact
And in turn, forgetting to feel anything?
Maybe I had it wrong
Maybe hope is harder than living jaded
And thus courage implies flying my hopes high
Like the flag I pledge my allegiance to
And if I'm dashed on the rocks,
My ship is too
But at least I'll have learned how to face the waves
Instead of numbly turning away, settling down and
Accepting they bested me

Surrender
Let go of predicting bad
It's better to fall than merely survive
It's better to live than deny
You have my good in mind

And if I had it wrong, oh well
At least I know I'm human now

WITHER'S RECKONING

HANNAH CARTER

"WHO DOES SHE *think she is? The daughter of a villain, trying to be a hero?"*

A punch hit me square on the cheek, smacking my head against the road. Fingers tightened around my throat, and I struggled to breathe—an all-too-familiar feeling.

Decay's superpowers activated. I gasped as my fingertips began to shrivel and turn black. He'd really use his wither power on me.

He'd really *kill* me, his own daughter.

Better me than innocent bystanders, though. They staggered out of cars and fled into nearby businesses. Some dashed into Central Park to find safety in the trees.

All the while, my father's vice-like grip tightened against my neck. Using his withering power against me might be new, but strangulation wasn't. He'd done that for as long as I could remember. *Punishments,* he'd called them. Whenever he got drunk, whenever he lost to a hero, whenever one of his schemes backfired. I had always been there for him to take his problems out on.

I kicked at his thighs and knees as I squirmed. The wither—that awful, destructive power—crawled past my wrists. My hands curled and grew decrepit, like a zombie's.

A part of me wanted to fight back, but my hands shook when I tried.

Prejudiced words from schoolmates echoed in my head, opinions that had made me an outcast. *Wither is an ugly, villainous power. It can only corrupt.*

"You're a traitor, Arielle," Decay hissed. His grip threatened to crush my esophagus while his words did the same to my soul.

I wheezed and beat at his thick arms with my blackened fists. I guess ten years in prison hadn't lessened the sting of my disloyalty. When the heroes had raided our home, I'd told them where my dad was hiding. I'd always been terrified he might kill me one day.

And that day might be today.

Tears leaked from my eyes. The world grew dark around the edges. He should have been my protector. The man who loved me most. He was my *father*.

But blood didn't matter in the face of betrayal.

Was it destined to shape my fate though? If I dared to fight, would I be like him?

"Arielle!" a deep voice bellowed. Tangles of ivy erupted from the ground and snaked around Decay's throat, throttling him while he held me.

A man with unkempt black curls hurtled into view. He slung his arms forward. More vines broke through the pavement and wrapped around my biological father. The plants tried to tear the two of us apart, but even as they hoisted Decay into the air, he kept his grip on me.

My frantic eyes landed on the newcomer—one of the heroes who had rescued me ten years ago.

The hero who had adopted me, a villain's daughter, an outcast shunned by most people. Who had packed lunches for school and made sure a traumatized eight-year-old girl had a nightlight. Who kissed me goodnight and wiped away many tears.

I didn't want my dangerous powers, didn't want to be a monster who hurt people like my biological father had.

But I didn't have to be like Decay. I could choose.

My dad—my *real* dad, reminded me every day.

I could choose to be like him. I could choose peace, even if my powers brought destruction.

"*Fight*!" Dad bellowed. "Don't let him take you!"

Another of Dad's vines pounded Decay's side. A third grabbed his feet. A fourth wrapped around his eyes.

I thrust my zombie-fied hand against his face and tried to shriek.

No sound escaped my oxygen-deprived lungs. I could hardly see, but I channeled every frustration, every fear, and every bit of my anger into my hands.

It's terrifying. Wither works with her emotions to steal the very life force out of someone—what good can come of it?

A black vein slithered up his face. His face shriveled and sank under my power.

I screamed until his stranglehold slackened. As Decay released me, Dad's vines held me in the air like I could fly, like how he played "airplane" with me as a kid.

A crowd gathered below. The sound of blood *whooshed* inside my ears, and I fought for deep breaths. My vision cleared, and my fingers began to regain their coloring without Decay's poisonous touch.

"Don't *ever* come back here again!" I held out my hands, but they trembled as years of mental blocks fought against me.

No. I could be stronger.

Decay ripped the vine off his eyes. His gaze met mine, full of malice and pure hatred. His wither raced up the plant, which shriveled and turned black.

He didn't have to say anything. I knew he intended to rip away the very person who had replaced him in my life.

My heart sputtered, and I dove for Decay in mid-air. My wither crept down his neck and past the collar of his prison outfit.

"Leave—us—*alone*!" With one final screech, my powers exploded out of me. Wither shriveled up Decay's body, and the vine dropped from his hand before he could infect my Dad.

Decay and I both dropped to the ground. He twitched on the cement. My shoulders drooped as the anger drained from my body.

I held up my hand and watched the last bit of the blackness fade away. I hadn't killed him, so there was a good chance he'd regenerate. But with a blast that powerful, he wouldn't be able to return for a very, very long time.

The onlookers shoved closer to me. Whispered.

"Isn't that Decay's daughter? Is she a villain, too?"

Wary eyes watched as I sank into Dad's arms.

"I'm not the daughter of Decay." My throat hurt from my screaming, and I swallowed. "Because blood doesn't determine who you are. My name is Arielle, and I'm..." I choked and met Dad's eyes. He nodded. "I'm the daughter of a hero."

Dad squeezed my shoulders. "Yes . . . but also a hero yourself."

A PRIZE WORTH SEEKING

ALI NOËL

If only life's doors
were as crystalline water
lucent and cool to the touch
O, that I could sail through
a spray of sea the only mark
life could leave on me

Alas, by flame my path is set
Who am I to fight it?
A freedom worth having
A prize worth seeking
will demand refiner's fire
And faith has not failed me yet

DAY IN AND DAY OUT

ANNE J. HILL

EVERY MORNING HE clocked in. Every evening he clocked out. His hands covered in earth. His brow drenched with sweat. Liam moved dirt for a few coins under the beating sun. And under the moon, he pushed bottles of beer across the counter until his shift ended. Four hours of sleep until he hit the dirt again. Weekends came, and the excitement of *five* hours of sleep got him through the long monotony of bagging groceries.

Day in and day out.

Each month, he placed a wad of cash in an envelope and slipped it into her mailbox. Liam never left his name and made sure Haley wasn't home. If she knew it was him, she'd tell him to stop or burn the money in front of his face. But he had to do this.

Liam only kept enough to pay his bills and food. He couldn't live with himself if he didn't right his wrongs, and she'd refused every offer of help he'd given her.

So there he stood, on a warm summer evening, staring at her mailbox and feeling the absence in his wallet, again. He noticed her fence was fixed. It used to look like it might cave in at any moment but now it stood nobly. His money must have done that. Liam smiled, admiring it. But then he winced. He wasn't allowed to enjoy this. It was supposed to be torture. He *deserved* torture.

He climbed into his red pick-up truck and stared at his steering wheel. Each time he'd gotten behind the wheel since that violent thunderstorm, Liam turned his phone off and put it in the glove compartment. He would never make the same mistake again.

Liam froze when he saw her Prius roll down the street. It was a different model than the one he'd crashed into, but he'd still memorized it to make sure he stayed out of sight.

She certainly wouldn't forget *his* truck anytime soon.

Liam turned his engine on, ready to speed away, when he saw her park and open her door.

He would make himself watch. He hadn't seen her since the hospital, where he'd tried to pay for her heart surgery, the only thing that kept her alive. He deserved to see the shambles he left her in.

There was some shuffling around in the car, then she set a wheelchair out of the door and opened it. Then, carefully, she gripped onto something he couldn't see, twisted, and lowered herself down like a pro. She rolled to the back door and pulled out a box of groceries, whistling and—

Was that a smile?

Liam blinked. She looked happier than he'd felt in a year.

Her bright eyes danced around the neighborhood, looking as if only memories of love and happiness lay behind them, and then they settled on his truck.

Liam couldn't peel his gaze away, but he knew he should go. Before he could, she was wheeling over to him and waving.

Liam swallowed hard and pushed his door open.

"Hello, Liam. Would you like to come in for dinner? It won't take long."

Liam blinked at her. Dinner? He should be the one making *her* dinner. "I . . ." How could he say no? He owed her his life. "Okay. Yeah." He turned his truck off and slid out. "I can carry that for you."

She smiled. "No need, but you can open the front door if you like."

Liam nodded fast, rushed to the door, and held it open. He stepped in behind her, his stomach twisting. Pictures of her before the accident littered the living room. Doing things she could never do again. All because he'd been too busy cussing out his ex over text instead of paying attention to the road.

He deserved every restless night and every grueling day.

Haley set her box on the low counter and wheeled around the kitchen. "So, Liam. When are you going to stop leaving me money?"

He shoved his hands into his pockets. "I don't know what—"

"Oh, come on. I'm not stupid." She set out a cutting board. "Every month, you drop off more money than I'm sure you can afford. And frankly, more than I need. You need to stop."

He shifted his weight. "I can't. You deserve so much more.

She peeled a carrot over the sink. "And you deserve to live."

He frowned. "How can I when you—" He caught himself short of calling her life not living.

She arched an eyebrow at him. "I'm just fine. Better than you, I imagine." She gave a pointed look at his sorry state before placing the smooth carrot on the cutting board and snapping the knife through.

Liam shook his head and brushed at a tear in his jeans as if he could wipe it away. "I didn't mean . . . I . . . I ruined the life you wanted. This is the least I can do."

Haley smiled softly. "Yes, you did. And I was angry with you for quite some time, I'll admit. Threw out the first two months of money."

Liam's gut churned. He'd almost starved those first two months getting her that money.

"But then I figured, hey, if he's going to throw money away, then I'm going to put it to good use." She brushed the sliced-up carrot into a bowl.

"The fence looks nice. And your new car." He nodded. She *had* put it to good use.

Haley chuckled. "No, I paid for those myself. I have this beautiful thing called a job." She pointed to the mantle above her unlit fireplace. "Get that urn for me, would you?"

Liam hesitated but brought down the blue and silver vase.

"I've been saving your money in this urn for someone who needs it more than I do. And Liam, stop it. Stop blaming yourself so much that you're not living. I forgive you. Go live your life before I have to move because some stranger keeps illegally tampering with my mailbox, okay?" A smile tugged at the corner of her lips.

She forgave him? "But . . . how can you?"

Haley studied him hard, then said, "I couldn't spend forever hating you, so I prayed a heck of a lot until I didn't."

Liam looked at the urn in his hands. That was it? That was her grand secret?

"Liam," she said, and he looked up. "Move on. I have."

He blinked back tears. Was he allowed to move on just like that? "I don't think I know how to."

Haley smiled and said, “Well, start by deciding you need to, and the rest will follow. It’ll be hard.” She paused a moment and stared at the urn, *past* the urn, and then a smile returned to the corner of the mouth. “But start small.”

Liam ran his thumb over the cold metal in his hands. He nodded slowly. “I’d . . . I’d like more sleep at night.”

Haley smiled. “Then sleep.”

“I work . . .”

“Quit your job.”

Liam winced. “I can’t afford to.” Not with all the money he’d lost to a blasted urn.

Haley shrugged. “Like I said, the urn is for someone who needs it more than I do. Take it, Liam. And move on.”

Liam inhaled. He couldn’t undo everything he’d worked for to pay his dues, could he? To make all those long hours and sleepless nights meaningless.

Haley watched him. “It’s okay, Liam, to need help. It really is. I think we both needed that lesson.”

He really did need the money . . . if just to get a full night’s sleep. “You’re sure?” Everything in him cried out against this. Run. Flee. Keep her away. Keep the money away. He didn’t deserve this.

“I’m sure.”

Liam rapped his finger on the metal. And for the first time in a very long time, he made a small choice to put aside his pride, and he opened the urn.

UNMARKED GRAVES

KELLY HELLMUTH

I took each step carefully
Feeling my way through the dark
Shifting this way and that
So as not to step
Upon the mounds of dirt
Covering the ground

As the fog rolled in
Obscuring my already limited view
I could only trust
That my feet knew the way
Through this precarious field
Full of things once holy
And precious

I knew each mound
For each one had been made
By me
For me
I had not attempted to cross
This place in a while—

A cemetery of my hopes and dreams—
It brought too much pain
To remember
What never was
And what might have been

But I could stay away no longer
The way forward was through
So I tread lightly
Careful not to crush
That which was already dead and buried
Every so often, my toes
Would brush up against a memory
And it would cascade over my bare skin
Threatening to bury me then and there

But I kept moving on

Each careful step
Brought me closer and closer
Through the unmarked graves
Of what never was
So I could run freely
Full of life
And light
On the other side

PART TWO: THE SACRIFICE

THE MERMAID IN THE LIBRARY

ANDREA RENAE

DALTON WHITFORD SLUMPED in the library's window seat and watched the minuscule figures move across the beach below. The ladies glided over the sand, their silken skirts ballooning behind them, and the jacketed men bobbed black top hats in respectful greeting. Beetle-like bathing machines crawled into the windswept waters on one end of the beach, carrying noblewomen out to bathe in modesty, while the men's stark white specks galloped unencumbered into the waves along the other.

He sighed.

Every holiday since the age of eight, he had been shipped off to Aunt Persephone's manor on the cliffs. His mother would dismiss him with an airy wave and say, "*You need to get better, darling,*" claiming the only hope for his sickly countenance was the English seaside. His father hardly even spared him a glance from behind his crisp, ever-present newspapers.

The whole thing was a farce. Dalton wasn't sick—at least not in the traditional sense. Moody, yes, but not ill. His parents merely wanted to attend their high society events without the burden of parenthood. Of *him.*

Was it his fault their disinterest made him melancholic?

All his protests fell upon deaf ears, however, and he was sent to the coast with unfeeling regularity.

Now seventeen, manhood pulled at his bonds with maddening insistence. He came to the coast resolved to make the most of his confinement. After all, it had to be better than the indifference of home. Perhaps he would try sea bathing this time or attend the public balls at the resort village. He was old enough to start making his own social connections.

But upon his arrival, his aunt had interpreted his determined expression as proof of the fabled "illness." She'd commanded a course of rest and recuperation, forbidding him from so much as a stroll along the beach.

Weeks in that miserable situation, with nothing but a neglected library and the same decrepit wolfhound for distraction, had drained Dalton's spirits further. He rested his forehead against the window's leaded bars and watched water spray over the rocks in the bay.

In a year, he would be released from this suffocating existence, without his apathetic parents and his aunt's reproachful looks condemning him. Maybe he'd even meet a pretty girl—someone who fancied the brooding type.

That was not very likely.

Despondent, he took in the untouchable scene until the setting sun dipped into view below the window's casing. He exhaled, his breath fogging the glass.

"All right. What delights will it be tonight?" He slid off the window seat, sending dust motes swirling. The wolfhound raised his grizzled head, groggily regarding the young man's movements. Dalton patted his head, then crossed the thick carpet to peruse the books.

"*Man's Intransigence* . . . *The Mathematics of Money Changing* . . . *Matters of Decorum* . . ." Dalton groaned. His uncle had the driest collection of books imaginable. But when his finger fell upon a small book, oddly out of place among the other weighty tomes, he prised it from its hiding place in the shadows.

Camborne's Compendium of Mythological Creatures, the title read. Its illuminated cover glowed in the evening light. Dalton turned it over in his hands, brushing away the thick layer of dust that blanketed its gilded pages.

Curiosity piqued, Dalton opened it.

The pages contained nothing he hadn't seen before in English fairytales—dwarves, elves, and even grindylows. But the illustrations were vivid, spilling enthusiastically over the pages as if they had been printed yesterday.

Glancing back inside the cover, Dalton found two cryptic words—*Never Again*—scrawled next to a signature he couldn't interpret. He scanned for the date. *1579?* His jaw dropped. Was this volume really two centuries old?

Finally, something interesting.

He thumbed its pages until the book fell open at a well-cracked spot.

A depiction of a riotous sea tinged with violet and sapphire hues greeted him. Clinging to a rock jutting from the waves was an otherworldly entity, who gazed at him with penetrating eyes. Her hair was a mahogany tangle of oarweed strands. Viridescent scales, brilliant as emeralds, spilled from her collarbones, encasing her body from chest down until they merged with a spreading tail draped luxuriously over the rocks. Silken fins trailed from her wrists like the sleeves of a medieval gown, adorning arms the color of sparkling champagne.

She was a mermaid unlike any rendering Dalton had ever beheld.

Hungrily, he devoured the description.

A heartless creature that inhabits rough seas. Lures unwitting souls to watery graves with a siren's call.

Dalton frowned. That couldn't be right. She looked more sad than heartless, and the familiarity of it twanged within his chest.

He touched a finger to the image but withdrew it with a start.

It felt . . . *damp?*

He bent, scrutinizing the paper. It looked perfectly ordinary. He dared brush the depiction again. Yes, it was definitely wet. *Very.* His fingertips dripped with moisture.

Dread filled Dalton, and he slammed the book shut. Streams of liquid exuded from the old pages—first a gush, then a geyser. He dropped it. Soaking the carpet, its waters sent the dog howling out of the room. As Dalton fled, salty spray hit him in the face. Aquamarine swells gamboled around him, now at his thighs, now at his chin. He gulped air moments before the deluge dragged him under.

After a disorienting moment of fighting the undertow, Dalton broke the surface. The coffered ceiling of the library was now a sky luminescent with twilight. He clawed desperately for purchase as powerful waves threw him against lacerating stone. Mercifully, he managed to grab a hold on the rock and heave himself out of the water's reach.

Exhausted, he rested his forehead in battered hands and gasped for breath.

"Aubrey?" A hopeful voice drifted through the air like a morning mist. Startled, Dalton straightened and glanced around dumbly for its owner.

There she was, the mermaid from *Camborne's Compendium.* Flesh and blood.

Dalton's mind clouded with confusion, with questions he couldn't convince his lungs to voice.

Had the book turned the world into a vast ocean, or had he been miraculously transported elsewhere? And how could a simple drawing turn to life? Was the mermaid even real?

He stared, mouth agape, at what Camborne had unfeelingly classified as a "creature." Fear and curiosity warred within him. She was most definitely real, and her beauty was even more haunting than the illustration. As if she was not beholden to time's demands, she looked to be near Dalton's own age, yet at the same time strangely ageless. Shimmering droplets trailed down her pale skin, and she tilted her chin, revealing thin slits along her neck. When he looked at her black opal eyes, Dalton's apprehensions melted away. She seemed just as astonished as he was. Intelligence mingled with the bewilderment in her gaze.

And sadness.

"You are not him."

There was a note of disappointment in her voice, like Christmas had been canceled or an especially beloved pet had died. It was a knife to Dalton's heart.

"Since I don't know who *he* is," he replied, swallowing hard when his words emerged as sulky and pathetic things, "obviously I am not."

The mermaid regarded him thoughtfully for a moment, as if he was a puzzle she considered solving, but then sighed resignedly and turned away.

She was brushing him off, and the sting of it was just as acute as every other rejection Dalton had experienced in his life. He clenched his jaw and called upon anger to chase away the pain. It didn't seem right that a mythological creature would treat him with the same indifference as every other ordinary human in his life. Like he was an unwanted thing that didn't merit a second look. Dalton's chest thrummed with anger, but it quickly shifted to desperation when he realized she was going to leave him. "Wait—please! Won't you even tell me your name?"

The maiden glanced back, seaweed hair trailing in the brackish wind. Instead of the indifference Dalton expected, her eyes were laden with compassion.

"Leida." As the name melded with the roar of the sea, her expression grew uncertain. "How came you to this rock?"

Dalton raised his chin. "I found a book—an old one, full of fantastical creatures—and when I touched your page, it . . . well, this world sort of appeared around me."

Leida's severity evaporated, her voice lowering to a trembling whisper. "It is not possible. Aubrey said . . ." She stared out at the glimmering water, lost in her own thoughts.

"I'm sorry—*who* said *what*?"

Blinking, Leida focused on Dalton again, as if she had forgotten he was there. She looked at him curiously. "How can you possibly be the one?" Her fins twitched, as if she longed to disappear into the sea and leave this conundrum behind.

Dalton didn't know how to interpret her question or whether he should be offended by her incredulity. All he knew was that his only chance at companionship was a few feet from disappearing from his life forever, and he could not bear the thought of facing the rest of his vacation alone. "Do you think—" He licked his lips, feeling much more like a school boy than someone on the brink of manhood. "Can I see you again?"

Except for her heaving shoulders, she stilled. Her eyes fell on a rectangular shape, washed up on the rocks. *The book.* A peculiar emotion Dalton could not identify passed over Leida's features.

"I think not."

With a powerful thrust of her tail, she plunged into the sea.

Dalton stared at the darkening waters. Fumbling for the strangely unharmed volume, he let it fall open to her page. The mermaid within had turned her back, now facing the ocean beyond. When he raised his eyes to compare the image to the real thing, the dry, shelf-lined walls of the library stared back at him with an air of boredom.

He let out a shaky exhale and closed the book.

As soon as the sun had dawned the following day, Dalton cracked the compendium open—this time prepared for the forceful waters. He clambered up the rock and prayed Leida would return, despite the previous day's unpromising meeting. The sun ascended, bearing down without mercy, and the tide rose around the rock until he only had a small footing. Suffocating despair pooled within him hour by hour. The tide retreated, and still, she did not come.

When the golden rays had almost vanished from the horizon, Dalton held the book between shaking fingers.

Was he truly destined to be alone?

It is what you deserve, a voice whispered in his mind. And he believed it.

"Why have you returned?"

Dalton's heart jumped into his throat when Leida's porcelain face emerged from the waves. He scrambled to his feet, despondence forgotten, and offered her his hand. She merely raised an eyebrow.

Chaffed, Dalton folded his arms. "Not for your pleasurable company." He meant the words to bite, but they were childish and desperate. And absolutely untrue. He pressed a hand to his forehead and let out a slow breath. "I'm sorry."

The mermaid regarded him with confliction as she bobbed in the swells, shadows circling her eyes. "I must warn you against growing attached to me." Pain flitted across her features as she turned away. "It will surely lead to trouble."

Caution thumped in Dalton's chest, begging him to listen. "I-I don't care!" he shouted over it, and the words tore his throat. He quieted himself with a quick breath. "I don't care. Can't you see? There isn't . . . I don't have anyone else."

But her jeweled tail slipped beneath the surface.

Dalton sagged and blinked back tears. He thought he had hardened himself to rejection, but this one slipped past his defenses, cutting him where he could still feel. He grabbed the book and flipped through the entries slowly, unwilling to leave but finding no reason to stay.

Just as the enchanted page turned over, he heard her musical voice.

"Tomorrow. At twilight."

He stood in the library, alone.

For the next several evenings, Leida met Dalton at the rock. He was sheepish, feeling keenly that he didn't deserve her company. But the sea maiden was gracious, even if she was only humoring him. Her kindness was pure sunshine to his light-starved soul. She didn't pry into his life or make him feel like he had to prove himself to be worthy of her attention. For the first time in years, Dalton felt seen. As they sat above the deafening swells, the old scars of neglect began to soften.

Aunt Persephone soon noticed healthy color in Dalton's cheeks, which she attributed to her ministrations. He smiled as if he agreed but kept the secret of his mermaid to himself.

After a week of sunset meetings, Leida also began to change. Her reservations melted away, and the "heartless" mermaid's true nature bloomed. The first time Dalton saw her smile was like spring's dawn, awakening something tender inside him.

Still, Leida gave him another gift. She invited him into her world, sharing her air with him when his weak lungs burned. It had a peculiar effect on Dalton, strengthening his body so that the crushing pressure of the depths did not harm him. Something new coursed through his blood, igniting in his core, making him feel alive in a different sort of way.

Together, they raced through bottomless chasms and explored brilliant coral reefs. Brazen fish nibbled at Dalton's toes while Leida called them by curious names in a language he did not know. Thousands of species of anemones, sponges, starfish, urchins, and invertebrates all vied for his attention, and try as he might, he could not take everything in. The sea held a myriad of colors he never knew existed—purples richer than figs and golden ochres that smarted to behold. Nothing above the surface could ever compare.

Dalton drank his fill of wonder.

Each day, they ventured further and further into the heart of the ocean, into mysteries that lay concealed from the world above. Leida showed Dalton tempestuous underwater volcanoes that shot lava through the glassy ceiling, birthing new lands waiting to be claimed by intrepid seafarers. When the two of them came upon sunken ships, they became like children, plundering pirates' hordes and flirting with the danger of sharks' teeth and rays' barbs. And when Leida brought Dalton to the secret waters where blue whales courted each other with songs that pained the soul, she made him promise never to reveal where to find them.

"It has been so many years since I have been able to travel far enough to hear them," she said in a hush as they sat on their rock again.

Dalton tucked a strand of her seaweed hair behind her ear and gave her a quizzical look. "And why is that?"

Her face was troubled, as if she was unsure of what to tell him. "The book does not simply bring you to me," she said, keeping her eyes fixed to its cover. "I am bound, like it is physically tethered to my body, and I cannot stray far from the one who holds it."

Horrified, Dalton thrusted the book to her. "Then you should have it!" he cried, sickened at the thought that he had kept her like some sort of prisoner.

Leida tentatively ran her index finger along the spine of the compendium, then quickly removed it as though she had been burned. She bit her lip and pressed her hand to her chest, tears gathering in her eyes. "It appears I cannot touch it."

The book was heavy in Dalton's hands. Finding it had seemed like such a gift, but now it felt more like a curse. "If I destroyed it, would that free you?" He could barely whisper the question.

"Perhaps," Leida answered softly, slipping her hand into his. "But how would you find your way back to me?"

Dalton exhaled. "Then it is a good thing I have every intention of staying close to you." He squeezed her hand. "I will go anywhere you want."

The clouds that had darkened Leida's eyes lightened, and her smile emerged, warm and genuine. In that moment, Dalton knew she was exactly what he needed, but he also wondered if he had been what she needed too.

As he spent more time in her company, however, his constitution began to suffer. He craved the sea more than the sun, and the old house suffocated him. He felt like a captive within its drab walls, not really alive. All the advances he had made in Aunt Persephone's estimation vanished. He grew truly ill for the first time in his life.

The magic—whether from the book or the mermaid herself, he did not know—was poisoning him.

After a fortnight, Dalton's downturn was alarming. Worry tugged at Leida's lips as she laid a cool hand against his flushed cheek to delay him from opening the book and returning to the library.

"Please, Dalton." Leida bit her lip and glanced down at the opened cover. Her brows lowered when her eyes landed on the name scrawled within. "When you return to your home, you must not come back to me."

All Dalton's childhood hurts reasserted themselves, swirling into a fury. His voice emerged strained. "Haven't you been enjoying our time together?"

She smiled sadly, brushing a thumb across his cheek. "More than I dared dream."

Dalton caught her hand. "Then why would you send me away?"

Her gaze drifted to the burning sunset waters. "Long ago I used my song to lure men to me, as all my kin have done for thousands of years, until the day I chose to spare a man named Aubrey. I did not lead him to his grave as I had been taught to do, although it meant banishment to forsake my people's ways. But I did not care. For once I wanted to share in a life, not steal it forever."

She inhaled slowly, the slits along her neck widening. Dalton bit his cheek, trying to sift between the feelings of jealousy and horror rising up in his chest.

"He became obsessed with me, with this life. I pretended he loved me, but it was only a result of my manipulation, my indelible song. I craved something real, something that was impossible while he was under my enchantment. When I lifted it, I hoped he would see me for who I really was, that I would be enough."

Leida's brow flickered with pain. "Instead, he became angry, as was his right. I had stolen many days of his life, treating him like nothing more than an entertaining pastime. And he left me."

Guilt spiraled through Dalton's core, and he fixed his gaze to the churning waters. Hadn't he only thought of Leida as a means to endure a lonely summer? But she was so much more than that to him now.

"In penance," she continued, seemingly unaware of his discomfort, "I spent years resisting the urge to sing my siren's call. It was a terrible burden, for it is in my nature to draw men in, just as it is in man's nature to take. But I was determined I should never again be the cause of a human's pain. The suffering would be only mine. And I learned to bear it."

Dalton's heart broke. "Oh, Leida . . ." he whispered.

She sniffed and straightened her back, as if determined to bring her tale to completion. "Decades later, Aubrey appeared on that rock, just as you did. He was so much older, holding that same book in his hands. Anger still burned in his eyes. He said he found a way to bind me and my magic into a single page—I know not how. '*Only someone as twisted as you will ever find this place,*' he said, '*and I will make sure to hide this book where no one will look.*' He meant to hurt me, but it was a strange relief. It freed me to sing again without harming anyone. And even though I became his captive, I finally felt released from him, from the burden of my nature—at least until the book would be destroyed, if that day ever came."

Her rigid posture weakened, and she slumped forward. "But two hundred years is an eternity to be alone."

Fondness eased her features as she turned to Dalton. "Somehow, you found me." Tears slipped from her eyelashes, splashing onto her iridescent scales. "And it had nothing to do with my curse."

A dry laugh shuddered out of Dalton, and he could not meet her gaze. "I only wanted something to amuse me."

The corner of Leida's mouth quirked in a wry smile. "As I once did. But I also desired to be known—to be seen—for who I really am. And that, Dalton Whitford, is why the book brought you to me. We are the same."

She gripped his hands, her expression now somber. "But this is not where you belong. You are unwell." Her dark eyes pleaded with him to accept her words. "If you stay with me, this magic will kill you. Does your family deserve that heartache?"

A chill spread through Dalton. When he met Leida, she gave him a chance to pretend his whole rotten history didn't exist. Desperate for escape, he had basked in this beautiful stranger's attention. But Leida had given him much more than distraction. Setting aside past hurts, she had offered him undeserved kindness. Was he supposed to give that up for the sake of a family that didn't want him?

Maybe he was just as flawed and jaded as they were.

But the realization of what she was asking hit him harder than an ocean breaker. "If I do what you ask, I'll never see you again." His breaths came in gulps. How could she even suggest something that would bring him so much pain?

Holding his hands even tighter, Leida made no reply.

When he witnessed the regret in her eyes, Dalton's anger melted away like mists on the waters. "You would be alone."

"But you would *live*."

Hers, he realized, was the real sacrifice.

Slowly, unwillingly, he nodded.

He pinched his eyes shut and didn't open them when her soft lips brushed his, when her hand trailed over his features, or when he heard the gentle splash of her retreat.

When all was quiet, he sucked in a breath and stared at the ocean. It was calm for the first time since he had come.

He opened the book, and the library unfolded around him once more.

Tears blinding him, Dalton clutched the book tight. It was proof of his adventure, of Leida's love. He would keep it safely hidden to remind him of what he'd lost.

But as he ran a hand over its illuminated cover, the draw to flip it open and call her to him again became unbearable. And yet, Leida's words still echoed through his mind.

It is in man's nature to take.

The book may have been precious to him, but to her it was as confining as the old coastal house. As long as it existed, then someone could claim her. Yet even though she faced an uncertain future, her appeal had not been for her freedom: it was for his well-being.

She deserved to be as free as the sea.

Dalton approached the library's hearth, courage growing. *I will not be the one who takes.* With a fitful jerk, he fought his flesh and tossed the book in.

The flames rose to embrace it.

Far below the Atlantic Ocean, the mermaid dove. Deeper, deeper still, as far away from the wretched rock as her bonds would allow, where light couldn't penetrate and warmth feared to tread. Without the book's keeper by her side, she would not be able to stray far. Still, she pressed on. As the fathoms rushed past and each thrust of her tail became more difficult, her tears joined their comrades in the salty sea. She cried out against the hold of the book and the pain in her heart.

A ripple passed through the depths—gentle, like the wake from a bloom of jellyfish. When it reached her, something snapped from her chest as if an invisible tangle of bull kelp had been cut loose. She turned skyward and stared at her trailing fins, her unencumbered tail, the moonlight cascading in broken beams overhead.

She understood.

Dalton Whitford had set her free.

When summer ended and Dalton returned home, he never spoke of the mysterious mermaid. His health returned to him, but he had changed—had *been* changed—and even though it must surely have been obvious to all around him, his parents refused to see it. They continued to sluff him off as another person's problem.

But as he imagined Leida shifting through sapphire waters with oarweed hair drifting around her lovely face, the desire to punish his family like he used to diminished. He knew Leida would never again use her song to manipulate another, even though it meant bearing through the pain. If she could spend an eternity denying herself, then maybe he could do the same, one moment at a time.

Perhaps that was the secret to true freedom.

SLEEP, OH CAPTAIN

ANNE J. HILL

Waves crash and rock this ship of ours
You wear the captain hat and stand
At the helm with shaking hands
Stressed eyes wide with terror

Pirates, all of us, swimming upstream
We've set out to down the vessels
That threaten to wreck our bond
Plunder the seas; take back what's ours

You shout commands with a quiver
Blood stains your hands and heart
Making hard choices for us all
Our Fearless Leader, full of fear

With the wheel in your hands
You order the sails to your command
Unsure if you're staying the course
Or leading your loved ones into an abyss

But this I know, this I believe
The compass in your shaking hand
Is fair and holds fast, oh my beloved captain
It points true north through any storm

With weary eyes on the compass
Blood and bones ready to crumble
You grit your teeth and point this ship
Straight into our enemies with a prayer

Your crew readies their arms
Cannons are filled, and fires are lit
We wait your order, oh my captain
To down the ships of lies

For as long as your eyes
Stay firmly on the cracked compass
Then I will hold your hand up
And help you steer through the fog

Pirates, all of us, fighting the current
Following the path you've blazed
Through enemy lands with guns at the ready
Waiting for your shouts to fire

Shots crack through the air
Cannonballs slam through masts
Blood is spilled into the sea
You grow weak against me

But with my arms around your waist
And a crew following orders
Our ship makes it through
The enemies left in shambles

You slump against me, exhausted
I slip the wheel from your grasp
Pull the compass from your fist
And I take this ship to shore

I tuck the crew into bed and
Kiss sleepy little foreheads
Our crew drifts to sleep with
Teddy bears in their arms

Oh, captain, lay down your hat
Rest your head on my lap
Close your eyes and breathe in the sea
Don't forget you're only mortal

Slipping into bed with you
I stroke your hair and whisper prayers
Of peace over your body and mind
So tonight you can rest and

Tomorrow steer this ship again
With me by your side to lift your head
And our crew under our wing
But for tonight, sleep, oh captain

A SPRINKLE OF PIXIE DUST

HANNAH CARTER

OUTSIDE THE RAIN-splattered porthole, thunder rumbled and lightning streaked across the sky. The frothing waves of the Great Neverland Sea slammed the Jolly Roger against the rocks, and I shrieked as I tumbled out of Wendy Darling's hand.

"Tink!" she cried. She snatched me up, holding me against her chest. "Are you okay?"

"Fine," I chirped, though my light flashed gray with anxiety. Outside the window, I could hear the tick-tock of Pan's loyal croc—the prison guard that kept anyone from reaching the Second Star portal and leaving Neverland.

Hook burst into the room, startling me. "That blasted crocodile bit a hole in the hull!" He staggered. The room tilted at an unnatural angle. The open door banged against the side of the wall repeatedly. "We have to get everyone off the boat, or else we'll lose more than our hands to that beast!"

"Tink, can you fly us out yet?" Wendy asked. I shivered in her hands, my teeth chattering together. But even when I wrapped my arms around my tiny frame, I couldn't keep the chill off my body. Another violent wave slammed into the boat, and Wendy staggered against Hook's desk. A blazing lantern fell to the floor and shattered; flames raced across the wood as it rolled.

"Tink!" Wendy backed away from the flames and huddled against Hook, as though the pirate could shield us from the flames like he'd been protecting us from Peter Pan.

She wanted me to fly. Such a simple request for a fairy . . . right?

I flashed a bright, pulsing crimson, but no pixie dust accompanied it. "I—I can't."

The foul aftertaste of poison rose in my throat—the poison Pan had forced me to swallow when he found out that Wendy and I planned to free Neverland's inhabitants and return them to their home worlds. Wendy had nursed me back to life with her belief, but I couldn't make enough pixie dust for *her* right now, let alone all Neverland's captives.

"Don't worry, Wendy-bird." Hook scooped Wendy up, bridal-style, into his arms. "I'll get you out of here."

The boat lurched again. Hook slammed against the wall. I collapsed on Wendy's palm, and Wendy looped an arm around his neck. My stomach turned as the people on deck uttered frantic cries. Around us, the flames rose higher. Smoke filled my lungs and made the three of us hack and wheeze.

Curse that Peter Pan. He didn't care at all for the people who got hurt in his wicked games. And he'd kept me next to his side for too long, manipulated in fear and living for the bits of praise that he sometimes gave me, no bigger than a sprinkle of pixie dust.

Hook shoved himself from the wall and staggered like a drunkard to the last ladder. "Hold on tighter, Wendy." Louder, he added, "*Abandon ship*!"

The *tick-tock, tick-tock* grew louder as we surfaced on the chaotic main deck. Lightning flashed. The loose sails snapped loudly as the wind whipped them about. Nausea boiled in my stomach, and my light flashed gray again. Neverland should be a safe place, full of dreams and childlike wonder. But here I was, clinging to Wendy's thumb, fighting for my life while the wind, rain, and waves lashed out with a vicious fury at Pan's behest.

Tick-tock. Tick-tock. Tick-tock.

The boat crunched.

I screamed as planks of wood drifted away in the waters, rent apart by Tick-Tock's massive maw.

The three of us rolled like a barrel overboard. I couldn't see—the world was a blur of sky, deck, water, *chaos* before we plummeted into the frothy waves. My lungs instinctively gasped for oxygen, but water answered their pleas instead.

Panic set my nerves on fire, and my hand reached up, like I could pull all of us up to the surface. But I was the tiniest and weakest there, even if I wasn't poisoned, which just increased my feelings of helplessness.

Bubbles escaped my mouth as I shrieked. *Don't let me die! Oh, please, stars above—don't let us die!*

Through the water and my own emotions, it took me a moment to realize that Hook was swimming. We broke through the surface, all gasping as he swam us ashore.

His captain's hat was long gone, and his hair lay limp against his shoulders. I'd lost one of my shoes, and my flower-petal dress sported a handful of new rips and tears. Wendy collapsed, her hand falling in front of her. I bounced out of her hand and rolled against the beach. Sand stuck to my body, my blonde hair, my mouth.

"Oh, no—oh, no," Wendy murmured. She crawled over to me. "Tink, are you okay?"

I spat out sand, saltwater, and any other number of fluids. "It's fine. I'm fine."

Wendy plucked me from the sand. Thin scratches decorated her palms, elbows, and freckled face. Her red hair had long ago fallen out of her braids, and hung now in tangled, wet clumps that brushed against me.

Behind us, men screamed from the waters as the mermaids laughed. I squeezed my eyes shut, but my brain created horrible images of the mermaids tearing their victims apart as blood filled the water.

More noises filled the air as a handful of survivors crawled out of the waves. The Lost Boys, pirates, Tiger Lily, and her tribe. All of us, dripping and defeated, our lot much smaller than it had been minutes before.

Hook rested a hand on Wendy's shoulder. She glanced up at him, her face fierce, like she thought it might have been Pan who dared to touch her. But upon seeing his face, her expression melted into one of softness.

"Thank you," she said. "I promise, Tink and I will still find a way to get everyone back to their home worlds."

Hook patted her head. "Don't worry about me. It's my job to make sure *you* get home safely."

Wendy sighed. Tears gathered in her eyes. "Don't—don't say that. I don't want anyone to feel responsible for me. This whole plan was my idea, and I convinced Tink. I'm so sorry. This is all my fault."

"None of this is your fault," I snapped. My soaked wings trembled as I shook them off. "This is Pan's fault. His fear of growing up traps him here, but that gives him no good reason to make the rest of us his slaves. I'm with you, Wendy Darling. Even as useless as I am without pixie dust, I'm with you until the very end."

A rooster call filled the air.

In a sparkle of pixie dust, Pan perched on the sinking ship's crow's nest, which barely bobbed above the waves. "I see a bunch of yellow-bellied codfish!"

A smattering of whispers and exclamations flew between the survivors. We huddled together on the shore helpless as Pan, his crocodiles, and the mermaids circled the waters, all with murderous intent.

"Let us go, Peter," Wendy begged. "Please."

Pan left his perch, and it slid beneath the waves. The only proof that the last hope of Neverland ever existed was the splintered debris being churned on the waves. "Why do you want to grow up?" He stomped toward us. "Can't you see I'm helping you?" His visage twisted. "Grown-ups are boring. Stay here. It's always fun here."

"It's only fun for you." Wendy jerked her hand away as Peter tried to reach for it. "Not for everyone who has to do just as you say when you say it. You control everyone and everything."

"Yes?" Pan chuckled. "That's why it's so much fun!"

"It's not!" Crimson light burst from me. "You kill the Lost Boys if they disobey you. You cut off Hook's hand and fed it to Tick-Tock. You tried to poison me. You tried to get the mermaids to eat Wendy! Neverland was supposed to be a refuge—you've turned it into a prison!"

Pan's face twisted into a sneer. "You're the one that brought me here, Tink. And now *Wendy-bird* has convinced you to abandon me?"

Wendy flinched at the mocking tone he used on her nickname.

I flew in front of her, like I could protect her from Pan's wrath, even as minuscule as I was. "I would have followed you anywhere. Until you showed me that you don't have to grow up to lose your innocence."

Thunder tumbled through the skies. Beneath our feet, the world rumbled.

Teeth bare, Pan whipped his dagger out of its sheath, lowering it toward us. "You'll never leave."

Hook unsheathed his cutlass. He sliced it toward Pan's weapon, and they met with a loud *clink* of clashing metal. I buzzed back and settled on Wendy's head, gripping her red locks for balance.

"Go, Wendy!" Hook bellowed.

Peter spun around. With a grunt, Hook intercepted the blow once more.

Neverland itself seemed to revolt.

The ground pitched beneath our feet, and the other inhabitants cried out. One of the pirates tumbled into the water as a fissure split under him. The mermaids swarmed the poor fellow before anyone could help, their voices raised with excited laughter. The crocodile's great jaws snapped in the air as it scoured for another victim.

Tick-tock. Tick-tock. Tick-tock.

The chasm raced toward us. It tore the ground asunder faster than anyone could move, a wicked earthquake.

The world collapsed around us.

My stomach flew into my throat. Wendy shrieked, one frantic hand shooting out for the cliffside to find some kind of hold. She latched onto a thick vine, her momentum cutting off, and slammed into the wall of dirt. The blow almost dislodged me again, and I let out a piercing shriek. I grabbed onto Wendy's hair, dangling precariously from just a few measly locks. Below us, water rushed into the newly-formed canyon, as did prowling mermaids.

"Come swim with us, Wendy," one called with a giggle.

"Wendy!" Hook yelled. "I'm coming!"

Pan cackled. Their blades clashed again, but I couldn't get a good view of the fight from there.

"If you save her, Hook, I'll gut everyone here and no one can do anything about it. You can't kill me or this whole world dies too. I'm the host of Neverland, and you'll all *do as I say*!"

Wendy grunted. Her hand slipped a bit further. "No, Hook! Keep holding him off. We'll handle this!" She adjusted her grip on the vine. "Tink—I need pixie dust!" Her feet slid across the cliff face but could find no hold. With each move, more dirt fell into the depths below.

The storm buffeted us, as if it, too, wanted us to join the mermaids down below.

Snap.

I screamed before my mind could register the situation, and everything blurred together. Neverland shook. Part of Wendy's vine cracked. Though it didn't sever, we fell a few more inches. The shock stole my breath for a heartbeat until I cried out even louder than before.

"Aren't you going to save your Wendy-bird?" Pan jeered.

Hook and Pan's swords met with a *clang*. "Maybe I'll kill you instead," Hook rasped. "End it once and for all."

"You can't!" I yelled. I clung to Wendy's hair still, like she hung to the vine, both of our holds precarious and feeble. But Hook couldn't kill Pan, or else—

"Do it," Pan taunted. "Then you'll never get free. Without me, all of Neverland will disappear in an instant. *Give up*, Hook. You can't win."

Wendy grunted and reached up higher, but the vine twisted. The plant fibers frayed more, and I could feel the certainty of our death in my bones.

"I need pixie dust, Tink," Wendy begged. "Please."

My light flashed ashy once more. "I can't—"

"You have to!" Wendy's eyes filled with tears.

"It'd take a miracle," I said, my voice thick and clogged. Rain blurred my vision, or perhaps it was the tears that rolled down my face. "Pan almost killed me."

"I believe in a miracle," Wendy murmured. "I believe in you."

Her warm words settled inside my chest, just like magic. They blossomed inside me as one child's belief took hold, filling every crevice in my body. My tears dried as the death in my bones thawed away. Her belief shone out from deep within my soul, and—

A flicker.

A solitary sprinkle of pixie dust floated down onto Wendy's freckled nose.

Another one . . . then another . . .

Wendy laughed as her body started to lift. She soared into the sky with childish glee on her lips, a stark contrast to the chaos as Hook and Pan's swords collided with metallic *shings*.

Quiet as a bird, Wendy alighted behind Pan and captured his arms from behind. He kicked and bellowed, legs up in the air, like he intended to fly off with her in tow. Wendy grunted and wrestled him back down, receiving an elbow to the face for her efforts.

"*Don't*." Hook wrenched Pan away and wrapped his arms around the struggling boy. Trapped in Hook's immobilizing bear hug, Pan could only batter Hook's shins and spew empty threats. "It's over, Pan. Tink is free now. We can make it to the Second Star."

"Can you?" Pan stilled in his arms. "Go on, Tink. See if you can make everyone fly." His beady eyes locked with mine, and I saw a malicious glee on his face that chilled my bones more than the rain.

My sprinkles started to falter.

"Hurry, Tink." Rain plastered Hook's dark hair across his brow. "We have to help everyone."

I could do it. I had helped Wendy. I *would* save the others.

I darted among the survivors. From Tiger Lily to the Lost Boys, I spread my pixie dust as far as it would go, spurred by the belief of my friends.

"The more pixie dust you use, Tink, the less effective it'll be!" Pan screeched with laughter, like a child so pleased with a new toy. "I'll fly faster. Higher. There won't be a place you go that I won't hunt you down!"

The golden pixie dust that decorated Wendy's freckled face started to fade. The specks turned gray around her. "Don't listen to him, Tink! He's lying. You can take everyone and go."

"But Pan—"

"I'll hold him down." Hook tightened his grip on the squirming Pan. "You girls have to go and lead everyone. I'll handle Pan . . . I'll stay."

Wendy shook her head. "No—*no*! We're not going to leave you behind. We're not escaping unless everyone can!"

My heart hammered in my chest, and my light flashed an anxious gray. "I—I'll try harder. We'll . . . we'll tie him up. *Something*."

"There's no time and no supplies. And if we tied him up, he'd just escape." Hook grunted as Pan landed another hard blow to his knee.

"I'll kill you *all*," Pan snarled. "I'll hunt you down. Nobody can escape from *me*! I'm the cleverest, the fastest boy alive!"

Wendy ignored him. "Hook, we can do *something*." Tears flowed freely down her cheeks.

Hook's gaze softened, and his voice carried a soft tone as he said, "I told you girls. It's my job to make sure *you* get back home safely." He nodded to me. "Tink, you have to go now. We all have to do our part."

Pan snapped his teeth at Hook's arm. Hook grunted when a bite landed, jerked his arm up to punch the boy back, and squeezed his neck in a chokehold. Pan spat in our direction, but Hook had his forearms and neck caught now.

Casting a sorrowful glance to Wendy, I buzzed closer to the survivors. With a dusting of my magic, the Neverland natives took to the skies. Few of them would wait around to see the end of the battle, and I did not blame them. With so many using my recently-poisoned magic, I had no idea how long it would keep them aloft.

"But . . ." Wendy croaked.

Hook shook his head. "Fly, Wendy-bird. This is how it was always meant to end. Hook and Pan, Pan and Hook. The first Lost Boys, the last two to remain."

Behind us, the mermaids and Tick-Tock lashed out in futile attempts to snag the escaping survivors from the air. My anxious gray melted into a deep, sorrowful blue as I landed on Wendy's shoulder and latched onto her ear.

"Hook . . . what if I gave you some pixie dust . . ." I began.

"I can't leave. Ever. Not if it risks him getting out." Hook grunted as Pan elbowed his stomach and kicked his shin. The perpetual youth flailed about, biting at the air until his face turned red. "Please, *go*. I can only hold him down for so long."

"Promise me you'll come find me in London. Somehow, someday." Wendy sniffled, and I patted her cheek, though tears burned in my eyes, too. "*Promise*."

A wisp of a smile passed across Hook's face, though his mouth trembled, and red rimmed his eyes. "Fly, Wendy-bird. Second Star to the right and straight on 'til morning."

Wendy choked on a sob, and my light flashed a despondent blue. Hook grunted as Pan landed a heavy blow to his chest. We couldn't even give him a goodbye hug. Wendy and I rose to the sky with hearts so heavy it was a wonder we didn't sink right into the Neverland Sea. The storm intensified above us. Pan cursed and raged below us, but Hook held firm.

Ahead of us, the Second Star grew brighter on the horizon, beckoning us home.

To home.

To family.

To *freedom*.

"It'll take a miracle for him to escape," Wendy whispered, her voice hollow. "We'll never see him again."

I glanced back over my shoulder. I could see Hook and Pan, two smudges on the horizon, forever locked in battle. It seemed impossible that he would escape . . . but not too long ago, it had seemed impossible the rest of us would escape, too. "We've already received one miracle today. You have to believe in a second one, too."

Maybe every one of us could live free—and all it would take was a miracle, a sprinkle of pixie dust, and a single child's belief.

UNKY

ANNE J. HILL

LANDON SAT UP in bed, sweat dripping down his back. He panted, eyes darting around his room. His mind was foggy after such a rough night of little sleep, many tears, and a few drinks. He rubbed his face, wishing his sister's death had been a mere dream.

Sunlight trickled in. He swore. He was late for his meeting with a new client . . . one who had a reputation of not being so forgiving.

Throwing his blanket to the side, Landon jumped out of bed and tugged on fresh jeans. He went to grab the same shirt from yesterday that lay right beside his bed, but pulled back.

He'd thrown up on it last night after seeing his sister zipped into a body bag.

Landon tossed the shirt toward the hamper, missing. The closet door squeaked on its hinges as he pulled it open and threw on the first shirt he saw.

He headed for the door, but stopped to shove socks and shoes on. The coffee maker drew his attention, but he shook his head. *No time.* He pulled his phone off its charger and stashed his car keys in his pocket.

As he reached for the apartment door, he froze.

"Unky?" a small voice said.

He glanced over his shoulder and let out a long sigh. *Right. Mia.* His four-year-old niece was his responsibility now, after his sister . . . He shook his head.

The little girl was sitting on the couch, rubbing her eyes, Mr. Teddy in her arms. "Where are you going?"

"Nowhere, beautiful." He couldn't very well leave her here alone, and there was no way in all of the world that he would bring her along to meet with *this* client, who was prone to acts of violence. Landon swallowed. In fact, none of his *alegal* lawyer work was well-suited for children. It wasn't well-suited for *anyone* who valued common safety. A particularly nasty threat letter came to mind—one that included a severed finger and writing in blood. He shuddered at the memory. He'd handled that situation well enough, but he couldn't have dealings with murderers with Mia around.

He sighed, moving over to the couch. How had he had forgotten about her? It was his *job* to remember the details, but one day in and he was already failing at this guardian thing.

He sat on the edge of the couch by her feet. "How'd you sleep?" He brushed away bright blonde strands of hair from her face. *She looks so much like—*

"Fine." She hugged her stuffed animal tighter.

"Are you hungry?"

She shook her head, paused, then nodded.

"Cereal?"

She frowned. "Pancakes."

"Pancakes it is." His response surprised him. He wasn't usually so quick to accommodate inconvenient requests . . . "Want to watch TV while I make them?" He picked up the remote.

Her eyes widened. "I'm not allowed to watch shows before breakfast. Mommy says—" She winced and looked down.

Landon swallowed. Her mommy wasn't around to make the rules anymore, or to talk to her little girl. Neither of them said anything for a few drawn out seconds. They didn't need words to express what they both were feeling and thinking.

She's gone . . .

Landon cleared his throat. "But do you want to? Watch a show?"

Her face scrunched, and then she nodded. "Yes, please." She rubbed at her eyes.

He leaned over and kissed her forehead. "I love you, Mia."

She just smiled at him and nestled in to face the TV. Landon flipped to some cartoon with a dog and a bear in uniform, then moved to the kitchen. His sister had once told him to make pancakes in bulk and freeze them. She had always given unsolicited advice like that, and that morning he was glad she had. Making food was the last thing he wanted to be doing.

Beats meeting with a violent client, I guess.

He pulled the pancakes from the freezer and dropped two into the toaster, another trick from his sister. Mia's eyes were glued to the TV as he thumbed his phone and texted the client. "*So sorry. Can we do tonight instead? Emergency came up.*"

Landon studied the back of Mia's head. He was going to have to figure out what to do with her. Nothing about his life was set up to accommodate a child. Besides, she'd be safer with someone else. Someone with an honest job. Not someone who worked with criminals under the table to sway cases the way he wanted—*needed.* Someone who didn't get the occasional death threat in the mail.

His phone buzzed. "*This happens again, and I'm finding a different lawyer. Don't mess this up for me, Landon. 6 p.m.*"

Landon blinked at the text. That had gone much better than expected. "*6 p.m. sharp,*" he replied. Now what to do with Mia come 6 p.m. . . .

The toaster popped. Landon plated the pancakes, doused them in butter and syrup, and set them on the table. "Breakfast, honey." He paused the show, getting a scowl in return.

"But the show . . ." She pointed at the screen. Her bottom lip quivered. Landon knew if he pushed her, this could turn into a melt down. He'd seen it before at his sister's house and, after yesterday, he was sure her little head was a minefield of confusion ready to explode.

"You know what, if you come sit and eat your breakfast, you can watch the show as you eat, okay?" He was sure his sister would have a million resources telling him how that was not good for her, but so was not eating breakfast . . . and Landon was just trying to survive this morning.

Mia's face wrinkled. "Okay." She jumped up, hugging Mr. Teddy, and wiggled onto the dining chair.

"Thank you." Landon pressed play. He sat beside her and dug into the toasted pancakes. Mia deserved better than this. Someone who knew what they were doing and how to care for her better than he ever could.

Mia finished her pancake and stared down at her syrupy plate. "Unky?" Her voice cracked.

Landon tensed. "Yes, honey?"

She wiped her face and looked up at him with watery eyes. "Is mommy gonna come back?"

Landon's stomach churned. His jaw tightened and he forced his mouth open. "No, baby. She's with your daddy."

She seemed incredibly small as she hugged Mr. Teddy to her chest. Her eyes glistened as she said, "Are you gonna go away, too?"

He'd never been more gutted by any question in his life. This poor girl had lost her father when she was only a baby, and now her mother. She'd never met her grandparents. Landon was the only family left, and he'd been so busy wondering if he should have someone else care for Mia that he hadn't even considered the fact that she was his only family left, too.

He pinched his eyes shut and breathed out. "No, honey. I'm not going anywhere." He felt a few tears trickle down his cheeks. But he knew he couldn't raise her like this, and not here. Landon opened his eyes and ruffled her hair. "Let's wash up those sticky fingers and get back to your show, yeah?"

Mia nodded and squirmed off the seat. Landon followed her over to the kitchen sink. He sat her on his knee as she washed her hands exactly how her mother had taught her. The pair curled up on the couch with blankets and pillows. "Unky?"

"Yeah?"

Mia wrapped her arms around his neck. "Love you," she whispered into his ear.

Landon pulled her closer. Something in his chest snapped and he planted a kiss on her head. "I love you, too, peanut."

When 6 p.m. rolled around, Mia was busy cutting paper snowflakes at the table, and Landon scoured the internet for a new home and job. Somewhere his old clients couldn't find them, and a job that didn't get him threat letters.

At 6:05, he received a text saying his client was firing him and taking his money elsewhere. Fear and uncertainty tightened around his throat. He'd been doing this job for years and wasn't sure he knew how to move on, but when he looked up at Mia taping paper snowflakes together with her tongue out in concentration, he knew the struggle would be worth it.

MOTHERHOOD

ALI NOËL

I would save you from yourself
and I try, a million little times
You hate me for a minute, or two
but it's a sacrifice I'm willing to make
To love you better
To help you see
True freedom comes with restraint
denying the flesh, self-control
I'm still learning this myself
In a perfect world, I'd give you everything you want
break boundaries down, indulge without limit
But my desire is the freedom of your souls
and only through surrender
will you truly be free
I look to the Father, *show me how to mother!*
that my children would believe
mercy is good, grace is enough, we are perfect in weakness
The path to freedom is paved in sacrifice

4,380 DAYS

ANDREA RENAE

4,380 DAYS traveling away from the sun instead of around it.

My fingers trace the small tin in my palm.

As many nights, I've laid awake wondering if something more permanent than sleep would find me. Listening for the sounds of traffic, for a distant siren, for rain on the roof. For my husband's deep breaths beside me. Anything other than the vacuum of space.

Those are things I only hear in my dreams.

I squeeze the container tight. It buckles under the weight of my fingers, then springs back into shape with a *pop* that hurts my ears.

Seventy-two planets and breathtaking alien landscapes I'll never get to share with anyone. Ice volcanoes and diamond clouds dripping with razor rain. Soft ground that wailed when I touched it and poison fog-shrouded forests. I used to describe these things to myself, to pretend that any of it mattered, until the sound of my own voice scared me.

None of it was what I came to find, though I can't remember what that was anymore, or who I'm doing this for. I recognize nothing—not the constellations, not the ship. Not myself. Just this cold, aching loneliness.

The metal warms underneath my touch.

Warmth. Life. Wasn't that the mission? To find a place of new beginnings, where humanity stands a chance to survive?

To survive *what*?

I card my thoughts like wool to tease out any useful strands. The heat of the metal in my palm triggers an image of sitting by a wood stove, and then I remember. The firestorm—a great calamity scientists predicted will hit Earth in three generations' time.

Three generations minus the 4,380 days I've spent in this spacecraft.

My eyes hitch on the lines drawn onto the titanium wall with permanent ink, one for each lonely day.

I hold the tin of salve beneath my chin. Crystalline tears drift out of my reach, splashing the faded photos taped above the consul. I blink, taking in the faces I once knew. A name drifts to me like a whisper.

Jess . . .

She will be a teenager now.

I twist the lid.

She will be a stranger now.

The mingled scent of coconut, rosemary, and bergamot swirls with the reawakening of my grief, carrying tender images of cradle cap on a downy infant head and my husband's calloused hands as he gently rubbed the salve in.

This. This painful, precious jar of memory is the real reason I'm out here. Why I can't give up now.

A universe away and 4,380 days later, the fragrance still brings me back home.

BREAKING PROTOCOL

CRYSTAL BAILEY

I CAN NOW only watch the past, not move through it. It's part of my punishment for breaking protocol six months ago. For eight hours a day, I stare at the massive holographic screens which cover the walls of our semi-circular monitoring room and report any unusual or concerning activity I see to the Oversight supervisor. The rest of the time, I'm locked inside my living quarters.

Before I became the law-breaking pariah of Travel Station Two, I was a Traveler. Travelers are the ones who get all the prestige and attention around here: the local celebrities. Of course, that's not saying much with only four-hundred people per station. But time-traveling is an art, and not everyone can handle its demands—both physically and mentally.

The reason I now find myself in this predicament is because six months ago I broke protocol by going off mission in order to rescue a little girl from a kidnapper in the year 2042. Any unauthorized Traveler interference that is not part of the mission, or first approved by the council, is strictly forbidden. It's our most absolute rule, valued above all else by our superiors and our government—even above our very lives.

My mother, a respected training supervisor here, pleaded with the council on behalf of her only daughter for leniency. The council showed me mercy, sentencing me to various menial tasks around the station instead of reporting my conduct to the government, which would have resulted in my imprisonment.

But I also believe my reputation of being one of the best Travelers on this station played a part as well. If I play nice and continue to comply with the terms of my punishment, the council will allow me to resume my time-traveling duties soon.

I've done whatever was asked of me without complaint over these past few months and have finally earned enough of their trust back to work my way up to monitoring duty. My job now is to monitor our Travelers while they're on location in the past by watching their live bodycam footage sent from the tiny cameras they wear to the corresponding screen here in the monitoring room. Every aspect of our program focuses on guiding our Travelers toward strategic, yet subtle, encounters they can have, or missions they can carry out that will hopefully result in a shift of the Earth's societal trajectory, rescuing us from our past mistakes.

A surly guard stands at the entrance of my monitoring room, watching me like a hawk to make sure I don't break any rules. He has no comprehension of what my job entails. He just knows I can't leave this room until my shift is over, at which time he will escort me back to my living quarters and then lock me inside until my next shift begins.

I sigh, studying the wall screens in an alternating pattern, looking for anything unusual and making occasional notations for my daily report when something warrants it. I turn at the sound of hushed voices behind me to find it's time for the changing of the guard. Mac, the friendly older guard, smiles and winks at me as the surly guard stalks out of the room, the door automatically sliding shut and locking behind him. Now that it's just us, Mac greets me. "Hey, Isla. How's it going today?"

"Oh, it's going," I say without enthusiasm, slumping lower in my chair.

"Well, if you don't cause any trouble for yourself, you'll be back at your old job soon enough."

"Yeah, I know," I mumble.

Something on one of the holo-screens catches my eye. I focus on screen nine and zoom in. This one holds a personal interest for me. My ex-boyfriend, Bennett—the jerk who dumped me as soon as I was stripped of my prestigious job title as a Traveler, then began dating another girl two weeks later—is on assignment in California, attending an important conference that took place in 1997. Bennett's camera shows him walking down the alleyway behind the building where the conference will be held soon, but something happening at the other end of the alleyway looks suspicious.

My eyes widen as three people from my timeline approach Bennett. I recognize them. They used to be Travelers assigned to Travel Station One. A couple of months ago they went rogue, along with a group from Travel Station Four. These rogue Travelers no longer believe what we're doing is the right course of action. They are now convinced that altering the past will result in devastating, unforeseen consequences, and are determined to put a stop to our program by any means necessary. They've kidnapped three Traveler's already, giving them the choice to either join their cause, or die.

One of the rogues draws a stunner from inside his coat. Bennett reaches for his own stunner, but he's not quick enough. I crank up the volume on Bennett's holo-screen just in time to hear the rogue order Bennett to keep his hands in the air, turn around, and walk toward a parked van at the other end of the long alleyway.

I jump out of my chair and bring my portacom to my mouth, ready to alert the Oversight supervisor just as I've been instructed to do in a situation like this. He will then contact the council.

Instead, I pause, heart pounding, biting my lip, watching as Bennett continues walking toward the van with his arms up. At this moment, I realize a small part of me still loves Bennett. I don't want him back or anything, it's just that he used to be a really sweet guy before he let all the attention and fame that Travelers get go to his head. I still remember that old Bennett, so falling out of love with him is going to take some time, even though it's for the best. This unwanted, lingering love is what's about to force me to defy my orders and ignore standard protocol. If I don't, Bennett is as good as dead.

The moment he gets into that van, the rogues will no doubt work quickly to remove the small chip located just underneath the skin on his left shoulder, eliminating our ability to retrieve him from the past, or even locate him. Just like they did with the other Travelers.

I spin around. "Mac, I have to retrieve Bennett before the rogues remove his chip. You know the council almost never grants permission to intervene. They only care about the mission and maintaining a low profile. Bennett's life is disposable to them." I hear the desperation, the panic, in my own voice.

If Mac helps me, he could be fired, or worse. Me? I'll never be a Traveler again, and I'll probably face several years of imprisonment down on the surface.

Mac surprises me by removing his key card from his jacket pocket. "You'll need this to access the transport rooms. I'll say I forgot it was inside my pocket, took off my jacket, and left it on the table. You stole it and escaped."

I take the offered key card with a brief smile, ready to break into a run.

"I still have to alert security," Mac adds, just as I'm about to take off.

I nod in understanding, then sprint into the corridor and head straight for the transport rooms.

As I round the corner, I stop short when I almost slam into another Traveler—a young woman named Elodie. "Sorry," I mumble, head down, attempting to go around her. She grabs my arm to stop me.

"You're not supposed to be out here alone, Isla. Where's your guard?" Elodie narrows her brown eyes at me, digging her bony fingers into the soft inner flesh of my arm.

"I don't have time for this," I growl, then use my free arm to deliver a hard blow to her face. Elodie cries out in pain and releases me, reaching for her nose. I sprint past her just as the sound of several pairs of standard issue security boots pounding against the linoleum on the other end of the corridor warn me that my time is short. I slide to a stop at the entrance of the first transport room, remove the key card from my back pocket with a shaky hand, and scan it.

The door unlocks and opens. I breathe a sigh of relief to find the room empty and rush to the transport pad, entering my mother's access code in the panel next to it since mine has been revoked. When I gain access, I quickly bring up Bennett's Traveler profile and enter return instructions as fast as I can. I just hope I'm not too late to bring him home.

I scramble to put on some eye protection just before a blinding flash of light covers the entire transport pad. Despite the thick, dark glasses, I still look away. When I turn back, Bennett is standing on the transport pad. I remove my glasses and look him over. His sandy blonde hair is disheveled and he has a giant red welt on one cheek—probably from putting up a fight inside the van—and his shirt has been cut away to expose his left shoulder. I brought him back just in time. He also looks disoriented, which is normal for the first few seconds after time travel—but he's here, he's safe.

"Isla?" Bennett steps off the transport pad. He's still a little wobbly, but he walks toward me, closing the gap between us. "You saved me from those rogues. How did you—?"

Security is outside the door. A second later, they burst into the room, weapons drawn, and shout at me to step away from Bennett and get on the ground. I look at Bennett once more, then lower myself to the floor in compliance.

While the other security officers keep their weapons trained on me, one of them holsters his stunner and moves toward me. He grabs me by my elbow and roughly lifts me to my feet. "Come on, let's go," he barks. "Now!" He doesn't even bother to cuff me, just yanks on my arm, dragging me to the exit.

"Hey!" Bennett shouts at the officer. "She's cooperating. No need to be so rough."

The officer mutters a few curse words under his breath, but relaxes his grip a little.

"I'm sorry, Isla. About everything," Bennett says as I'm led away.

I look over my shoulder and hold his gaze until I pass through the doorway, out of sight.

My feet are heavy as I walk down the corridor, like they're made of lead. My heart is heavier. I fight against a rising panic and overwhelming sense of loss the further I get from the transport room because I know I will never travel through time again. Since as far back as I can remember, my solitary dream was to become a Traveler. But saving Bennett was more important than living out my dream.

I paid a high price for Bennett's freedom, for his very life. And though it's a very hard pill to swallow, I choose to accept my fate without bitterness because I understand those things never come cheap.

FOR BABI

BEKA GREMIKOVA

In the beloved memory of my grandmother, Tatiana,
who passed away July 4, 2016

She smiles softly at me, this grandmother
I have never known
A black and white photograph
Her lips dark, perhaps from

thick red lipstick

I like to think we have—had—

have

that in common.

She is maybe twenty-five years old
(I am almost twenty-four)
If you misread her name, you would see a fairy queen

If you read her name correctly, you couldn't possibly see
everything.

When did she last smile at me, this grandmother
I knew for twenty-three years
Soft thin lips trembling as they grinned
Her voice high, thick with the accent
of a war-torn motherland who pushed
her out of a womb and across a sea
into the arms of a husband
into the toil of farm life and children
into a Canada that didn't know Russia
from Ukraine, didn't know Ukraine from Poland—
didn't care, as long as taxes were paid.

I knew nothing about her for twenty-three years
Didn't know she had sneaked food into her labour camp
Didn't know she had worked in a circus
Didn't know she had given my father her adventurous spirit
Didn't know that spirit of his had first belonged to her
Didn't know that my ability to adapt through heartbreak
Perhaps started with her,
in her soft sweet smile.

When she last smiled at me, this grandmother
I knew and never knew
was slumped in a hospital bed, her mind
gone back to that motherland, clawing to get back in.
Asking for friends, sisters, I had never heard of.

I wonder if, before she died, she saw Ukraine
as she might have remembered it. I wonder if
I will ever be able to visit that place, and see it
as she would have wanted me to.

I wonder if, one day, I will see her in Heaven
and see her as the woman in the photo
(or the woman in the hospital bed)

or as someone completely new—

the woman I loved and never knew.

NOT ENOUGH

JESS BRADY

THE HMSA ROMATANIA sailed west through the sky, her massive solar-powered sails absorbing the rays from the setting sun. Reginald Van Litber leaned over the airship's ornate railing and gazed at the mountain tops beneath him protruding through orange-tinted clouds. This luxury passenger ship allowed him the quickest air voyage home. A moment of quiet reflection away from fellow passengers was just what he needed after a tedious day. As a prestigious ambassador serving in Her Majesty's court, Reggie always attracted attention. This past week on board had been spent dodging political conversations from the men and unwanted flirtations from the women. For years, his consuming ambition was to negotiate peace between his beloved country Romatania, and the neighboring I.S.N. He patted his brocade vest pocket containing a ruby-studded band. Evelyn, his secret sweetheart, had waited long enough. *I've finally succeeded, now it's time to turn over a new leaf. One more day, Evelyn . . . I cannot wait to hold you again.*

Reggie's mind wandered as he twirled the ring between his fingers. Footfalls soon interrupted his musings. He turned to see his valet approaching with a black evening coat draped across his arm, top hat in hand. Martin was a loyal friend, and although not much older than himself, a wise confidant. "You left these at dinner sir," Martin said as he held out the garments.

"Blast. Thank you, Martin. I'm distracted tonight."

"Will you be needing anything else, sir?"

"No, thank you. Go and enjoy your dinner."

"Very good, sir . . ." Martin lingered a moment. "It will be good to be home again."

"Yes. Yes, it will."

Reggie watched Martin descend the main stairs at the center of the ship just as a stream of first-class passengers ascended from the dining hall. Servants followed, carrying bright lanterns to set the ambiance for a leisurely evening. He donned the hat and coat, preparing to feign sociability. As he strolled around groups of conversing passengers, he noticed a strange whirring noise off to his left. *Must be the backup engines.* The young lady he was introduced to at dinner approached him in a corseted, blue evening gown and began to chatter coquettishly. *What was her name again? Her hair is the same auburn as Evelyn's.* That whirring noise grew, distracting him from her conversation. The sound morphed into mechanical vibrations and Reggie saw more people turn their heads to listen.

An explosion wracked the far side of the ship and the deck shook. Smoke filled the air and the lady screamed before fainting away in his arms. *What the blazes is going on?* Social pretenses were dropped as everyone shared shock and panic. Adrenaline coursed through Reggie's body as he carried the lady amid the throng until he spotted the white uniform of a medical aid who could revive her. The buzzing came again, another boom sounded, and debris from the *Romatania* launched into the air. Crew members seemed to appear out of nowhere wearing bright vests and goggles, directing screaming passengers to remain calm and move away from the damage. *I must find Martin.*

Reggie turned against the flow of the crowd to head back to the main staircase. He lost his footing when the airship suddenly pitched portside. He slid across the tilted deck and smacked into the railing, saved from careering overboard. The pain from the impact spread across his chest as he watched his top hat tumble into the cloudy sky. Screaming men and women piled around and on top of him. He tried to cry out, but couldn't even draw a breath. *God help me, I'll be crushed!*

Momentary relief finally came as the *Romatania* leveled. Freed from the crushing weight and bony elbows, he sucked in a deep breath. Another explosion resulted in the deafening crack of splitting wood. Reggie scrambled to get away as the ship's mast crashed against the deck. The humming noise zoomed by again, louder, closer. He looked up to see the unmistakable outline of a sleek

I.S.N. airship of war cutting through the darkening clouds at an astonishing speed. He cursed to himself. *It can't be . . . Why would they break our treaty?*

Two other enemy airships circled the damaged *Romatania* and fired their cannons. Their shriek and subsequent boom consumed Reggie's thoughts as he crouched down among the passengers with nowhere to hide. The firing ceased, the ships disappearing as quickly as they had come. Reggie stood and looked around, overwhelmed by the destruction. Acrid smoke billowed from below and more passengers crowded the deck, seeking to escape lower levels. *Martin, where are you? There's no way I'll find you in this chaos.* Reggie pushed aside the panic and focused on what he could do: help those trapped underneath the sails. As he wrestled with the heavy material laced with solar-absorbing wires, men and women were able to crawl free. Other men followed his example and joined in, adrenaline fueling their heavy labors. A familiar voice stammered between coughs, "Sir, are you all right?"

"Martin! Thank heaven! Yes, I'm unhurt. What—"

"I'm fine . . . fire below deck . . . Who would attack an unarmed ship?"

With a tremor in his voice, Reggie answered, "The I.S.N."

Martin's coughing stopped for a moment and worry clouded his usually stoic eyes. "But . . . the treaty?!"

An announcement interrupted over the loudspeaker. "This is Captain Wilton ordering evacuation to starboard for all passengers. The fire cannot be contained much longer. Women and children first. May God have mercy on us all." Uninjured crew members raced to prepare the emergency sky rafts and unlock trunks containing glider packs. Reggie, Martin, and the other passengers chaotically maneuvered through the smoke and around debris. Women and children lined up first to cram into the sky rafts. Reggie watched the operators start up the small steam-powered engines of the rafts. *These blasted things don't look capable of flying anyone safely to the ground.* The men clustered around him, waiting to see if there would be room enough for escape.

These moments of inactivity, after the adrenaline rush, drove panic to the front of Reggie's mind. He heard another explosion as the fire caused more damage below deck. *We have to get off this ship before the engines fail . . . and we fall out of the sky!* He turned to Martin. "So many left to evacuate!"

Martin had no answer but placed a reassuring hand on Reggie's arm before suffering another coughing fit. They watched as the last of the women and children piled into the sky rafts. *God help them make it to the ground.* These emergency aircraft were safe enough, though notorious for unreliable landing mechanisms. *No telling where they will end up.* Reggie noticed the now disheveled auburn hair of the lady he helped not a half hour ago. *Seems like hours ago.* The image of a more familiar auburn adorned head flashed in his mind. *Oh Evelyn, how you will worry!* He realized word of the attack would reach her sooner than any accurate information regarding survivors. As he mused, injured men were assisted into the remaining rafts.

Crew members wearing glider packs began distributing packs and goggles to the waiting men. Reggie strained to listen to the rapidly shouted instructions for pulling the glider wing's deployment cord. Martin strapped on his glider and just as Reggie reached for one, the *Romatania* lurched and all the men tumbled to the deck. The warships had returned, firing their cannons. The grinding shriek of metal ripped through the air. Shock prevented audible speech, but one thought overwhelmed Reggie's mind. *engines gone, it's over.* The whirring warships sprayed machine-gun fire haphazardly across the deck before disappearing again. A man fell at Reggie's feet, his crumpled body askew in an unnatural position. Pain shot across Reggie's shoulder as he stared, horrified, into the eyes of the dead man. Then everything went dark.

Moments later, Reggie awakened, and Martin's face slowly came into a hazy view. "You've been hit. I'm taking you to the raft." Reggie struggled to stand on the leaning deck, grinding his teeth as pain throbbed. Blood streamed from the wound in his shoulder. He leaned on his friend for support and stumbled to the railing in front of the last raft. As they approached the operator yelled, "Taking off now! Room for one more!"

Martin moved forward to load Reggie when a hysterical young man shoved past them and leaped into the raft. It launched, and it was Martin's turn to curse. He helped Reggie sit down and ran to grab another glider. Reggie slumped, face in hands, desperate to clear his foggy mind. Martin soon returned, empty handed. He crouched to Reggie and desperately murmured, "Not enough." Martin looked around, counting a dozen or more men without means of escape. Those who did have gliders already jumped overboard. He unhooked the glider from his own back and reached for Reggie.

Those fatal words echoed through Reggie's pain-addled consciousness. *Not enough.* Reggie looked up and realized what Martin was doing.

"Martin, you have a daughter to think of . . . put it on quick!" He shoved the glider back towards Martin. *Before it's too late.*

“I won’t leave you.”

“You must go! And take this . . .” Reggie reached into his blood-soaked vest pocket and pulled out the ring. “Tell Evelyn . . . I love her, and I’m sorry.” Martin took the ring with shaking hands and managed to secure it inside his vest pocket. Voice heavy with emotion he said, “Grab onto me . . . We can glide down together.”

The *Romatania* tilted forward and plunged toward the mountains. Screaming men careened into the night. Reggie and Martin struggled to find a hold as they slid down the deck. They were stopped by a tangled piece of the solar-sail bunched against the railing. Martin repeated desperately, “Grab onto me, I won’t leave!” Martin clasped Reggie’s left forearm.

“We are too heavy . . . won’t make it.”

Reggie reached forward with his right hand and yanked Martin’s deployment cord. “Goodbye, my friend.” Reggie choked out the words and let go of Martin as the glider wings unfolded and caught the wind, sending Martin gliding into the night. For a desperate moment, Reggie’s injured body screamed to jump in a vain grasp for survival.

Lord, have mercy. I love you, Evelyn.

The *HMSA Romatania* hurtled to her demise, a blazing streak against a dark sky.

THE PRICE OF GOING

B.R.R. CANNON

I LIE ON the battlefield and stare at the cloudless sky. My limbs feel cold, but my chest is warm from the growing pool of blood. The din has faded into a gentle roar that reminds me of the sea. My home. A place I will never see again.

When the war began, my wife Genevieve hunched over the table, face hidden in one hand while our newborn daughter snuggled in her other arm. She told me with a quivering voice that her aunt and uncle had been killed. Their village on the border with Rovania had been burned.

"Will you go, Silas?" she asked, red eyes meeting mine. Her fingers wrapped around my hand, as though she were afraid I would slip away.

"I couldn't leave you two." It was true. How could I march to the other side of the kingdom and leave Genevieve and little Emmeline without me to guard them? To care for them and provide for them? They were my first duty. My most important duty. We had a large army and a strong king. They would handle it.

Days wore into months. The harvest was hastily gathered ahead of the advancing Rovanian army. The bulk of it was stored here by the sea in hopes that the lack of food would slow the enemy come winter. However, even the bitter winds didn't faze them. They continued to press forward, warming themselves with burning villages. As the ground thawed, they gained speed. By spring, our lines of knights and soldiers dwindled. The capitol was taken, and the king and queen were killed. The princess escaped with a remnant of the army and regrouped not far from our town.

"I saw a placard in the market," Genevieve said. "The princess is pleading for help."

She set a copy of the hurriedly written message in front of me. *Join our forces. Protect Cordovia.*

Silence hung heavy in the air between us. We both knew what it could cost us. I may never return. Emmeline would grow up without a father. Genevieve would have to find a way to provide for them herself. I couldn't bear the thought of leaving them forever.

But I also knew what would happen if I didn't go. It was the same fate that Rovania had inflicted on the rest of Cordovia. The Rovanian army would eventually reach us. They would drag us out of our home and burn it. They would take a sword to each of us as smoke choked the sea breeze. Even with all my courage, my lone sword would not be enough to protect us against so many. But if I went now, my wife and daughter might have a future, even if it was without me.

Though I did not speak, Genevieve knew and she nodded. I would do this for them.

Two days later, I stood before the threshold with a pack on my back and a weight in my chest. I held Emmeline, taking in every one of her tiny, round features. Her mother's eyes and lips. My nose and brows. Her rosy cheeks. She grabbed my face with her soft hands, and I memorized the feel of each little fingertip. I kissed her forehead over and over then held her close.

"I love you, Em. I love you more than you will ever know."

As I pulled her back, those sea blue eyes met mine, and I fought back the ocean of tears that slowly blurred my vision.

Genevieve grabbed my arm. As soon as I set our daughter down, my wife buried herself in my arms. Her shoulders heaved as she sobbed into my chest. I held her close, forcing back my own tears. When she finally calmed, I took her face in my hands and we shared a long kiss.

She looked up at me. There was so much I wanted to say, but the words caught in my throat. Thankfully, she knew what was in my heart. She nodded, gripping my hand in both of hers.

"I love you more than anything," I choked out.

"And I love you."

I scooped Emmeline up again and held both of my girls one last time. Then I handed Emmeline back to Genevieve and clenched the straps of my pack. Words failed me again, but Genevieve understood. She forced a smile as fresh tears welled in her eyes. Mustering all of my courage, I turned away from everything I loved and towards the road I must take.

"Dada!" little Emmeline called as she waved.

I turned and kept a brave face as I waved back. Then I forced my feet forward. All the way to the camp, I wept. By the time I arrived, my sleeves were soaked and my feet felt as heavy as my heart. I dreaded that I might never see them again, but my love for them steadied my hand as I wrote my name on the roster of new recruits.

I spent the next four months with the army. Spring warmed to summer, and the unseasoned troops, comprised of husbands and fathers like me, have become determined soldiers. We do not fight as the army used to. We slip through the familiar forests and surprise the Rovanian army. We hunt them like deer instead of fighting like a trained military. It has worked to our advantage. The Rovanian army has dwindled, and those who remain have been beaten back toward their own lands.

This morning, we launched a fresh offensive in the open farmlands. But it is here, in the middle of a fallow field near the Rovanian border, that I was finally struck down, run through with a sword from behind. Far from home. Far from Genevieve and Emmeline.

Now, the blue sky above is growing dim and my fingertips are numb. The pounding of feet around me is faint, but I do not know if it is because the fighting has spread out or because I am fading—fading from my family's life. I pray it's been enough.

Drifting over the plain like a gull's call, I catch a sound repeated over and over. I force my mind to focus, but it is hard to hear beyond my labored breath. Then, like a crashing wave, I understand. *Victory.* They are shouting, "Victory!"

As I close my heavy eyes, I smile and gentle waves of darkness wash over me. Genevieve and Emmeline will live. They will have a future. And one day, we will be reunited. With one last breath, I am at peace.

MY OLD KENTUCKY DERBY

HANNAH CARTER

LEAVE THE DEAD *to their derby, and they'll leave the living to theirs. The ghosts don't hurt anyone; they come, celebrate, and leave at midnight once a year. Horse races mean a lot to folks around here.*

That's what the old hillbilly had said as he pumped Reynolds's gas earlier that day. But leaving ghosts alone was hard to do as a paranormal investigator, exorcism division. He'd traveled all around the world to send ghosts on, and now, his occupation brought him to Louisville, Kentucky.

Reynolds shuffled through the excited derby crowd as ragtime music drifted on the wind, carried from a bandstand. Smoke lingered in the air, thick as fog.

Everything here was tinged in shades of gray, like a vintage movie from some bygone era, and filled Reynolds with a sense of nostalgia for a time period he had never lived through. To be fair, though, Reynolds's job made him a bit more familiar with the not-so-dead-past.

Sometimes *too* familiar, given his past dating history.

From the press box, a man in a waistcoat and jacket leaned over a microphone until his handlebar mustache almost touched it. "At the gates, ladies and gentlemen, we have Man o' War—a familiar favorite." The fast-talking announcer continued his string of names: Kincsem, Sir Barton, Seabiscuit,

Citation, and Secretariat, among others. They numbered twenty in all, the pride and joy of yesteryear.

Reynolds lifted a cigarette to his lips as a girl with a feather in her hat sashayed past. The fringes on her flapper dress shook as she batted her eyelashes at him.

He flicked the ashes onto the ground. The red embers, as vibrant as the atmosphere, burned in bright contrast to the ghostly surroundings, drained of all color.

He couldn't let a dead girl distract him . . . *again.*

"This your first time at the Kentucky Derby?" A woman sporting a sensible suit and a wide-brimmed hat settled next to him, leaning on the railing. She toyed with the short ends of her hair framing her round cheeks.

Reynolds admired her out of the corner of his eye. She didn't look like a poltergeist who wanted to eat his soul after their date—just a regular old ghost caught in an eternal time loop. A man would only make that mistake once. "Yes, ma'am."

She smiled. "Welcome. It's always the event of the season."

Reynolds nodded. "'The greatest two minutes in sports,' I hear."

"Are you betting tonight? My money's on Seabiscuit." She pointed to the once-bay thoroughbred. "It's surreal, getting to see him race in person. I just wish my brother was here, but he's working under FDR's New Deal. I'm grateful he has a job, but . . . I do miss him when he's so far away."

So this girl still thought it was the Great Depression. Interesting. "Sorry to hear that." Reynolds took a puff of his cigarette. "Maybe you'll be reunited soon." He flicked more ashes onto the ground. Wherever they hit, the ghostly gray faded, revealing the bluegrass underneath. If he circled the whole race track with the embers, this Kentucky Ghost Derby ordeal would be over.

So why dawdle and fraternize with this girl? Why did he let this nostalgia tug at his heartstrings? She was a beautiful face, nothing more. A beautiful *dead* face, as a matter of fact. Her brother had probably long passed from the world, too, even though she was unaware of the passing years.

Behind him, souls crowded in, singing along to "My Old Kentucky Home" at the top of their lungs.

Leave the dead to their derby, and they'll leave the living to theirs.

"What's your name?" his pretty guest continued.

He shouldn't fraternize, but . . . "Reynolds."

"I'm Eliza." She held out her hand. "Look! The race is about to begin."

The horses pawed the ground, kicking up clumps of dirt. The jockeys shifted on their mounts, expressions inscrutable behind their goggles. The band reached a climax, a gunshot piercing the air. The horses burst out of the gates, and the crowd's cheers swelled over the music.

It means a lot to folks around here.

Beside him, Eliza cheered for her steed. Tears glimmered in her eyes, like her hope for her brother lived on, even though *she* didn't.

Reynolds cleared his throat and tucked his cigarette into his mouth. He just wished he could blame the sting of his eyes on the burning nicotine instead of any show of compassion.

"Oh—oh!" Eliza clasped her hands together as Seabiscuit rounded the curve first, just a neck ahead of Man o' War. "He's doing it!"

The hoofbeats increased their frenzied pace. Reynolds imagined none of these legends wanted to lose, but there could be only one winner of the Derby. Seabiscuit's lead shortened. Eliza gasped. The horse's lead lengthened—she cheered.

They don't hurt anyone.

The Derby was too big, his boss had said. If the ghosts tried to escape, Louisville would be doomed. Reynolds ought to finish the job and go. He shouldn't be so enamored by the atmosphere, by Eliza's wholesome sweetness—

Seabiscuit crossed the finish line a nose ahead of Man o' War.

"He did it!" Eliza cried. "He did it!"

She grasped Reynolds's face and planted a kiss right on his lips, like a gentle brush of wind against his skin.

Breathless, she pulled back, her hat askew. Her eyes widened, like she realized her impropriety. "I am so sorry!"

"Don't be." Reynolds cleared his throat and rubbed his flushing face. "I hear this race means a lot to people. Emotions are bound to run high." He could hardly hear their conversation over the wild music and cheers as people rushed the gates to get a glimpse of their champion.

"I just—my brother. He will be so excited! He might get to come home with these winnings!" She chattered about what her family might do with the money, what they must be thinking. Her love and excitement made Reynolds choke up once more . . . though it could have been smoke inhalation.

"I'm very happy for you, ma'am." He dipped his head and shuffled his feet.

They disappear at midnight.

He only had a few more minutes to exorcize this bandstand of people forever—Eliza included—or risk them going rogue one day and escaping into the real world. His boss wanted him to. That was what Reynolds had been *paid* to do.

But was it what his *heart* still wanted to do?

Eliza hugged her winning ticket to her body. Tears sparkled on her cheeks. "You have no idea how much it means to me."

Drat.

With a sigh, Reynolds flicked his cigarette onto the ground and extinguished it with his leather shoe. As the ashes faded, Reynolds watched his job go up in flames. His boss wouldn't be too happy about this disobedience, but Reynolds couldn't bring himself to care about whether or not his boss canned him. Perhaps the old hillbilly had been right about the ghosts being harmless, or maybe Reynolds had succumbed to his weakness for pretty girls once again.

"I think I do." Reynolds tipped his fedora. "I'm glad you enjoyed it."

She beamed. "You too."

"Go find your brother." Reynolds nodded as the clock struck midnight, and Eliza and the ghostly derby began to fade. "I'll see you next year."

KINGDOM

DENICA MCCALL

They didn't know what their unrest was leading to
That it was calling them to a homeless man
A small town craftsman
With cosmic dreams and
Deep, deep love
They didn't understand that
All their action plans had the wrong aim
They targeted empires and
Those who profaned their God's name,
But all the same, empowered the powers that be
To have a say in their lives
When freedom came as a man with dirty feet
Walking the shores of Galilee
Walking from town to town, teaching
Because he was seeking hearts

They didn't know that the need they felt was not for safety
But rather, a wild freedom
That only one Kingdom had ever offered
And for those with eyes to see and ears to truly listen,
They would know

The curious, the misunderstood,
The zealot and the harlot alike,
They would know
Their restless hearts led them home
To rest, not by the world's definition
But this astonishing kind of burden-less work
A freedom to be, to give, to submit
To a king who didn't demand it, but
Only invited
A king who *saw*
A king who offered his own identity
As the rock on which to form our own
So some knew
This paradox of living
Open hearts and bound hands
Ear to ear grins and bloodied backs
Their king, Messiah
Overthrowing not empires, not kings, not evil men,
Oppressors and wicked schemes
But death itself, and any way of thinking
That sought to thieve
Exposed, earnest, hurting, and hungry hearts
Of life
A kingdom beyond the powers of men
Beyond, but among
Bending down, he washed our dust, our grime, our tears
Laying down his own worth, his rights, his name
Bleeding, as he unveiled eternity
Many didn't know, but some caught on
This king, he longed for his family
And wasn't that
Worth everything?

WHO I DIE BESIDE

ANNE J. HILL

MY CHEST HEAVES as a cry worthy of shaking the earth tears from my throat. My skull rests back on the wood, on this cross. I can barely fathom what is happening to me. I've seen it done before, even cheered when they tied other criminals to the cross—some people I had dealings with in the past. Scum of the earth that got what they deserved.

And here I am, hanging on a cross at Golgotha.

I wish I could plead with the God I've never loved. But I know I deserve this. Every time I push myself up just to catch a breath, I see flashes of my mistakes. My sins. By law, I should have been here years ago, if they had caught me. I have no idea how many times I promised myself I'd steal just one more time, and then I'd get an honest job, settle down. And now it's too late.

Sweat drips down my brow and stings my eyes. I squeeze them shut and let out a pathetic wail. That's what I am now. Pathetic.

The man on the cross beside me turns his blood-stained head to look at me. His back is torn to shreds, and I can make out muscle and bone—things I've never seen on a living person before. His eyes are filled with agony, and I feel it in my soul. We are in these final hours together. Me and the one they call the Messiah and someone else on the third cross that I don't know.

I chose who I spent my life with, but I have no say in who I die beside.

There's something fitting about dying next to a religious fraud. For a man who's never given God or religion much thought, the irony stirs something akin to humor in me and I smile. But then I feel it in my gut—a feeling I won't be able to find the words to explain.

His eyes are locked with mine, and his face twists in a pain I hope I'll never have to feel. Fresh blood trickles down his skull. His head slumps and tears—or sweat—glisten on his cheeks. I can't take my eyes off of his. And even though there's suffering like I've never seen before written on his very soul, there's light in his eyes. That's the only way I can explain it. Light. Not light that hasn't seen the dark, that hasn't screamed in agony, but still—

Light.

I feel my own eyes shrouded in darkness. That feeling curls in my gut, and for a brief moment it overpowers thoughts of pain, but then it's back. And I'm once more face-to-face with my death—something I somehow thought I wouldn't have to worry about for a very long time.

I don't know who this man is to think he's the son of God, but right now, I'm desperate. What if they're all horribly wrong? What if this *is* God dying beside me?

My heart races. What happens to the world if God is dead?

But it doesn't matter, I realize. Not for me. I won't be a part of this world soon. But what might come next terrifies me. I rack my brain for what I was taught as a child, but I've worked hard to avoid such thoughts for years.

I hear laughing below us, but it hurts too much to look down. The man on the third cross laughs haggardly with whatever was said down below, and adds, "Aren't you the *Messiah?* Prove it, Jesus of Nazareth, and save us." Jesus does nothing. The man scoffs. "That's what I thought."

I am no better than this man, but something in me snaps. What right does he have to mock someone else in his same position? And if this *is* God, I might not have lived a God-honoring life, but I'll be damned if I'll mock God to his face. I push myself up by my feet, wheeze, and sputter, "Don't you fear God?" I get no reply, so I shout it. The man tilts his head toward me. My head is dizzy and I'm desperate to breathe, so I push myself up again, gasp, and add, "We deserve this. He's done nothing wrong. Will you mock him still?"

Will *I* mock him still? I have no proof that this man named Jesus is who he says he is, but I saw the light in his eyes. Jesus looks at me again, and despite the pain on his face, I feel a wave of something I can only explain as love wash over me. Or, what I always imagined love ought to feel like. A shudder runs through me, and I might be losing my mind, but before I can fully comprehend the thought, I whisper, "Jesus, remember me . . . when . . . when you come into your kingdom . . ." I know he can hear me, and I expect him to laugh, even if he is God.

But instead, he says softly, "Truly, I tell you, today you will be with me in paradise."

Tears well up in my eyes. A dying man has no reason to still pretend he's someone he isn't. This is the Messiah, I'm sure of it now. My soul feels splayed out for all to see, but only He can see it. I don't know what I did to deserve such love in my last hours, but something tells me that's the whole point.

And I know when I breathe my last, I will see the Messiah again.

RYDINGER AND THE WOLF

ANDREA RENAE

RYDINGER FLIPPED THE hood over his head as a chill wind whipped around a corner. He clutched the waxed fabric parcel closer.

"You sure about this, Red?" His insides twisted at his cowardice. Nessa deserved better.

The shadow in front of him didn't slow.

"I guess that's my answer," he muttered, quickening his pace to match the towering woman's stride.

"Get the Goods to Old Mother," she finally grunted after they'd passed under the last bar of manufactured green light. "Don't get caught. What else is there to be sure 'bout?"

Rydinger peered behind him. "What exactly am I smuggling?" The alley was empty, but that didn't mean anything. The Wolf could be anywhere.

Just think about your sister. Think about Nessa.

Red turned abruptly, her wiry hair escaping in a haze from under her cap. "That ain't your business. Got it?" Her shrewd eyes landed on Rydinger, as if she could read his insecurities like a computer code. But her gaze eased. "If the Wolf finds you, run. The rest is on you, kid." She jerked her head toward the yawning darkness. "Old Mother's waitin'. Now, *scat.*"

Four steps into the shadows, Rydinger's confidence flatlined. "I'm not sure I'm ready . . ." He turned to the last Light District, but Red had already vanished.

Going through the Black Out Zone was the only option now.

Fumbling to hold the Goods, Rydinger dug inside his jacket. He pulled out a rattly torch and swore when it didn't click on. He smacked it a few times on his knee, sweat beading on his brow. A feeble beam shuddered into existence.

The Boz was a labyrinth of dead ends and dilapidated buildings. All the smugglers had been given a rough map to study. Very rough. Incomplete.

He gripped the electric torch. It was one thing to find something like it, and quite another that it still worked. His sister had chanced upon it years ago, but she was too young to know what it was, or that having it was dangerous. Rydinger had quickly confiscated it.

Now, he was glad he had. With a light to guide the way, the Boz would be just like any other district. Or so he told himself.

He stood straighter.

An hour into climbing through rubble and spooking at several blasted rats, the torch began to flicker.

"No . . . no, no, no!"

It went out.

Darkness swooped in. Rydinger gulped, trying to control his rampaging heart. Why couldn't he remember the map? Nessa had helped him go over it a dozen times. A hundred.

A clatter sliced through the pounding in his ears. He spun toward the sound. The Goods slipped out of his hand, rolling into the surrounding darkness.

The noise again.

"Who's there?"

Footsteps crunched in response. He felt for the cold metal of his pocket blade, flipped it open, and swung it around.

"Peace, child." The voice was feminine. "You'll hurt yourself."

Rydinger flushed but kept the knife raised. He honed in on the stranger's position. "You're the Wolf." He used the name as a weapon.

She sighed, and something heavy scraped against gravel. "Do you know what this is?"

She must have found the Goods. "My ticket out of this hell," he spat.

A soft laugh brushed his senses. "And what if I told you the thing you're using to negotiate freedom is what ensures this city will remain a 'hell?'"

There was a slicing sound, and the Boz filled with impossible light. Rydinger struggled to make his eyes focus. A slight-framed woman wrapped in layers of gray came into view. Her hair was a shimmering cascade without pigment. Countless cares etched her face.

This tired, unassuming woman was the Wolf? The legend that put fear into every smuggler who entered the Boz?

Her street name did not suit her.

"You have a choice." She held out a glowing sphere and dropped the thick fabric that had concealed it. "Take this and work toward purchasing an escape . . ."

He eyed the orb hungrily. All the threats, all the secrecy surrounding the Goods finally clicked into place. "Or?"

"Or give it back to the ones who cannot leave."

The Wolf approached and gently pushed the blade aside.

One choice between freedom and the fate of a cursed city.

"What will you choose?"

Rydinger's eyes lost focus on the dazzling spectacle. It would only take a few orbs to earn his release, but how many more would he need to secure Nessa's? His sister was deteriorating rapidly from the Shadowblight that ravaged the poorer districts, where true light was scarce. And he had been about to hand over the very thing she needed most of all.

His efforts to save her could be the reason she would die.

The untruths and the guilt swirled so violently, he felt sick. But he grasped at one sure thing.

Old Mother was stealing light from the city—light that sick kids needed to survive.

Hot anger cut through his immobilizing thoughts. He grabbed the sphere and hurled it against a wall. It shattered into a thousand luminescent fractals, and he threw out a hand to snag a shard before it could escape. His breath caught as he watched the rest float to the sky. That single orb already made an infinitesimal difference in the gloom. Maybe with enough of them released, light—*health*—would no longer be a privilege for the wealthy.

The woman's illuminated face spread with a smile before she faded into the Boz's oblivion.

Rydinger returned to the Light Districts, armed with truth that left no room for cowardice. He sheepishly reported another victory for the Wolf.

Red was furious, but she bought the lie.

When he returned home to his sister trapped in her Shadowblight sleep, he retrieved the shard from his pocket. The blinding thing burned in his palm. He raised a fist and let the Wolf's gift drift to the ceiling.

Nessa's eyes opened.

Rydinger would do everything in his power to ensure more of them would follow.

UNDERGROUND

KELLY HELLMUTH

GWEN SWALLOWED HARD. Outside the door of her first-floor apartment, a member of the Gestapo pounded and ordered her to open up in German before repeating himself in Dutch. His accent was harsh and his tone offensive, as if he were spitting the words out with disgust. It made Gwen's skin crawl. She couldn't afford to open the door, but she couldn't ignore it either. She had been reckless, and now it could cost everything.

Gwen was a proper Dutch girl who had been raised to look out for those less fortunate than her. That's what put her in this situation in the first place. She had confronted Pieter on their way home from work. He was her best friend for years, but ever since the German occupation, things had changed. Pieter had started hanging out with a different, more arrogant crowd.

These boys would attend meetings hosted by the Reich. Pieter insisted the meetings made him feel like a part of something more important than himself, but Gwen was skeptical. The boys relentlessly harassed weak children while Pieter stood by. Gwen never let Pieter get away with it, and he always promised he hadn't changed. And she believed him. This situation shouldn't have been any different.

But today, Pieter had punched a small girl who accidentally bumped into him on the sidewalk. The girl couldn't have been more than seven. Gwen was absolutely horrified, pulling Pieter off the girl as he pummeled her with all his strength. He turned and swung at Gwen, missing her, before running off in a rage. Gwen knelt before the girl, and that's when she noticed—a yellow Star of David on the girl's coat.

Gwen should never have been so naive. That was only a short time ago. Not nearly long enough to completely relocate the children hidden in the space underneath the floorboards.

Gwen could almost feel their tiny eyes stare up at her between the wooden slats, waiting in terror for instructions. The nook was not deep, but it spanned the entirety of the ground floor, where each resident was part of the Underground resistance. It had served them well up to this point, but now Gwen had brought the Gestapo straight to her door. She hoped the children moved to the space furthest from her apartment at the first sign of trouble. Some might say they were not worth her life, but she knew better. They mattered to her. The pounding continued, and Gwen decided it was time to move quickly.

She turned on the lamp and placed an empty flower vase in the window, signaling to the Underground that she had been compromised. Hopefully, her father would see it and know to avoid their apartment until she was gone—this was no time for him to be a hero. She ruffled her clothes and hair, making it appear as if she had been roused from sleep, and headed for the door. She stopped in her tracks as she heard a tiny whimper underneath the floorboards, and her heart dropped. The youngest boy was crying softly just beneath her. Gwen knelt down, placed her cheek against the floor, and whispered softly to the space underneath.

"Stay silent. Stay strong. Go find the others."

She had to trust that he heard and listened, but it was no longer something she could control. Gwen's stomach dropped as she stood. Her heart beat loudly in her ears, almost drowning out the pounding on the door. She took a deep breath, silencing the building panic.

Gwen considered fleeing. It was possible to follow the children to the exit point. No. That would only endanger them more. She was sure that she was being watched, and her absence would only provoke them to investigate further. It was better for everyone if she faced the soldier alone. One last shudder traveled down her spine before she told herself that it was time. The soldier pounded again. Gwen opened the door.

The man in front of her was formidable. His mouth was set, straight and emotionless, in jarring contrast to the ferocity of his knocking. The cold gray of his Reich uniform matched his unfeeling and distant eyes. Gwen took note that he did not look at her immediately but scanned the room behind her. Her knees threatened to buckle, but she stood as firm as possible and forced herself to yawn.

"Are you Gwen Brouwer?" the soldier barked in his native language.

"I'm sorry, I don't speak German," she responded, rubbing her eyes.

"Why didn't you answer the door? What are you hiding?" He switched to poorly-spoken Dutch, not bothering to repeat himself.

"I was sleeping. I am sick." Gwen faked a cough, praying that it was convincing enough. It caught in her throat for a moment and set off a fit. The soldier stepped back in disgust. Good. A reason to stall.

"We have received a report that you are not loyal to the Reich. Did you stop one of our recruits from doing his job this afternoon?" So it was Pieter for sure.

Gwen bit her lip, the pain of his betrayal mixing with escalating fear. She might break at any moment. "Not on purpose. I am feverish. I didn't know what I was doing."

"Our source says this is not the first time you have been sympathetic towards Jewish scum. You must come with me for questioning."

Gwen glanced behind the soldier and almost collapsed. Her father had come in from the alleyway and had stopped just within view. His eyes were wide, sad, and glistening with tears. He mouthed, "I love you," before turning the corner silently, hopefully making his way to the apartment at the end of the hallway. If the children had all made it, he would usher them out through the city sewers.

She opened her door wide. "Would you like to come in? I can show you there is nothing to hide." She coughed again, hoping to discourage the invitation.

He let out a quick, disdainful snort, the edges of his mouth curling. "I do not want to enter this disgusting place. My subordinates are on their way. If there's anything to find, trust me." He gripped Gwen's arm tightly, and she let out a little yelp. "We will find it. Time to go."

As the soldier dragged her through the hallways, all of the doubts and questions came crashing down inside Gwen's head. How much did Pieter actually know about their involvement in the Underground? What if her father couldn't get the children out in time? And what would become of him and the others? It was only a matter of time—hours even—before the entire operation was uncovered. What had she done? Gwen could not help it, and she began to cry.

A jet-black car was parked on the street. As the first soldier shoved her into the backseat, another vehicle pulled in behind them. A swarm of soldiers raced into the building. Gwen could feel everything breaking. She breathed in deeply and exhaled slowly. It was up to her father now. She had to trust he could handle it. Gwen looked straight ahead as the car drove away, wiping away a tear rolling down her cheek. If even one of the children managed to escape, it would be completely worth it.

A MOMENT TO REMEMBER

ELAINE WELLS

Little socks packed away in cardboard boxes,
little shirts and skirts and pale blue dresses,
pacifiers and rubber ducks,
all the things we couldn't live without,
too much to fit in two boxes,
too much to go through before you get home,
a stuffed lion your mother made for him,
a doll you gave her for Christmas,
books and toys and beautiful things,
my favorite things,
the things I held onto on the bad days,
when I hid from you,
when you tore paintings off the walls,
and ripped the earth from under me,
I held onto little moments like these,
how you'd smile at our daughter,
and hold our son swaddled in that blue blanket,
you told me you'd never hurt them,
and I held onto that too,
I kept that promise like a picture in a locket,
I wanted it to be true so badly,

that portrait of a happy family,
and on the good days,
it was so easy to believe you,
that you were a good man,
a role model,
the kind-hearted surgeon,
the man I thought I married.

You gave everything to me,
and I deserved none of it,
but this isn't about me,
or what is deserved or earned,
it's about them,
because children need more than a father
who beats his wife,
I have to choose better for them,
so I will show my daughter how to leave men like you,
I will teach my son to be kind,
my children will know what love is,
they will know what it looks like,
they will know when they've found it,
because it won't hurt,
or make them feel guilty or ugly,
or broken,
you said you would never hurt them,
but you already have,
without laying a hand on them,
you did more damage than you can imagine,

but it ends today,
because sons often become their fathers,
but they don't need to,
my children will know
it does not have to be this way,
I will not let this cycle continue,
I am choosing better for them.

As I set my wedding ring on the kitchen table,
and help them out the door,
I know this is the best thing,
even as she asks me why I am crying,
even as I cannot find the words to tell her,
as my throat closes around the thought
of what I am about to do,
I know I am doing what I need to,
I do it so they can heal,
so I can heal,
and one day,
I know this will be a thing they hold onto,
a moment to remember.

EMBER

YAKIRA GOLDSBERRY

ALL IT TAKES is opening the door. Violet's left hand hovers inches above the brass knob. The magic that keeps it locked stings her palm. Her fingers shake as she takes a deep breath to calm her racing heart.

There is a prophecy. One that shook the world and upended Violet's life forever.

Violet's very first child born will either save the world or destroy it. And Mikhael wants to be the one to control it.

She never dreamed things would end this way. Six years ago, she believed she'd found the love of her life. Mikhael was the kind of man who charmed his way into her heart with sweet words and gifts. A mighty sorcerer with riches and political power, how could her parents say no when he came to the door to ask for her hand? How could *she* say no?

It was like a dream come true.

What a naive fool she had been. Taking his words at face value. Believing that he was the escape she needed to get away from her drab life. What she hadn't seen until too late was the manipulation. The abuse. How he had drawn her in like a lamb to slaughter.

"Mama?" Ember tugs on Violet's other hand. Violet's daughter looks up at her, wide eyes half hidden by her copper-red curls.

"Yes, darling. Don't worry." She gives her little girl a trembling smile.

It was three weeks ago when she had discovered the real truth of Mikhael's secrets. Why he had lured her in.

There is a prophecy Violet thought long forgotten. One that was spoken in whispers at her cribside, just after her birth. Her parents kept it a secret, but it wasn't long until word spread like wildfire. Violet became a child of prophecy, though instead of being praised in wonder, she was shunned and pushed aside. Violet was determined to believe it wasn't real. After all, some prophecies had been proven to be wrong before. Her parents planned to hide her away, to keep her from ever speaking to another soul until she died.

How suffocating they had been, those three months in isolation. She lived in that tiny cell inside a tower tucked away on the edge of the country, the sea waves beating constantly against the rock below. The memory of it burned into her mind, refusing to let her forget. But then, Mikhael came along. Crouched outside her cell door, saying sweet words and boasting how prophecy meant nothing to him. How he was the only one who believed her, how everyone else was wrong.

How he was the only one who loved her.

She was foolish to ever believe him.

No. She will not allow the prophecy to happen. She will do whatever it takes to keep Ember from turning down that path. To keep her away from her father. Violet grits her teeth and clamps her hand around the knob. Magic races up her arm like electricity—burning her skin, her bones—but she ignores it.

It had taken hours, months, years until Violet finally discovered a way to counter the prophecy. Now she has finally found the courage to escape.

It won't be easy, but Violet is willing to cross a thousand oceans if it means Ember can have any semblance of a normal life. Of course, she never will. Not as a child of prophecy. But Violet wants to give her a home that Ember can feel safe in—a place to grow and thrive without fear of turning into a monster.

The magic glows blue as it crawls up her arm. Violet whispers the counterspell under her breath. For weeks—months—she had carefully, secretly, listened at the door for the counterspell. The moment she heard the words spoken, she repeated them to herself, over and over, lest she forget. Until the words had become engraved in her mind.

Slowly, the magic dissipates, leaving the door free to open. But as she grips the knob tight, her stomach churns.

He will hunt you, a voice whispers in her mind. *He will hunt and kill you. You'll never be safe.*

I will gladly take that risk, Violet growls in her mind. If being hunted means keeping Ember safe, then it is worth it.

He will take ember from you. He'll find you, kill you, and take her. Mikhael will rule the world through her.

I won't let that happen. She looks at her daughter once more. *I've protected her for five years. I can, no, I* will *protect her for more.*

Ember turns away from watching the pendulum swing in the clock. She turns her beautiful, amber eyes up to Violet, her gaze full of precious innocence. One look is all she needs for every fear and doubt to fly away.

She can do this. She has to.

Violet turns the knob. She opens the door. The sky beyond is streaked with brilliant purple and red. Her heart skips a beat. Mikhael will be home soon. If she's to run, it's now.

Firming her grip on Ember's hand, Violet takes her first step toward freedom.

It will be a journey wrought with fear and sorrow. She could even be leading them to their deaths. But at least they will be free. Free to face the world on their own two feet, and decide for themselves how to live their lives.

For the sake of her child, for the sake of the world, she needs to try.

That's all she really can do. One step at a time, she will lead them both to freedom.

ELEANORA AND THE DREAM COLLECTOR

ALI NOËL

I'VE FOUND IT.

The ancient roof moans above me as its crooked shingles whistle in the wind like loose teeth. Upended furniture is strewn across the small, dark room. Its damp floor is littered with tufts of moss creeping through the breaks in the wood. The stagnant air tastes old, and I can't help but wonder the last time human breath disrupted it.

The mirror almost escaped me. Its cracked frame and blackened glass are as aged as the forgotten room which keeps it. Some say it predicts the future. Some claim it shows our deepest desires. Others insist the mirror's reflection is whatever you need it to be.

That's why it's dangerous.

But my reality has become more than I can bear. Whatever the mirror holds for me, it has to be better than my god-forsaken excuse for a life. I should have known better than to make a deal with the Dream Collector.

"'Tisn't a matter of cost, lovey. 'Tis a matter of *worth.* You give a dream to get a dream. That's the deal," she'd said. I can still remember her unnerving violet eyes boring into me from behind a filthy curtain of jet-black hair.

My mother had tried to warn me against visiting that wretched woman. I'll never forget the look on her face as she told me, "Those roadside thieves walk away with your dream in their pocket, and dreams aren't meant for trading, Eleanora!"

I should have listened.

Another savage wind howls over the decrepit roof, as if annoyed with my reluctance to look inside. And so, I take a deep breath and step directly in front of the fractured glass. The dreary room fades away, and I shield my eyes with my hand as a brilliant light shines out from the mirror. Tears stream down my face as I force them to stare into the light. It takes a few seconds, but finally my vision clears.

A woman sits at an elegantly set table within a stunning palace garden. I watch as she arranges a bouquet of wildflowers before tilting her face towards the sun. Even from a distance, with her face turned away, it's clear she possesses a peace altogether foreign to me. The kind of joy that seeps into the bones, filling in life's marks. Little wonder. Hers is a world untouched by the gnarled, merciless hands of tragedy and bondage, neglect, and shattered dreams. It couldn't be further from the world that awaits outside this dilapidated ruin.

There's a likeness to her, but I can't quite put my finger on it. She's like a memory, but I've never known a palace or woman like this. Another older woman joins her with a tea tray, her back turned toward me. I watch as they go about their motions content and unbothered amongst vibrant flora and gentle sunlight. I envy them. They don't strike me as women experienced in crawling through muck and mire like a beast, scouring for scraps of food wherever they can find them. I can't imagine those delicate hands faring a winter in the bowels of the Trench or the foul creatures of the Clearing.

A crow squawks behind me, making me jump. At the same moment, the sitting woman snaps her face in my direction. I frown as unease settles along my gut. She stares straight at me, sending my pulse into a frenzy. I try to make sense of what I'm seeing.

I take in her high cheekbones and wide-set mouth. She lifts a hand and tucks her long auburn hair behind her right ear, exposing a thin scar running the length of her neck.

The same as mine.

Her sapient eyes study me, with what can only be described as pity. The thought sets my teeth on edge. I don't want pity from anyone, least of all some imaginary, alternate *me.* I'm so furious I curl my hand into a fist to punch the cursed mirror.

"I wouldn't do that, lovey."

I whip around. Standing in the middle of the room, as filthy and bedraggled as the day I met her, is the Dream Collector.

"If you value the air you're breathing, old woman, I'd keep a fair distance between you and me," I warn.

The grimy hag cackles as she leans down on her walking stick. It takes everything within me not to yank it from her grubby hands and beat her with it. She shakes her head and *tut-tuts.*

"Such violence, princess," she sighs.

"So, you invade the privacy of people's minds as well as steal their dreams?"

"Steal? I think you know very well I didn't steal a thing from you, lovey. *You* came to me. Against the wise judgment of your poor mother, as I recall. *We* made a deal."

"You weren't honest. You didn't tell me what—"

"They were *your* dreams, lovey," she says, cutting me off. "Perhaps *you* should have spent a little more time considering the ripples of those dreams before hastily trading them. But you have always been an independent one, haven't you? It's the headstrong who fall the hardest. And what you have learned, like countless others before you, is that even dreams have a price. And sometimes, the price is . . . costly."

I want to rage. To tear her limb from limb. Scream at her. Inflict unimaginable pain. I've spent the last ten years fantasizing about the day I'd see her again. The excruciating ways I'd make her pay for her deceit and clever omissions of the deal we made.

But even in the darkest recesses of my mind there is one impenetrable truth I can't escape: I did this to myself.

I sought her out. I made the trade. I made the deal.

I got my mother killed.

I got what I wanted. Or, so I thought.

Eleanora.

I turn back towards the splintered mirror, to the woman whose face might have been mine in another life. And standing behind her, looking right at me, is my mother. Just as she once was. Beautiful and healthy. Radiant and strong. But her eyes are filled with the same knowing-sadness as my strange lookalike.

"What is this?" I ask through gritted teeth. Between my scalding hatred of the Dream Collector and fierce longing and guilt at seeing my mother again, tension pulses around the base of my skull.

The Dream Collector hobbles her way across the room and takes her place beside me.

"It's what *would have been*, princess."

"Don't call me that," I snap. "I forfeited that title a long time ago. Would have been, what?" But I already know the answer, and I hate myself for it.

"What would have been, if you had kept the dream you needed and given up the dream you wanted."

The Dream Collector's hovel flashes in my mind. I'd been so sure at the time. Eighteen years old and so certain I had control over everything. Convinced it would all work out exactly how I wanted it to. All too eager and foolish to believe I knew better than my wise and loving parents.

Now, which dream do you need and which dream do you want? Remember, lovey, even dreams require sacrifice. What looks like freedom today, could feel like bondage tomorrow.

Oh, I gained my freedom that day. Freedom from my arranged marriage to a foreign prince from the other side of the world. Freedom from my parents' overbearing ways. Freedom from the chains of the crown and everything attached to it—the overwhelming responsibilities I resented at the time. I forfeited my crown for the sake of my own willful independence. It only added insult to injury that the handsome, cunning young knight I actually wanted to marry vanished soon afterwards, taking what little remained of my heart with him.

And I've paid for it every moment since.

"Dream Collectors shouldn't make deals with children."

"Ha! Come now, lovey. You were eighteen. By law, you were within your every right to make a deal. At the time, your father was the most powerful man in the realm. What hope would I, a humble Dream Collector, have if I upset the sole heir to his throne?"

"Since our deal, you've never been wealthier. It's amazing how dreamers show up in droves when the country is in shambles."

A loaded silence falls between the two of us, and I'm aware of every detail. The slightest shift of her hands upon her walking stick, the breeze rushing through my mother's hair from her world within the broken mirror, the tick of my pulse within my wrist.

Coming here was a mistake. What little semblance of peace I had, the mirror has now obliterated. Not that I don't deserve it. The high of being my own master, of relying on nothing and no one, had been exhilarating, but fleeting. I single-handedly drove our kingdom into dust, taking my mother down with it. I close my eyes, willing the hissing shame I've craftily dodged for so long to be silent.

What I needed was my mother getting better. But in my foolishness, I believed I could find a way to heal her *and* get the freedom I wanted. And now, I'll spend the rest of my days having *what would have been* hounding me whether I'm awake or asleep. I could have avoided all of this had I been more selfless—more like my mother.

"Why are you here?" I ask.

The Dream Collector laughs weakly before lifting her cane and tapping the mirror with it.

"It's been three hundred summers since a soul gazed into that mirror. Do you know what happens to those who look upon it?"

"They get to live in torment with the knowledge of what would have been."

She shakes her head. "Another choice."

My blood runs cold.

"I'm not interested."

"Hastiness has always been your downfall, lovey. Perhaps you should listen to the offer before you make up your mind."

"I made up my mind a long time ago that making any kind of deal with you isn't something I'm willing to do."

"I understand your anger, but—"

"Do you? I very much doubt that." I laugh bitterly as I turn away from the mirror. It hurts too much, seeing my mother as she would have been. *Alive.* And healthy.

Despite my best efforts, I can feel myself unraveling. All the years spent dodging every condemning thought, every well-deserved ounce of shame, have finally caught up with me. And for the first time, I don't have a shred of strength or desire to fight it. Mother is gone. I forfeited that pretty life in the mirror for a hollow reality I can't bear to face.

I pick up a broken piece of tile from the ground and wind my arm to hurl it at the mirror. With a mighty whirl of her cane, the Dream Collector strikes my hand. I cry out in pain as the bit of tile shatters on the floor.

"What's one more crack going to hurt?" I seethe as I rub my now swollen hand. "Don't tell me you've grown a conscience since we last met."

"I don't suffer tantrums, lovey." The Dream Collector sighs as she steps over and peers into the mirror herself. I watch as her expression shifts, surprised to see a deep sadness settle in her violet eyes.

"You have a choice to make. You've tasted and seen what you wanted and now, you've seen what would have been. Now, you must choose. Will you continue with what has been, or take a risk on what you've seen in the mirror?"

I glare at her. It can't be as simple as that.

She turns around, her back to the mirror. Her knuckles are white from clutching her walking stick and she suddenly looks weary to her very bones.

"The last person to find the mirror was a prince of this once legendary castle. The choice drove him to madness. He wanted both. What was and what would have been. In the end, his own indecision held him hostage. He tried to break the mirror and set the castle ablaze, killing himself in the process."

I rub my temples as I try to process the story, to understand the implications.

"So, I can continue life as I know it or I can step into the life I see in the mirror."

"Yes." She nods.

"What's the catch? Will I remember what the last ten years have been? Or will it be as if I chose the dream I needed from the start?"

"You will remember everything, but you will lose what you cherish most," she says pointedly. "Time will be as if you made no other choice. Your mother would never know you initially chose something else."

I frown. There's nothing left I cherish. My parents are gone. My gallant knight ran off the moment the kingdom's foundations began to crack. As if reading my thoughts, the Dream Collector urges, "Take another look in the mirror, lovey."

I sigh but do as she says. My mother is standing behind the woman I now know to be me in another life. Mother laughs about something as she braids my hair. Once she's finished, she places her hands on a set of handles I hadn't noticed before. I watch as she maneuvers me out from the table and down towards the gardens in a chair fashioned upon polished, wooden wheels. I remember seeing a similar contraption in the city, but a frail old man sat upon it, his legs spindly from lack of use.

My heart drops.

Am I paralyzed?

Tears stream down my face as I watch my mother push me along a pathway. We stop and pick a couple roses from a hedge before continuing on. The image changes and I now watch as my mother and I make our way back into the castle. We're in a spacious foyer when a man hurries in, a smile on his face. He's undeniably handsome, but more than that, he looks kind. I reach up as he bends down and scoops me up into his arms, and my mother follows us up the grand staircase and disappears from sight.

I wipe my face and step back, my head pounding. If I choose the mirror, I'll be dependent on so many. Unable to walk or run or scale the stairs. A wave of shame washes over me as I think over the more personal and private endeavors or tasks I may need help with in this other life. I'll exchange one kind of freedom for another. I'll lose my independence but gain, from what I can see, a joy and peace beyond understanding. I'll get my mother back.

"Can you see what I see?" I ask.

The greasy, old woman shakes her head. "I see nothing, lovey. Dream Collectors cannot dream. Not that I haven't tried."

"Will it be just as I see it? If I choose the mirror?"

"Just as you see it, lovey. The mirror doesn't lie."

"No wonder the prince went mad."

"Will you?"

I peer down at my filthy boots. My pants torn and tattered from months of relentless searching for the fabled mirror. What would it be like, to never stand or walk again?

"I'll only go mad if I stay here," I say at last. "I choose what would have been."

The Dream Collector smiles as she taps her stick into the ground.

"So be it."

"Come now, Eleanora, the day is going on without you."

A dream. I tell myself. *It was all a dream.* I force my eyes open, scared of what I'll see.

Sunlight spills in from a wall of enormous windows onto the spacious four-poster bed on which I find myself. I'm buried beneath a glorious, goose-down blanket covered in a velvety, crimson cover. A cabinet shuts to my left and I look over to see my mother laying a dress out on my bed. I suck in a sharp breath, startling her. The light catches on her silvering brown hair as she beams at me. Her smile quickly fades into a frown. She bends down and wipes the tears from my cheek.

"What is it, dearest?"

I force myself up onto my elbows, but my legs feel weighed down. I panic for a brief second before the Dream Collector and blackened mirror flash in my mind. I reach out and grab my mother's hand, overcome with emotion as I press it to my cheek.

"You're real," I whisper.

"Well, of course I'm real. You silly girl." She laughs as she takes a seat beside me. "What else would I be?"

I reach over and wrap my arms around her, bury my face into the nape of her neck. I breathe her in until my lungs hurt, the familiar scent of lavender soap and sundried cotton, and then I weep. Tears of regret and shame. Tears of relief and joy.

"Eleanora, whatever is the matter? You're acting as if I've returned from the grave!"

I laugh, knowing she can't understand the poignant irony of her words. But I break my arms from their iron-clad grip around her and lean back to see her face.

"I'm just happy you're here with me, mamma. I have everything I ever wanted."

And everything I need.

A LIGHT IN THE DARK

HAILEY HUNTINGTON

FOUR YEARS, THREE months, fifteen days. That was how long it'd been since I'd seen the sun.

I slammed my pickaxe into the cave wall, scattering bits of stone and minerals. Grunting, I did it again, and again, and again. The movement was subconscious and automatic, ingrained in my muscles by repetition.

Above my own huffs, I could hear the echoing clangs of the other miners. Occasionally, there was a brief cry of pain, or a faint sob. Those typically came from the new ones. The darkness hadn't sucked the soul out of them yet. Their skin was still soft enough to bleed.

I could barely remember what the sun was like. There was just a brief, hazy memory of warmth and brightness so intense it'd hurt my eyes.

The rank air was full of soot and sweat. Dust coated my mouth, and grit matted my beard. I tightened my grip and swung again. My calloused palms barely felt the metal handle.

Swing. Adjust. *Swing*. Adjust.

Sometimes, when it was just me and the darkness, the memories of Before crept back in, and there was nothing I could do to keep them at bay.

I'd had a family once. We had lived in idealistic—*idiotic*, if you asked me now—happiness. Then the goblins had broken down the wall. And the darkness had stolen everything.

My sweet Emmaline's face flashed through my mind, followed by little Charlie's. Then blood coated the memory.

With a guttural cry, I swung the axe. Rock cracked beneath the blow. Raw pain seared my heart, a reminder that I was still alive. Sometimes, I wondered if it'd be better if I wasn't.

I gritted my teeth and closed my eyes. Taking a deep breath, I shut away the pain, forcing myself to be as unfeeling as the walls around me.

When the goblins collected us at the end of the "day," they chained all us miners together. We stumbled through the tunnels, the clinking of metal and skittering pebbles the only noise. I kept my head down. I'd stopped looking at my wrinkly, bruise-colored captors years ago.

Like always, we were deposited in a large, open cavern. The air was choked from the sputtering, smoking fire. But there was a stew pot bubbling over said fire. My stomach rumbled at the prospect of something other than just bread.

It was when I was getting my bowlful that I bumped into the boy.

He was crouched right in front of the flames, and I nearly tripped over him. Muttering a curse, I righted my bowl just in time to not lose any food. "What ya doing sitting in the way?" I growled.

Normally, the goblins didn't take young'uns to the mines. They never lasted. The boy was new—his blond hair hadn't been dyed from coal yet. As he looked up at me, my breath caught. It was like a ghost of my own lad looking at me.

But Charlie would have been years older now, if he'd still been alive.

"I . . ." the boy stuttered. "I just miss the light. Everything is so dark and hard down here. I want to watch the fire dance."

"Best get used to the dark." Hunching my shoulders, I shuffled away into the shadows.

Five months, one week, and two days. That's how long the boy had been there. I couldn't escape him. Every morning and evening, he was there in the cavern. And he'd always be talking about some nonsense belonging to Before.

He sat several feet away, speaking in a low voice to several others gathered around him. "I used to just sit outside in the sunshine, watching the world," he said.

I couldn't stop myself. He and his words were like a splinter that'd started to fester. Chains rattling, I leapt to my feet. "Stop blathering about the light!"

The entire cavern went silent for a moment. Not even the fire dared to pop.

"But the light can't be extinguished. It's here, even in this darkness. And to have light is to have hope." He looked up at me.

I scoffed. "Hope of what?"

"Of an end. Of a return to the sun, regardless of what pains it might bring. Of freedom."

The same invisible splinter throbbed. My jaw clenched. "You're mad." Turning, I left him to his fantasies.

One year. That was when you'd know if a miner will last, if they're still healthy enough a year later.

After that one night, I'd finally managed to avoid the boy. Him and his nonsense. I'd settled back into the mindless pattern that'd kept me here these nearly six years.

When we were chained together at the end of the day, there were plenty of coughs and wheezes, more than usual—new miners that wouldn't make it. Morbid curiosity gripped me, and I tried counting how many.

I stopped when I saw the boy, doubled over hacking. *Charlie*, my memories whispered. They'd been more frequent lately, bringing me back to the days Before, trying to stir up sparks of dreams that had long died. Now, the embers of memories flared.

Charlie wading in the sparkling creek, trying and failing to catch a fish with his bare hands. He and Emmaline flying kites. All of us sitting on the fence, watching the sunset, carefree.

The chains yanked me forward, nearly sending me tumbling. I shook away the cursed thoughts. But my gaze was stuck on the boy, his back hunched from hours of mining, his wasted frame with scarcely more substance than a ghost's. The light was gone from his eyes.

Later, like that very first day, I found him by the fire. His expression was gaunt as he stared into the flames. "I don't want to die in the dark in chains," he whispered. A tear marked a path through the grime on his face. "I thought, dreamed . . . that there would be an end."

So had I once.

That invisible splinter stabbed deep and hard. And this time, it pierced my heart. Raw, aching pain crumbled the walls I'd hardened around myself. I didn't rebuild them this time.

I looked down at my hands, scarred and worn. The goblins didn't check my work anymore. It would be hard, back-breaking work to tunnel upward, to dream of climbing to the surface, but it'd be possible. Once I'd breached the surface, I could find the boy and we'd take an axe to our chains. We could feel the sun on our skin once again. Even if the world above was scarred and ruined, it'd be better than this living death trapped in the darkness.

But if the goblins discovered I was mining an escape . . . I'd heard the echoing screams and torture.

Swallowing, I brushed back the boy's ashen hair. He flinched at the touch before relaxing. More tears washed his face as he looked up at me, a flicker of hope back in his eyes. For all his blathering about light and the world of Before, he himself had brought a piece of light into this pit. And that, maybe, had restored a little bit of my soul.

I'd fight for there to be an end to the darkness, to be free of the chains.

"Don't give up your dream just yet, lad." I rested my hand on his shoulder. "You might be free again."

ROPE

VANESSA E. HOWARD

If only I could haul you back
Like the man on the dock who pulls the boat in
To tie it off

If only I could walk this with you
Take the treatment, swallow the pills
See the shrink

If only I could throw you
A life ring on the sea of addiction
To keep you afloat

Reach, my friend
Reach through the pain
Reach through the shame
Grab on tight

I've got rope burns
On my palms
But

I'm holding the rope and
I'm not letting go

FOR ELLIE

LARA E. MADDEN

A BRIGHT-EYED girl skipped up the steps of a two-story suburban house, energy seeming to emanate from her in vibrant waves. Following a few steps behind her was her father, Nate. He was a slim man, with shadowed eyes that looked both kind and tired, and he was tall when standing at full height. He moved with his usual stooped posture and shuffling gait.

Nate held a suitcase in one hand, and in the other a pink backpack with the name "Ellie" embroidered in glittery letters. Ellie's short, messy hair flew out around her head as she bounced on tip-toes. She rang the doorbell over and over until the dog inside barked and someone called, "Just a minute!"

Nate smiled despite his inner sadness. His daughter was all the light in his world. And the pain of missing her was already gripping his rib cage like a vice. She would be safer here, and happy. His hand trembled. On instinct, he reached for his right jacket pocket and was comforted by the weight of the flask. A pang of self-loathing flooded his mind.

"Daddy, how long are you going away?"

Nate steeled himself, mustering all of his courage for the sake of the six-year-old girl, who couldn't possibly understand the gravity of the situation. He crouched down so he was eye level with her, and steadied his hand on the back of her head.

"I don't know yet, baby. But I'm going to come back for you as soon as I can, okay? And we're going to be together again, and we're gonna start all over. Does that sound good?"

Ellie's face scrunched in confusion, but Nate couldn't explain more. He didn't have the words. And anyway, there were some things his little girl shouldn't be made to understand yet. A lifetime of regrets swelled in his gut and crashed with nauseating waves.

"I want you to know," he said, pushing back tears, "that everything I'm doing is because I love you. So much. I want you to have lots of fun this summer, okay?"

Ellie nodded and smiled, but Nate knew his daughter. She was being brave for him. When he couldn't look in her eyes anymore without breaking, Nate pulled her into his arms. He hugged her tightly, afraid he would fall apart if he let go, and she squeezed his neck with more strength than he thought could possibly be in her small arms.

The door opened and Aaron came out of the house with a loud "Hey! Come on in!" Nate looked up to face his childhood friend. Aaron was jovial as always, still broad-shouldered and imposing, but now with a few shocks of gray through his black hair and new lines crimping his face. As soon as the big man was out the door, he was knocked off his feet by an energetic retriever. Sounds of children laughing and screaming came from behind him, along with the sweet smell of something baking inside.

"Uncle Aaron!" the girl squealed. She let the dog lick her face and held her arms out wide. Aaron laughed, threw her into the air, set her back on her feet, and crouched down to whisper that there were cookies in the kitchen. She gasped and gave Nate a wide-eyed look before scrambling inside.

The two men stood alone on the porch.

"Hey, Nate. Been a while."

The old friends looked at each other without making eye contact, neither seeming sure what to say. Nate scratched his beard and looked down at the porch. The wooden boards were worn and muddied with child-sized footprints, and lawn toys were strewn around. Near the spot where he was standing, chalk drawings of flowers were beginning to fade.

The two men's lives had started so similarly, and yet, they'd ended up in such different places. They were both hard partiers as teenagers. They even had their first drinks together. Somehow, Aaron grew out of the drinking and Nate grew into it.

Nate cleared his throat. "I packed all her things. There's more in the truck." He glanced back at his rusting red Chevy. "Sorry for all the luggage. I didn't want to make too much of a fuss, but she has all these stuffed zoo animals and she has to say goodnight to them all or she won't sleep . . ."

"It's okay, really. We're happy to have her."

"Um . . . I just wanted to . . ." Nathan took in a shaky breath. "It just means a lot to me, and . . . I don't know how to—"

"You're welcome." Aaron was quiet a moment, then added, "You're doing the hard part."

Nate glanced up and finally met his friend's eyes. He sniffed and put his shoulders back, and then looked at the ground again. He knew how much he owed Aaron and Cathy for this. They'd been trying to find ways to help him for years: planning interventions, sending him phone numbers for addiction counselors and AA meeting times, making many offers to take his daughter into their home while he went to rehab. It wasn't until Ellie had almost gone into foster care because of his drinking that he'd surrendered and accepted their help. Aaron's kindness was a debt he could only repay by getting better. Getting sober. For good this time.

"How much have you had this morning?" Aaron asked.

Nate winced, even though there was no judgment in Aaron's voice. *No more lies.* Discreetly, he pulled the flask out of his pocket and indicated an invisible half-full line. "Um . . . just enough to function. I didn't want her to see me sick on our last day." He slid it back into his pocket and placed his hand over it, hating the way its presence calmed him.

Aaron nodded. "You can throw it away here if you want."

"I'm not ready yet." Nate's hand trembled. "I'm going to throw it out when I get to the facility."

Aaron put a hand on his shoulder. "I'll drive you."

Nate nodded. His mouth was too dry to respond, and, once again, he was too ashamed to meet his best friend's gaze. Aaron squeezed his shoulder and lifted Ellie's suitcase onto his back. "Come on. Let's get these things inside."

Luggage was unpacked, cookies were eaten, and the stuffed lion, horse, giraffe, elephant, and monkey were arranged on the bed. Ellie pulled the tiger out of her backpack and gave it to her father. It was white with black stripes, a little line of thread for the mouth, and a pink plastic nose. The fur was worn, a hallmark of Ellie's favorite toys.

"You can talk to him if you're ever missing me," she told him, putting her tiny hand on Nate's arm.

Nate pulled his baby girl into a hug and held on tight, long after she had let go. He couldn't keep the stray tears from falling into her hair, but he brushed his eyes before she could see them.

"I'm going to miss you every single minute," he told her.

"Okay, Daddy," she said. "You should probably keep Tiger with you all the time, then."

It took all of his strength to pull away from her. He could hardly say goodbye, but Aaron urged him, with a gentle voice and a firm hand on his shoulder, that it was time to go.

The drive to the rehab facility took an hour and twenty minutes. Both Aaron and Nate were silent most of the way. As the miles ticked down, the nausea in the pit of Nate's stomach grew. He drummed out his anxiety with twitching fingers on a bouncing leg, and his breathing grew ragged. He tried to keep his facade hard and determined, but internally, he could feel the panic that was fighting to surface. He could hardly think straight by the time Aaron pulled into the center's parking lot and shut off the engine.

"You ready for this, man?"

Nate started to nod, but his head shook instead. The sudden stillness of the truck and the soft clicking of the cooling engine made him feel sick. His heart was racing, the blood pounding in his temples. He rubbed his brow and forced himself to inhale. "Honestly, I've never been so damn scared before." He mentally reached for the flask, and his pulse surged again. "Never in my whole life. . . ."

"Hey, Nate."

Nate looked up, letting the tears sit in his eyes this time, knowing there was nothing else he could hide from his friend. Aaron's face was kind and serious, free of accusations, and—for a moment a thousand boyhood memories seemed to pass between them.

"I'm really proud of you, man," Aaron told him.

Nate grimaced, but Aaron wouldn't let him brush off the comment.

"No," Aaron said. "I'm serious. You've been struggling with this for twenty years, and you've never gotten this far. You're going to do it this time. I really believe that."

"What if I . . ." Finishing the sentence would have made it too real. *What if I can't? What if this is all there is, and I'm stuck in a series of ever-worsening failures? What if this is all I am?*

Relapse haunted him like a death sentence.

"Then we'll begin again, as many times as it takes." Aaron waited for Nate to look him in the eye, then gave him a nod, and got out of the truck.

Nate hesitated before following him.

The men walked up to the entrance and through the sliding glass doors. While Aaron waited by the door, Nate went to the front desk and spoke quietly with the receptionist. He filled out intake paperwork with wavering letters that barely stayed on the line. He stared at his last signature, which he'd practically scribbled in his struggle to hold the pen steady. It didn't look like his name.

The final moment came, and Nate turned to face Aaron.

"I'm not going to come out of here the same person," Nate promised. He hoped Aaron couldn't see how much he struggled to believe it himself.

His best friend just smiled and held out Ellie's stuffed tiger. "I know."

The image of Ellie's lit-up eyes, her toothy smile, and wild hair gave Nate an injection of courage. He gripped the tiger to his chest and reached into his jacket pocket. As he pulled out the flask, his hand shook violently but held on tight. Aaron took the flask, almost casually, from Nate's hand and tossed it in a trash can. The metal-against-metal ring echoed through Nate's mind. He wasn't sure if it sounded like victory or death.

Before he could say anything, Aaron pulled him into a fierce embrace. For a moment, Nate knew with certainty that his friend loved him better than a brother.

"You're going to make it, man. You're going to do it for Ellie."

Nate exhaled all the air from his lungs and took a deep, new breath. He straightened his back and stood at his full height. It was time. "For Ellie."

PART THREE: THE STAND

SECRET BEAUTIFUL THINGS

LARA E. MADDEN

THERE WAS A knock at the door of the crypt. A series of soft raps—three, then two, then three again—spelling out "S.I.S." in morse code. The dimly-cloaked phantom pulled her hand back into her voluminous sleeve and pressed her body against the wall of the mausoleum, staying in the shadow. Under the hood of the cloak she wore a black mask which distorted all features except a pair of shifting eyes. Around the figure's waist hung a long, black-sheathed dagger, and in the pocket of the cloak was a pair of highly dangerous and illegal items: an undocumented hand-bound notebook and a ballpoint pen.

It was the darkest night of the month, but the members of the Secret Inscriptions Society all knew the route through the cemetery blind. As part of their induction into the S.I.S., they had each proven their ability to reach the meeting point from anywhere in the cemetery, and to find an exit within minutes. The patrolmen kept careful watch on this place from every point of entry, but no one wanted to patrol the inside after dark. Local legend said that the ghosts were known to be unkind here. Few people were daring—or stupid—enough to risk the wrath of either the guards or the ghosts. Whether or not the stories were true, they made for good cover.

The phantom didn't so much as flinch as the morse code tapped through the crypt door: *A.K.A.*

The cloak fluttered like a thick cloud as the phantom moved to the edge of the crypt, looked around each side to check for guards, and then knocked out the letters: *SCRIBE*. Her alias.

A single knock from inside confirmed the message. A few feet away, a false gravestone that sat in the shadow of the crypt pushed up from the ground and seemed to fall over. A head popped up from the mound, also hooded and masked. The head turned quickly in every direction, then beckoned to Scribe and disappeared.

Scribe walked slowly to the mound and dropped down into the hole in the ground where the gravestone had previously been. To a witness, it would have seemed that a ghost had floated through the darkness and simply disappeared.

Once inside the crawlspace, Scribe reached up to a rope, and yanked it hard to pull the false gravestone back into place. She tied off the rope to a hook on the tunnel wall, effectively locking the trap door. Finally it was safe enough to use a light.

Click.

Scribe turned on the flashlight and ripped off the suffocating mask as dim light flooded the crawl space, and midnight-black hair spilled down her shoulders. Packed walls of damp earth and stones surrounded her; close and musty and unventilated. Roots hung down from the ceiling and snaked through the walls while grubs and beetles squirmed through the soil. The way ahead of her was only slightly wider than her slender frame and high enough to walk through in a crouch. It split off in several directions, most paths leading to dead ends.

"You shouldn't take your mask off yet," Raven whispered from a few yards ahead of her. "You shouldn't have the light on either."

"I just need a minute." Scribe took some deep breaths, trying to steady her heart and push down her panic. Somehow this part was always the worst for her. The most dangerous phase of the meetings was traveling to the cemetery and slipping past the night watch. Breaking curfew without authorization and being caught in possession of any literature besides the government-issued nationalist booklet were crimes worthy of imprisonment. The crimes of carrying weapons, possessing literature with intent to distribute, and writing new literature of any kind were all punishable by execution. Even with these threats, though, it was crawling through the tunnels that made panic rise up in Scribe's throat. The dank earthy air, the thought of being buried alive, the close darkness that wanted to swallow her whole. She hated it so much that she would dread it all month until the next meeting.

"Scribe, come on!" Raven whispered harshly up ahead. Scribe filled her lungs one more time with the dank-soil air, pulled her mask over her face, and reminded herself of the importance of her mission. She had risked her life to get to this meeting place. There was no going back. She was not as brave as the other Society members, but she was stubborn. That would need to be enough.

Scribe clicked off the flashlight.

Darkness pulled the oxygen from her lungs and replaced it with lead. She forced her muscles to move past the freezing panic. Her fingers felt clammy against the cool tunnel walls as she pushed onward, following the sound of Raven's annoyed voice ahead of her, urging her to go faster. Blood pounded through her skull, pulsed behind her eyes, swished loudly in her ears. *Onward.* She fought the need to reach for the light again as she moved deeper into the tunnel. Being able to see the walls closing in around her wouldn't help her panic to subside. Instead, she tried to imagine the tunnel being wider than she knew it was, and avoided brushing against the sides. She thought of the notebook in her pocket. What it contained was too valuable; it needed to be shared. She couldn't turn back.

A faint flickering light glowed at the far end of the tunnel as it straightened out into a long, widening passage, giving Scribe just enough of a jolt of hope to breathe again. Her dizziness eased with every step closer she came. She hurried through the final portion of the tunnel, bursting into the threshold chamber with a relieved, tearful laugh. Three other cloaked members stood silent in the dark room. "We're just waiting for Psalm to open the door," said Poet, who was holding a torch.

"Did you have any trouble getting here?" asked Librarian.

"No," Scribe told her. *except for that godforsaken tunnel.* "It was unusually quiet tonight."

"But you were careful?" Raven's voice held a note of warning.

"Of course," said Scribe. "When am I not careful?"

On the other side of the chamber's metal vault door came a knock, requesting the password. Scribe stepped forward and returned it, tapping out the new safe word that had been determined at the previous meeting. A different password would have indicated that guards had infiltrated the tunnel, and that the most essential contents of the meeting place needed to be cleared immediately before the door could be opened. For every scenario, there was a protocol in place, as Raven was quick to remind them all.

The door opened and the cloaked figure on the other side passed lanterns to the other four, who lit them with the torch. Following the leader, whose alias was Librarian, they walked in formation and softly chanted the Society's verse. Psalm, following up the line, closed the door and slid three heavy bolts into place, then fell into formation. Flickering lantern light landed on floor-to-ceiling shelves of books, loose pages, stacks of blank paper, paintings, and an old-fashioned, manual printing press which completely filled one corner of the large chamber.

Five young women, inconspicuous and seemingly tame, made up the S.I.S., which locals simply termed "the Society."

The members marched in a circle until their lines were complete, then bowed somberly to each other and waited for the fifth member, Poet, to read the commencement verse.

With the meeting officially begun, the masks and hoods came off and the five sat on cushions around a low table. It quickly filled with notebooks, paper scraps, pens, and high-valued illegal literature. A book of Grimm's fairytales. A crumbling H. G. Wells science-fiction paperback. A pocket-sized New Testament. A poetry collection by Walt Whitman. A copy of *Fahrenheit 451*.

"How did you get *this?*" Librarian asked. "Bradbury was one of the first to be banned! I didn't think any were left at all."

Psalm knitted her fingers together and cracked her knuckles, satisfaction gleaming in her eyes. "Anonymous donation that came down the rumor mill. Someone had a twenty-year-old book cache that they wanted to pass on. They were too afraid to retrieve it themselves but gave me the location. I had to make multiple trips to carry them all. I saved some history books from it too—*and* a hymnal, a copy of *1984*, *A Tale Of Two Cities*, *Brave New World*, *The Crucible*—"

"That's *incredible!*" Poet said, wide-eyed. She was the youngest in the group, and often the most eager.

"Very good," Raven said. "We'll each take one book and carry it home to write a copy before next month's meeting." She held *Fahrenheit 451* and brushed her fingers across the cover tenderly, then passed it to Librarian at the other end of the table. "Your home has the most secure hiding places. You should take this one."

Librarian flipped through the pages for a long moment, and no one spoke, hoping she might read a few lines aloud. Instead, she shook her head and gave the book to Scribe. "My place is less secure than it was a month ago."

The slim volume felt heavy in Scribe's hands, and dangerous. She'd never read this one before; she was too young to remember a time when hundreds of thousands of copies existed. Now, she could very well be holding the final one. She opened it.

"It reads like poetry." Delight bubbled up across her face. "The prose is so rhythmic." She read a few lines aloud, and as she did, she remembered the feeling of being a small child, and the thrill of throwing piles and piles of books into the great roaring mouths of the public bonfires. The hot light had glistened off her mother's cheeks, making her tears look like rivers of flame. Scribe had seen the fierceness in her eyes, but she hadn't understood then. How could a five-year-old know that a book was more than pages and ink and a pretty cover? That it was freedom, thought—the human soul encapsulated? Now, she fought to bring back what she had once helped destroy. It was all she *could* do. For her own sense of hope. For her mother's memory. For the network of people who relied on the Society to locate and circulate literature.

Scribe closed the *Fahrenheit* and wiped her eyes. "I'll protect this with my life," she swore. She tucked it into her pocket as the others chose books to bring home.

"Raven, you're still working on the Gospel of Luke, aren't you?"

"Just finished the copy, but I'd like to make another before we distribute it. This one's in high demand. Here it is; I redid the binding. I'll take home James this month."

"I'm still working on King Lear," Scribe said. "I've had to be more careful about security recently, so the work is taking me longer. I've caught someone following me three separate times this month, and there are new police cameras up all over my apartment building."

"Pass me *The Crucible*," said Psalm.

"You just want that one because it's short," Poet teased.

The only person who claimed nothing was Librarian. She watched the books being exchanged with a far-away look.

"They're watching you closer, aren't they?" Psalm asked her. "Has it become too dangerous?"

Librarian nodded, swallowed, and gave a strained smile. "Isn't it *always* too dangerous?" Lamplight flickered on her pale face, making her dark eyes look pitifully tired. When they'd first come in, Scribe hadn't noticed how old and forlorn her young friend looked. After years of risking their lives for one another, she should have known her well enough to see it sooner. Librarian was carrying a heavy load.

"You're right," Scribe said and put her hand on Librarian's arm. Her friend stiffened at her touch. "It's always been too dangerous. But our work is worth it."

"Is it really?" Librarian mumbled so quietly that Scribe had to lean in.

"What do you mean?"

"Worth it." Librarian stared at the table. Her finger traced the grain of the aging wood. "Is it really worth the risks? How could it *possibly* be?"

"I've never heard you talk like this." Scribe studied her worn face. "What we're doing gives people a reason to live. We're preserving beauty. We might not be able to put food in our neighbor's bellies, but we can feed their minds and souls. Give them the chance to think for themselves, thoughts that weren't planted by the endless propaganda—"

Librarian looked at Scribe with an unwavering gaze. Her pupils were wide in the dark, irises intensely blue. She trembled in the firelight, her words punctuated with constrained emotion. "We are going to *die* for this. It's not even a matter of *if* anymore. Only *when,* and *where*, and how many *other* people we accidentally bring down with us."

"We signed our names in the registry book in blood. Remember? Because we knew the risks." Scribe searched her friend's face, trying to reach her. "We decided the day we were initiated that we were willing to die for this cause."

Librarian narrowed her eyes and leaned in close to Scribe. She whispered harshly, her voice masked by the others' ongoing conversation. "We're shouting into the void here. What if we change nothing? We come to the end of our lives and realize that nothing we did mattered to anyone? What, we just fight a pointless war that no one asked us to fight, and suddenly we disappear with no one to remember we were here to begin with?"

"*Yes,*" Scribe said.

Abruptly, Raven rapped her fist on the table calling all to attention. "Notebooks out. Who's reading first?"

Scribe pulled her notebook from her pocket and opened it to the most recent section. While pages rustled and each member searched for their own offerings of stories, local news, essays, and poetry, Scribe leaned toward Librarian again. She whispered, "What's really going on? I've never seen you like this before. You believe in this more than anyone I know."

"It doesn't matter." Librarian stared down at her own small notebook. "I was just asking questions. That's what we do, right? We ask the hard questions."

There was a scratching sound on the outside of the round metal door. Everyone went completely silent. Scribe froze. Her hands and feet tingled with paralyzing fear.

Librarian was holding her breath. The only sound in the chamber was the table, rattled by Scribe's trembling body. Raven reached over and pulled her hands down off the table. The rattling stopped, but Scribe continued to shake violently in Raven's arms, her breaths coming in fast, shallow gasps.

The scratching came again.

Psalm drew her knife from its sheath and held it behind her. She crept to the door and pressed an ear against the metal. The dingy clock on the wall ticked down a minute, then another.

She turned to the others and shook her head. "An animal must have burrowed into the tunnel. I heard it scurry away." She confirmed by looking through a handmade periscope that had been built into the wall.

Scribe tried to force her breathing to even out, but her heart raced every time she looked at the door. Desperately, she sorted through the dozens of sickening scenarios racing through her mind. She forced them apart while imagining what she would do in each, but they soon bled back together and drew her terror to the forefront of her thoughts.

"You talk a lot about courage for someone who panics over a rabbit," Librarian jeered in her ear.

Scribe glared up at the taller girl, who was clearly as shaken up as everyone else. Ignoring the cruel comment, she stepped away from the table and over to an alcove in the dirt floor beneath one of the bookshelves. A fireproof lockbox was tucked inside and covered over with a large, flat rock. Scribe took the copy of *Fahrenheit* from her pocket and secured it in the hiding spot, together with a *Bible* from the shelf above her, some loose pages of poetry, and a few sheets of music. She glanced back at the metal door, then walked over to the exit hatch on the other side of the chamber and placed her ear against it.

"It's okay," Scribe heard Raven telling the others. "Even if there was an emergency, we have protocols in place for a reason. We do drills."

Scribe rolled her eyes. Drills wouldn't be able to save them if the police ever found their meeting point. Aliases, exit plans, formations, a few daggers, some homemade explosive devices. They were up against a military superpower. Maybe Librarian was right. Maybe they *were* shouting into the void.

“I heard a rumor about a group that was caught distributing literature just two weeks ago. Maybe forty miles away, our same jurisdiction,” Psalm was telling the table in a whisper. Scribe walked to another bookcase and pretended not to hear.

“They were a larger group. Fifteen members,” Psalm continued. “They were taken out to the public square, and the executioner brought all the neighbors out to watch them face a firing squad. They left the bodies in the square to rot. No one was allowed to bury them for a full week.”

“I’ve heard worse things about what happens in the prisons,” Poet said quietly. “A firing squad would be merciful.” She looked around the chamber and wrinkled her brow. “It must be a pretty flimsy government if it’s so threatened by a few hundred books.”

“Not just books,” Librarian said somberly, glancing at Scribe and then staring down at the table again. “Ideas.”

Scribe opened a small chest on one of the shelves in the back of the room. She studied the contents.

“Scribe! Away from the explosives!” Raven said. “You’re too clumsy, remember the time you almost cremated us?!”

“Yeah, it took me three weeks to get my hearing back,” Librarian quipped.

“I was just checking them,” Scribe said. “I didn’t touch anything.”

“Well, just . . . step away from the box. You’re making me nervous.”

“All right ladies.” Psalm clapped her hands. “Party’s over. Let’s get back to work!”

For hours, late into the night, the members each took turns reading the things they’d written that month and critiquing one another’s work. This was an essential part of their mission, not only to keep and defend the stories that had nearly been lost to the world, but also to add to them. To continue the most dangerous and beautiful act of creation.

To write *new* things was good, but to write them *well* was now considered not only a profession, but a sacred duty. Their teachers were the volumes that surrounded them. They studied Dostoyevsky and Hemingway, Shakespeare and scripture, Longfellow and Dickens, *The Arabian Nights* and the *Canterbury Tales*, and Homer’s *Odyssey*—gathering vocabulary and form and concepts that would flow through them, mingle, and grow into something alive. They were the journalists, the teachers, the storytellers. Vessels for thought, builders of a small secret world which gave refreshment and escape to the hundreds of people they distributed stories to via the underground.

"I'm not trying to imply that your rhymes are *terrible*," Poet was saying of a few stanzas that Raven had written. "They just don't show any respect for the English language."

"Ouch," Raven said, pushing her chair backwards.

"Well, look, you asked for my honest opinion. And you can fix the problem if you dedicate yourself to it. You just need to study more of the masters." Poet jumped up to find a poetry book for Raven.

The clock on the wall ticked down the hours of darkness left. It was never enough time.

"We only have an hour," said Psalm.

The other four turned to look at the clock. Scribe's stomach churned. Back through the horrible tunnel soon, and then out into the dark morning, where no one could predict what they would encounter.

If only she could stay forever in this meeting chamber where she could forget the rest of the world—this place that felt like home, a sacred oasis. She thought of the irony of being so safe in a library, surrounded by enough incriminating evidence to condemn an entire town of people to a firing squad, or worse.

The lanterns were beginning to burn low. The Library was dimming and seemed to constrict as time passed, as if forcibly pushing Scribe and the others back out into the real world. Safety was only ever a temporary illusion, and this oasis could not last.

Librarian glanced nervously at the door. "I should . . ." Her voice trailed off, and she drew her cloak around her to stand. "I should probably leave early."

Scribe watched her movements, stiff and uncertain. Librarian's face looked vacant. Her eyes shifted, as if she were lost. Something was wrong.

"I'm really sorry I can't stay; I'm just worried. I'm being watched the closest right now, so . . ." She edged to the door. "I just need to get home."

"Okay." Poet nodded. "Be careful. Stay safe. We'll see you back here next month."

"Yeah," Librarian replied. She opened the door. "I'm sorry," she said once again. She turned and her eyes met Scribe's for a moment, then Librarian pulled the black mask over her face, put up her hood, and shut the vault door behind her.

Scribe fidgeted in her seat, her pulse playing loudly through her ears again. Something was very, very wrong. She looked around the table, but no one else seemed concerned. She tried to tell herself that the nausea in her stomach and the fear crawling across her shoulders were only overactive nerves.

She couldn't make herself believe it.

"I'll be right back," she said, shooting toward the door.

"What's going on, Scribe?"

"I don't know. Hopefully nothing."

After looking through the scope and listening to the vault door, she opened it, took a deep breath, and dove into the darkness. As she pressed through the tunnel slowly and quietly, her mind warred between fear and frustration at herself for being so concerned over what might be nothing. Far ahead of her, she heard the gravestone door open. It didn't shut again.

She came to the widened crawlspace and looked up through the hole into the star-bright sky. She pulled the mask and hood up to cover her skin and peeked over the lip of the hole. She turned her head, scanning the dark cemetery, and froze—

Night Guards. Four of them, standing in crisp dark-blue uniforms around a shadowy cloaked specter. A heavy weight dropped in Scribe's gut, at first because she thought they were arresting Librarian. Then, because she saw they were speaking with her. The Society's fearless leader pointed toward the tunnel entrance, and Scribe's head dove beneath the surface just as the guards turned to look.

She backed into the tunnel entrance, breathing heavily, trying to consider any other explanation. Then, she ran. Into the darkness, into the walls that closed around her body, back through the tunnel to the meeting place. Voices echoed behind her, and when she whipped her head around, she could faintly see flashlight beams in the distant tunnel entrance. There was no time. No time to think, no time to make a decision, to weigh costs. She came to the end of the tunnel and slammed her hand against the door, three times fast, then three times more. The warning signal.

The door opened for a moment and Scribe fell forward into the meeting room. Without hesitating she ran to the chest on the bookshelf and grabbed it, holding it tight against her body.

"They're coming!" she yelled. "Take what you can carry and go!" She ran across the room, pulled the lockbox from its alcove, and shoved it across the floor to Poet. "Use the emergency exit; don't leave by the cemetery."

Psalm took a duffle bag and pushed the contents of the table into it. She threw it on her back and ran for the exit door. She looked back once at Scribe, who was still tightly clutching the box of explosives. She gave a quick, somber nod and disappeared through the door.

Poet opened her mouth to say something, but Scribe shoved her toward the door. "Go. Go! *Run*!"

Poet's eyes widened, but she obeyed. Raven was setting charges outside the vault door. Without a word, Scribe held out her hand to take the detonator. Raven gave it to her and squeezed her arm. Her face was tear-streaked, but set like steel. Scribe felt her own determination rising. She stepped back through the main doorway into the tunnel.

"Do it," she said. Raven took a deep breath and followed the protocol.

The door swung closed like a casket lid. Heavy bolts thudded into place from the inside, sealing off the chamber indefinitely, and sealing Scribe's fate. She was alone in the dark. No matter what happened, that door would not open again.

Scribe's plan was to dart down one of the decoy tunnels, into the black maze, letting the guards pass her so they would be close enough to the vault to be caught in the explosion when she collapsed the tunnel. The extra charges, which she carried in the little chest, were to ensure that no guards escaped the tunnels if they got caught in the maze instead of going to the vault.

After the collapse, the tunnel would be left as a pile of rubble, but the vaulted library would become a time capsule that someone someday might come back for, might find a way to resurrect. For now, with the vault door sealed, their treasure at least wouldn't fall into the hands of the enemy. The remaining three Society members would have a shot at making it out. They would scatter to the designated safehouses and hiding places where they'd wait until the day they could come back together.

Scribe could give them that chance. She flew forward through the horrible darkness, feeling like a mouse running directly into the jaws of a snake. Her right hand was wrapped around the detonator, and with her left arm she carried the last few explosives.

Ahead of her, powerful flashlights beamed across tunnel walls and she could make out the profiles of men moving single file through the small space. She was close enough now to hear Librarian's voice, then a moment later she could make out individual words.

"Don't forget the deal," Librarian was saying to the guards. "I bring you to the books, and no one associated with us gets hurt." Her voice wavered, then grew urgent. "We have a deal, right? I got it from your commander in writing.

I *signed.*" None of the guards gave a response, except for a grunt from the one heading up the line. Librarian added weakly, "A confession for immunity." Her words disappeared into the void.

Scribe drew closer and brushed her hands along the wall until she found the opening to one of the decoy passages. She disappeared into it, slowly creeping into the even thicker darkness, trying not to breathe as the guards moved past her.

She tripped. Scribe caught herself without dropping the precious items she carried, but the motion was just enough to bring a small shower of soil down onto her head.

The flashlight beams stopped swerving across the tunnel and turned to train directly on her. Guards yelled and she heard the metallic scraping of guns being drawn. Scribe darted down the tunnel. She had only a few seconds head start, but she was also smaller than the guards and able to move more quickly. A mouse in a maze. . . .

Several large men barreled after her.

"No, wait," Librarian called in the distance. "This isn't the way—" But Librarian was being shoved along with the pack of guards now, down the decoy tunnel, deeper and deeper underground.

Flashlights illuminated a fork in the tunnel ahead of her, and Scribe made a right, then a sharp left. Gunshots rang out and echoed through the small chamber. A bullet exploded into the tunnel wall, just missing her, and another clipped the corner of the tunnel before the guards rounded it.

She could no longer hear Librarian's voice. Either her *fearless* leader had stopped trying to draw the guards back toward the true passageway or some had followed her.

Scribe wasn't sure of anything anymore. She had few senses to go on, and panic was beginning to override those. She glanced down at the digital watch Raven had given her. She wasn't sure how many guards were behind her, but if some had continued onto the vault, she would have to detonate soon.

She didn't know where this tunnel led anymore, or how near she was to the dead end. But she did know that she couldn't hold them off for long. The walls were becoming narrower now, and they brushed her shoulders as she squeezed through. Her pace slowed. Her panic grew. She could hardly catch her breath anymore, between the exertion, the fear, and the thinning oxygen in the small space. The stale, dusty air filled her lungs, and she knew she was nearly to the point where the tunnel would end and she would face her attackers.

When the flashlights caught up with her, she saw that the tunnel ahead straightened out to a dead end. With no more turns left to offer Scribe cover, the guards discharged their weapons again, and three bullets tore through the darkness. Nauseating fire exploded into Scribe's back. She screamed and stumbled forward. Before she hit the ground, another bullet hit her shoulder, and one more tore through her thigh. A stray bullet flew past her head and ricocheted off a stone in the wall. The chest flew from her hands and a dozen small explosive devices hit the ground in front of her. She pressed the detonator. There was a flash of light, and then all descended into darkness.

Librarian swallowed her overwhelming guilt as the guard who had followed her stepped closer to the vault door. She glanced around the chamber, silently noting the charges that had been tucked into a corner. So the others had escaped then. She wondered how much time she had left before the explosives would be detonated.

She knocked at the door of the library, knowing no one would answer. She knocked the password slowly as the guard drew close behind her. Closer. Closer. He was nearly pressed against her back now, his body large and imposing. In a practiced motion she spun and ducked away from him, snatching his gun from its holster and holding it out in front of her.

"Clever girl." He smirked and took a step nearer to her. Librarian aimed low and pulled the trigger, landing a round in the man's right hip. As he shrieked and cursed, she used the moment to dart back into the tunnel, out of his reach. He wouldn't get far before the bombs went off, but maybe *she* could.

Librarian was nearly to the exit when the first blast came from her left, knocking her off her feet. The tunnel filled with dust and debris, making it nearly impossible to breathe even through her mask, but she forced herself forward. She was so close to freedom. So close. She found her feet and stumbled onward, hoping—in her confusion—that she was going the right way, that there was still a possibility of survival.

Another blast came from behind her, this one much, much bigger. The tunnel roared, sediment rained down from every direction, and she surged toward the exit with every ounce of her strength, trying to outrun the collapse. In the past week she had been caught, tortured, and forced into a confession. She had betrayed her dearest friends and everything she believed in. And still, all she knew was how to survive. All she could do was get out of this tunnel, and maybe, *maybe*, see the sun rise at least one more time.

She came to the end, coughing and spitting up dirt and soot, and crawled up the ladder. Loud, disorienting ringing filled her ears. Librarian rolled onto the grassy cemetery grounds. She gulped fresh air and coughed again. She might be caught, but she didn't have the energy left to lift her head and look around for guards. She had the gun in her hand but might not be able to lift her arm to fire it. She closed her eyes and wondered if she was going to die of exhaustion. But no, even now, she couldn't. Her will to survive was too strong. There was nothing more important than continuing.

She took a few breaths more and let tears run down her dirt-streaked face. Her will to survive had come into conflict with every other good thing left in her life, and it had won. She thought of Scribe. Her body was somewhere in the tunnels now. She surely hadn't gotten out alive; it wasn't possible. Librarian had always been annoyed by Scribe's fear, and now she was shamed by her friend's courage.

She lifted her head, shoved the gun into the waistband of her cloak, and forced herself to roll onto her knees, then up to her feet. When she was steady enough, she stumbled forward, unsure where she would go. She had no more place in the world now that she'd betrayed the only family she had left. She'd just wanted to protect them. Now, she would go out into the world without them, and probably die alone for nothing.

The remaining three members of the Secret Inscriptions Society were never seen again—officially.

The investigators responsible for the takedown reported back to their higher-ups that the mission had been successful. The library was considered destroyed and the Society members presumed dead. The North American branch of the United Global Federation had fewer resources than civilians were led to believe, and the local government was even worse off. It simply wasn't worth the resources to excavate the cemetery and the land surrounding it just to locate a buried vault. The case was closed, and the secret police moved on with their attempts at tracking down the Society's extensive underground network. The escape tunnels leading back to the vault were never discovered.

As for the S.I.S., all reports of their work stopped completely for several months. Rumors spread that they had disappeared into the mountains, looking for a new secret place to write and regroup. They would return one day, when it was safer. When they'd been "dead" for long enough. In the meantime, the network of readers and freethinkers they'd painstakingly built continued to thrive in secret. Neighbors smuggled books, friends whispered lines of poetry, parents told stories to their children. Still, they thought of the forbidden library, and all the treasures of fiction and philosophy that were said to be buried there. It remained untouched for many years.

Until one dark night, in the middle of a cemetery, there came a knock at the door of the crypt.

WOULD YOU?

ANNE J. HILL

Would you die to save the books?
To save the art passed down from our
forefathers for such a time as this?
Would you stand on a pile of skulls
and bleed for a world unborn?
Would you jump the fence
and run through blazing grass
to save the least of these?
Would you do the right thing
even when everyone around you
screams at you to sin?
Would you skip a meal to feed the
child hiding in your walls?
Would you take up arms and march
into war to free those confined?
Would you stare the devil in the face
and tell him to go back to the Hell
from which he came because you
stand on the authority of someone
who created his chance to even exist?
Would you pen the words that

stir the hearts and minds of
generations to come, even if it meant
losing a few friends along the way?
Would you bloody your knuckles and
skin your knees to help a stranger escape?
Would you smuggle the Word of God with
the risk of losing your place on this Earth?

We've all shouted, "Yes! Yes! I would!"
But I ask you, think of where you are now

Would you find the courage to tell a friend
simply when they're wrong?
Would you call your sister and
offer to help her paint her walls?
Would you sip tea with your grandmother as she
told you story after story, and your legs fall asleep?
Would you give a stranger a compliment
as you're falling apart?
Would you sleep early tonight to
give tomorrow its full potential?
Would you pick up extra shifts to pay off that
credit card debt that keeps on building?
Would you stay awake an extra hour just to
clean the dishes for your family's sake?
Would you put aside your fickle feelings to
help out someone you call an enemy
as they spit in your face?
Would you climb out of bed even when
it feels like climbing a mountain?
Would you simply live each moment
for the dawn of a brighter day?

Would *you*?

THE WEIGHT OF FLOATING

EMILY BARNETT

LYRIC SIFTED THROUGH the stratospheric clouds with deft fingers. Her hands, once tanned, were stained a milky, iridescent white from the minerals she'd harvested since she was seven. Thirteen years later, she was doing the same thing.

Her fellow Collectors smiled faintly as they worked, as if they couldn't picture doing anything else. Lyric knew it was an important job. The silvery specks they collected from the clouds kept their people afloat—*if* they took the daily vitamin.

But recently, Lyric felt a gravity inside her.

Sitting back on her heels, she glanced past the cottony cloud fields to the city.

The towers—made of moon dust, lightning, and thunder rubble—scraped the stratosphere's dark ceiling, giving her a clear view of the heavens. Building the city had been a feat and true testament to the magic of her people. She used to be filled with pride for her ancestors whenever sunlight refracted through its glassy, almost billowy, façade, but now all she felt was a strange ache.

"You're daydreaming again."

Lyric jumped at the weathered voice of Greatmother, and she hastened to grab another handful of cloud fluff. Lyric pulled the thread-like fibers apart, plucked out tiny shards of frozen silver, and dropped the minerals into a basket to later be liquified into vitamins. She still felt Greatmother's gaze on her, so she sighed, looking back up.

"I'm sorry, Greatmother. It's just . . . the wind whispers again."

Greatmother lifted a white brow. "What does it say, child?"

Lyric hesitated. She knew the World Below was off-limits, even in conversation. But she couldn't stand it any longer. Every time she chose silence, heat built in her lungs, suffocating her. It was no use. She swallowed, her throat dry.

"I think Zephryns are ravaging the lands," Lyric said.

Greatmother's eyes cut like celestial winds. "And why does that concern you?"

"What if it's our fault?" Lyric studied the sparkling shards in her hands. "Zephryns are made of wind and malice, and . . . and *clouds*. What if our meddling has—"

"*We* are not to blame."

"But if we can control the winds, can we not control the beasts? Isn't it our duty to respond?" Lyric's stomach twisted at what she'd heard carried in the currents just this morning.

Screams. Cries for help.

Was she the only one who heard them? Or was she the only one who cared?

Greatmother turned her gaze on their city, as white and pure as the moon. "Our duty is to our own kind." She handed a vial of silver liquid to Lyric. "Take your vitamin, and do not dwell on those beneath." The old woman drifted to another field of clouds, her minerals buoying her up.

Lyric looked at the tincture. Her hand trembled.

It was a man she heard most often on the winds. His prayers ragged and raw.

Who did he pray to? Would *they* respond?

His voice had haunted her for weeks, along with countless others.

Lyric's gaze caught on the spotless towers and something in her grew sharp. What if all the beauty and peace her people valued had come at great cost? Had the World Below chosen to be left behind, shackled to dirt and violence, or had it been inflicted upon them?

The heat in her lungs and the cold bottle in her hand caused her to break out in a sweat. *I have to know. I have to . . .*

Lyric unscrewed the lid and poured her daily vitamin over the edge of the cloud. She watched it with a sinking feeling. But that's just what she needed to feel. She'd been floating her entire life without a care in the world.

The next morning, Lyric felt heavier.

Blinking, she looked around her small room of silk walls fluttering in a cool breeze, the stars hazy above. She blinked in confusion. Everything was white, foggy.

"What in the . . ." She tasted minerals. She clamped her mouth shut, understanding dawning. She had sunk into the cloud floor. Gravity was taking effect. Lyric was glad she'd thought to strap on her satchel the night before, not knowing when the minerals would gradually leave her blood stream and when the descent would begin.

She closed her eyes, telling herself not to panic. This is what she wanted. What she needed to do.

Further she sank, her room above becoming distant, blurry.

She was gaining speed now, and she gasped, grabbing a handful of unprocessed cloud and swallowing it, the mineral scratchy in her throat. It was less potent this way, but she only needed a small amount so she didn't crash to the earth below like a meteor.

Lyric slipped from the bottom of the cloud like a raindrop. To her relief, she did not plummet. She glided.

She had witnessed a few scouts leave their atmosphere. What they had glimpsed Below, she didn't know. Greatmother didn't divulge such information.

Each time Lyric met a cloud, it was thinner than the last. The air grew warmer, and she squinted, trying to see details of Earth. Her eyes watered, lungs overwhelmed with oxygen. But they no longer burned with unknowing.

Lyric pulled a breathing tablet from her silk bag and placed it in her mouth, dissolving on her tongue. It had been the trickiest part of her mission—stealing from the scout tent. But it would be enough to filter the oxygen until her lungs acclimated.

A few minutes later, Lyric saw Below in clarity.

Her breath caught.

It was saturated in color. More than the muddy greens and blues and tans she had glimpsed from above. The vividness and designs stretched below her like the tapestry hanging in their common space, woven from starlight and the silk of lunar wyrms, but *more.* A grand design not even her people could replicate in art.

Curling her fingers, Lyric finally called on her magic. She didn't want to use her power until necessary, not knowing how much she would need on her descent. Unlike the vitamins that kept her people listless and afloat, their wind magic did not come from a bottle. It was an innate gift, renewed with rest and refreshment. And now that the trace minerals in her blood were being depleted, she pressed on the winds, slowing herself slightly.

But still, Earth rushed up to meet her.

A new color bloomed below: *red.* It moved with the liquid energy of storm clouds and heat that licked up at her like the sun.

Below, houses and fields blazed with the fluid red, now orange. Swirling through it was a snake-shaped cloud. Lightning danced from its mouth and scoured the land. She'd never seen a Zephryn before. They were beasts of old, banished from the heavens by her ancestors. But she felt its malice and wind in her bones, and knew it instinctively.

Lyric landed roughly on a pile of ash and rubble, her knees jarring with the impact. She toed the ground curiously. How strange it was to feel something so solid. She did not bounce or float.

"Who are you?"

She turned. A young man with skin like pale dawn and a voice that echoed from her memories stared at her, slack-jawed.

"You're *him.*"

He looked depleted, confused. Terrified. And no wonder, his world was burning.

The heat made Lyric cough and she stumbled toward him, shaky on her weak legs.

How do people deal with so much weight *all the time?*

"I saw you fly." There was a sharpness in the man's tone, drawing her back to the moment. "Are you with *them?*" He pointed to the serpent cloud curling around a stone house, turning it to dust with a single squeeze. Bloodied people dashed around them, screaming and shouting for one another. Heat and noise wrought havoc on Lyric's mind. Tears streamed down her face as shock tried to consume her.

"This is not what I expected," she whispered, voice swallowed up in the chaos.

Lyric felt her brimming store of magic. One push and she'd float away from this hell.

Why did I think I could help anyone?

But Greatmother's avoidant words slid around her like an icy wyrm, and she thought of the carefree expressions of her people and their privileged lives amongst the stars. The contrast was more than Lyric expected. But this was why she'd dumped the vial—to know the truth.

Her people's backbones were soft. They were afraid to face what their actions of banishing the Zephryns had wrought. She knew with an innate horror that this world was not a place chosen. It was a place to be survived.

The man had moved on. She caught up with him, a new vigor pumping through her veins. She tripped but caught herself, and then helped him lift a sheet of something shiny off a woman. Lyric's arms shook with the effort.

But the woman did not look harmed.

"Get to safety!" he told the woman, and she limped away. Away from the burning. *The way we should be going, too.* But the young man was heading toward it. Lyric grabbed his arm and he rounded on her.

"Are you here to help or hinder?" he spat.

Lyric dropped her hand. "What is your name?"

"Grey," he said gruffly, then his focus shifted behind her, eyes widening. "Watch out!"

But Lyric already felt it coming, just as it surely smelled her star-cloud skin. She whirled as the beast rolled toward them. "Stay behind me!" she yelled at Grey.

"What?" he yelped.

"The Zephryn is mine."

The creature was a cyclone of power that spewed sunlight from its open maw. Its teeth, white and sharp as the turreted towers of her city. Clawed hands sprung from the serpentine body—a body that shifted like darkened clouds caught in a storm.

Lyric's heart caught in her throat. She'd been on Earth for all of a minute, and she was about to die at the hands of a beast born of her realm.

No wonder her people had fought them off.

But what of *these* people? They were trapped. Vulnerable. Gravity shackling them to their fates.

Lyric's sky-born blood whispered to her: *this is why you've come.*

Grey was behind her, his firm grip on her upper arm as if he were about to pull her away. Why didn't he run? She knew he had to be scared, but his courage strengthened hers. If only she could help them, the Below might have a chance.

With a cry, Lyric threw up her palms.

The winds obeyed.

A gale tore around the Zephryn, peeling back layers of consuming hunger. Thunder drowned out Lyric's hearing and light blazed, striking the dirt around their feet. Zings of electricity jarred her teeth. But her power held off the worst of it.

Heat grazed her skin as the Zephryn attempted to kill her with one last blow. But she squeezed the moisture from the clouds, dousing the beast in rain.

Lyric drew in the winds and clouds like many threads, tugging until they spliced the monster, fragmenting it into silvery shards and dew.

A loud sizzle and plume of white sent Lyric and Grey backward, choking on the last of the Zephryn's essence. A few moments later, the air cleared.

Silence rang strangely in Lyric's ears. It reminded her of home. A home she was no longer certain she belonged to—not yet, anyway.

She turned to Grey.

He was staring at her with disbelief. "I take it you're *not* on their side, then."

Lyric snorted, and her body trembled with overexertion. "There are more?"

Grey nodded. "Some from the skies, some that have clawed up from the depths. The dirt beasts we call Zoics." His night blue eyes swept over her, uncertain. "But with the Zoics came a magic of our own. A way to defend ourselves." He held out his hand and green light glowed faintly from the center of his palm. A sweetly rich scent tickled Lyric's nose and her eyes stung at the revelation. Just as her people had been given wind magic, those in the Below had been given a gift as well.

"But . . . why are you here?" Grey asked. "The Stars have never intervened before."

"Stars?"

He cleared his throat, running a hand through his short, black hair. "That's what we call your people: Stars. But seeing you up close . . . you look more like us than some ethereal being." His eyes flicked toward the flaky remains of the Zephryn. Grey had a large cut on the side of his face, glistening deep red. "Though what you did was not so normal. We haven't been able to kill the Zephryn yet."

Lyric sighed. "It's what should have been done long ago."

"So why now?"

"The winds carried your plea to me, so I'm here. To make amends."

Relief bloomed in Grey's face and his shoulders relaxed, as if Lyric's statement had given him back years of his life. And given him hope.

Lyric looked to the skies, surprised to only see blue, not the recesses of space. A lightness filled her in a way no mineral could. And it had taken her sinking in order to find it. To fight for it.

Perhaps it wasn't just those on earth who were bound. Ignorance had chains, too, and she had felt them tightening around her chest. For the first time, Lyric was free.

A rumble of thunder caught her ear, and she turned. In the distance, lightning illuminated a gathering storm cloud. Petrichor stung her nose, and she let it settle her nerves. Another attack was near. The Zephryn's rage within the air called her to battle. She wasn't here to save their world, but with her gift, maybe she could help.

She glanced at the skies. Maybe all her people could.

The earth quaked, causing Lyric to lose her already precarious balance. Grey steadied her, but he was staring at the battle beyond. Lyric stilled when she heard a far-off, guttural moan.

"What was *that*?" Lyric breathed.

"A Zoic." Grey's fists curled and she noticed something green growing from his wrist, its leaves as sharp as blades. He glanced at Lyric. "Care to join me?"

Awe quickened her pulse. What did Earth's magic look like in action? She imagined what hers could do beside it. What two people from two different realms could accomplish—together.

She followed Grey toward the storming skies, buoyed by purpose that bloomed open her lungs, and veins that rushed with celestial winds.

FREE AS A BIRD

ALI NOËL

I empathize with the zebra finch
this tiny, introverted bird
It does not wish to be handled
prone to fear and stress, when forced to be friendly
I believe the zebra finch
would choose the risk of briar-scarred feet
bent-belly feathers, weather-worn tails
Possess the marks of life in the great wide open
even if it meant its time was short
Prefer to drink deeply from green-leaf pools
collect thickened grubs, sing into the wind
To an extended life of pelleted seeds, watering tubes
its wings only ever expanding
to hop from plastic swing to shelf
The caged bird sacrifices freedom
The free bird sacrifices time
Beloved wouldn't you rather soar for a moment
than sit for a lifetime?

CRIMSON OFFERING

BROOKE J. KATZ

THE SEA CALLS for blood. It will not be denied.

The wheel of the *Black Vixen* slips from my grasp. My weather-worn hands are slick with warm crimson—the blood of my men. Gray menacing skies open, sending sheets of rain that whip me in the face. Lightning flashes overhead, and the voice of thunder rumbles and shakes me to the bone. The anger of Calypso tosses the *Black Vixen* to and fro.

I made an oath long ago with Calypso to save my brother from death's grip when we were just boys. The sea had tried to take him, but when I cried out, a beautiful woman emerged from the watery depths. She held him out to me. "Do you want him back?" her voice sang, inviting me in. I begged her to return him. He was my responsibility. She agreed on one condition: that I repay her with my soul on the day she called. I had no idea the magnitude that deal would have if I didn't follow through, how relentless she would be to get what I owe her. Today, she calls for my blood, a chill whisper in my bones. She has waited long enough.

Metal clashes with metal. Crimson tides slosh on the deck—souls slipping through the cracks. Men who were once our allies now hold the strength of Calypso, their hearts and the surrounding territories turned against us. They no longer accept our trades or our leadership on the sea. Enemy pirates who once feared us now pillage our treasures and our women. Calypso has even turned the ocean against us. The waves keep us from importing or exporting goods. Our formerly rich soil is nothing but mud and death. We were once a thriving island. Now we are starving, overtaken by Calypso—who will not relent until she gets what she wants:

My blood, my soul.

My men are before me, fighting with their last breaths. Dealing with this devil brought my crew into Calypso's murderous embrace. If we don't succeed, the pirates and the waves of her power and manipulation will slaughter the mainland. My brother is somewhere out in the carnage. I need to find him. I need to make sure he is alive and that everything wasn't for naught.

"Take the wheel!" My voice carries over the sound of death and chaos to my helmsman. He fights for both our lives as I hold the wheel tight. It's pointless. The waves are overpowering the vessel and it won't hold up much longer.

He skewers the heart of a pirate, then turns, passing me his bloodstained sword so he can take the wheel. I grab the hilt and spin around, plunging the blade deep into a man who came up behind me, twisting his guts before releasing him to join the others lying motionless on deck.

I know what I must do. I have brought this destruction on us all—but first I must find my brother.

I slash and slice my way to the stern, trying to save those who are left of my men. But there is only one way to truly save them. To calm the seas and cease this losing battle.

I have run long enough.

Every battle fought, her whispers snake around my soul. They remind me of my imprisoned demise.

I want to live. Foolishly I thought I could outrun this, but I need to stand by my sacrifice. My heart hammers in my chest. Soon it will cease its beating and rest in Calypso's collection.

Time seems to slow, and I long to see my brother once more. Through the thick rain, I glimpse him just a few feet away from me. Our eyes lock, and I see the little boy I saved from the sea all those years ago. I see us sword fighting near the cliffs back home, our laughter ringing in my ears. I see us wrestling outside in the damp grass, mud caking our clothes and Mother scolding us from the doorway. I see that goofy grin he gave me when he told me of the girl he fancied. I never allowed myself to fall in love. My love was for our land, our people and my family. I knew what awaited me some day, no matter how much I fought it.

Blinking, my brother comes back into focus as the man he has become: strong and healthy . . . unstoppable. He will make a great leader. He is already.

Tangy salt wets my lips and I can't tell if it's from the sea or my own tears. Copper and steel fill my senses; the smell of death encapsulates the ship. I nod my head in his direction when our eyes meet through the rain and chaos. He shoves the pirate he was fighting overboard. I swallow the pain of goodbye, turning away from life to face the pirate nearest to me.

As my nerve endings become numb, my grip loosens around the hilt of my sword. My blade clatters to the deck, taking my pride with it. I open my arms wide, welcoming death's sting.

"Do what you must!" I shout into the storm. The enemy's blade splits open my throat and warm liquid life oozes from the wound. Every ounce of blood that leaves my body takes with it all the worry and fear I have carried since that day I made the deal.

I feel a chain snap from my soul and I lean back over the rail toward my grave, my crimson offering mixing into the sea. The rain ceases and the sky starts to clear. A veil is lifted. The last thing I hear before the waves wrap their arms around me is the sound of victory . . . Silence fills me with peace. The sea calms, pulling me into its inky darkness, where I drift off to sleep.

UNRAVEL

MORGAN J. MANNS

MATT WATCHED AS the chasm grew, splitting the sky in two. His sister, Fen, hadn't been able to stop the gate between worlds from opening. He watched helplessly through her barrier of light. This was it—the end of their world.

Winged creatures circled the ship like carrion as if waiting for an unspoken cue to descend. Matt frowned, his fist tightening around his sword hilt. He didn't know why they hadn't attacked the *Windbreaker* yet. King Savok had promised that the summoned beasts would destroy their crew before wreaking havoc on the rest of the world. So, what were they waiting for?

He glanced toward Fen who still managed to keep a shield of light around herself and those nearest to her—Matt, the captain, and a few other men. His sister stared up at the sky. The crew mimicked her, waiting for the inevitable. Nobody spoke, unsure of what to say. Could a thousand-year-old prophecy be wrong?

Fen was the *Lightbringer*. She was supposed to have stopped the mad king's hoard of evil creatures from coming through the sky portal. But her golden power didn't drive the creatures back. They'd managed to push through.

Matt glanced back at the horrid beasts. From this distance, they resembled bats, but he knew they were much worse. After the creatures obliterated the *Windbreaker*, they would wreak wild destruction upon the rest of the kingdom. Savok's madness had deepened. He would destroy the land if he couldn't conquer it.

Perhaps the beasts weren't descending because they could sense Fen's power. If that was the case, and if her presence was enough to keep them from attacking, maybe their ship could make it to shore. They could find reinforcements and fight them off from land instead of sea. He clenched his jaw, determined. It was worth trying.

He opened his mouth to suggest the thought to the crew, but movement from his sister caught his eye, freezing him in place. Beside him, Fen tore her gaze from the sky and walked toward the center of the ship. She didn't meet Matt's questioning look as she approached the captain.

The sea became its own beast, rocking the ship treacherously. Fen widened his stance against the rolling waves. The storm around them was intensifying.

Matt couldn't catch the words spoken between his sister and the captain, but Klein's eyebrows reached high into his mess of windblown hair. Whatever Fen said caught him completely off guard.

Was his sister offering an apology? No, that wouldn't garner shock such as this.

As the wind howled its eerie warning, the men around him fell into old habits, securing lines, ensuring they wouldn't capsize. Matt was about to help when he saw Klein doing the unthinkable—he was tying his sister to the mast.

He held back a growl. Why was Fen being tied up like some criminal? He strode forward, ready to intervene.

"Stop him," Klein said, tightening the last knot.

Heavy hands gripped him. Two of his crewmates secured his shoulders, holding him back.

"Klein, what are you doing?" He struggled against them. "You have to let her go!"

The captain turned toward Matt, his eyes shadowed. "With the waves growing, we can't afford to lose her to the ocean. And . . ." Klein reached for his dagger. "She wants to do something else to ward off the beasts."

Suddenly, Matt knew what his sister wanted. The ancient prophecy was unclear, but its working suggested the *Lightbringer* could summon more power by—

"Fen! No!" he shouted. "It can't come to this!"

She looked up then, a worn expression across her features. "I have to try, Matt. This is the only way."

A flash of lightning cracked, and the sky filled with ear-splitting screeches. Everyone looked up. The beasts descended, becoming larger as they dove toward the ship. They rebounded against the shield of light, growling in frustration when they couldn't break through.

Matt cursed, pulling against the men holding him back. "Let her go!"

There had to be another way to save the ship and its crew without his sister sacrificing herself.

Amidst the growing storm, Fen's eyes fluttered closed, her raven hair plastered against her face from the unrelenting rain. Her head bobbed until it fell limp, sinking to her chest. The shield of light around them flickered. He didn't know how much longer she could hold off the wretched creatures still pouring through the gap in the sky. It was clearly using up the last of her strength to do so.

Heart pounding, he watched Fen tilt her head toward Klein's gilded dagger. "Just do it, Captain. I'm ready." Her voice came out in a tired rasp.

"You can't!" Matt shouted, pushing against his captors. "There has to be another way!" Matt pleaded, still restrained by the two men. His gaze turned to his sister. "Fen, you don't have to do this."

He couldn't lose her. Not like this.

Matt's ears rang with the turmoil around him. Thousands of membranous wings thrummed through the air, joined by screeches born from the depths of the creatures' obsidian-scaled bodies. Men screamed, their battle cries swallowed by the unrelenting storm.

Diving at the crew, one by one, the yellow-eyed beasts overwhelmed the sailors, quickly cutting down each man with fangs and claws. Matt cringed as men were carried away and flung to the frothy surf. But he couldn't worry about his crewmates. In this moment there was only one person he needed to save.

Fen's the only person who's ever been there for me. Who's seen me, for me, Frantically, he once again pushed against the men holding him. *She's saved me from my wretched self too many times.* "Let me save her!" he shouted.

"I can't do that, Matt," Klein shouted back, his tailcoat flapping in the wind. "She agreed to this."

Matt felt himself unravel as Klein stepped closer to Fen.

I need to stop him!

Matt lunged, intent on freeing her from the mast, but the men only held him tighter. "Let her go!" he screamed again.

"She's our only hope, Matt," Klein shouted over the battle. "Evil floods into our world! If she does this, she could still seal the gate!"

"I was born to do this Matt," Fen suddenly said, watching Klein raise the dagger.

Matt glanced at her, still bound to the mast. Her eyes had opened, brimming with resolve.

"The light has guided me here for a reason . . ." She formed a reassuring smile. "Let me save you."

No, no, no!

"Fen, let me help you! We'll find another way."

Trembling, she looked at him once more with those piercing blue eyes that reminded Matt of their mother.

"This isn't truly goodbye, Matt. We will meet again."

Words caught in Matt's throat as Klein stabbed his sister in the chest. She let out a shuttering gasp as blood poured from the wound.

No . . .

With her lifeblood draining, pooling at the base of the mast, his eyes widened in horror as the golden shield around them started to shrink. The dark beings converged, screaming and slicing against the glowing barrier, sensing it weakening.

"MURDERER!" Matt howled. Rain masked the tears flowing down his face. With another surge of strength, he strained toward her. His two captors, men he might have once called allies, held firm, forcing him down to his knees.

"You've killed her!" Matt set his jaw, glowering. "She doesn't deserve to die this way!"

Klein shouted back, "I'm sorry, Matt. If there were any other way, I'd—"

Fen turned her head to the storm-ridden sky as glorious light burst from her skin.

"Fen!"

Around them, the sailors released their swords, raising their hands to shield their eyes from the blinding brilliance. The evil creatures faltered, screaming in pain from the light as if burned. In that moment, the men released their grip on Matt. He fell to the deck and watched, helpless.

Fen . . .

Paralyzed, Matt could've sworn he was gazing directly into the sun. A shiver of awe ran through him as the dome of light Fen had summoned turned from dim to glorious. In explosive retribution it flared outward, pushing back the creatures of darkness, throwing them into a turmoil of wings and claws.

Wonderment beheld him as he strained his eyes through the brightness. The blast of light merged, becoming solid ribbons of gold, slicing through the air in pursuit of the deadly creatures.

Capturing demons in airborn snares, the light hurled them back toward the rift in the sky. The beasts screeched in terror and frantically beat their wings in their haste to escape.

With the creatures fleeing, Matt watched as thousands of golden ribbons changed course, gathering high. Merging together, wrapping and folding, they formed a massive thread. In a breathtaking display, they surged forward and began to knit together the impossibly large hole between worlds.

Fen had never been able to harness this much power on her own. This was nothing like he'd ever seen.

She's doing it, Matt thought. *She's going to seal the gate.*

Like a skilled seamstress patching worn fabric, Fen's thread stretched from one end of the horizon to the other, piercing the edges of the chasm. In and out the lines danced, tightening and sealing—a prison for darkness. They crisscrossed, preventing any more demons from entering through the shrinking gap. With a final tug, the golden thread completely sealed the dark void, leaving the heavens whole once again.

Matt blinked, hardly believing what he saw. No visible scar remained where the gate had once been. The sky was whole and Savok's demons were gone.

After years of watching his sister honing her skills and preparing for this very fight, she had finally done it. She fulfilled the prophecy and sealed the gate. They still had a chance to defeat the mad king. But, at what cost?

The remaining crew of the *Windbreaker* collectively breathed a sigh of relief. They had lived to see another day.

Menacing storm clouds quickly dissipated, and once raging waves danced gently against the hull, their rhythmic murmurs soothing the ship and her crew. Bathed in sunlight, the sailors turned their gaze toward their savior.

Matt crawled over to Fen, carefully freeing her lifeless body from the mast. Cradling her in his arms, his tear-stained face pressed against her pallid cheek. He whispered to his sister, "You did it, Fen. You did it."

Klein stepped up behind him and placed a hand on Matt's shoulder. "I'm sorry, Matt," he said, his voice heavy with remorse. "I'm . . . sorry."

Swallowing back tears, Matt almost shrugged him off. Instead, he gave no reply, simply rocking Fen gently in his arms.

She'd given her life to close the gate and protect their world from Savok's creatures, summoned from some hellish world. Only her, the most powerful, radiant person Matt had ever known could have saved them from the darkness—and she did. He would do everything in his power to make sure the world remembered her.

The sailors gathered silently around Matt and Fen, faces reflecting a mix of sorrow and gratitude.

Klein turned to his crew, addressing their tired and worn expressions. "In honor of Fen, we will continue the fight against the dark!" His voice boomed with confidence. "We will find Savok and make him pay for what he's done! Mark my words, the light will prevail!"

STAINS OF RED

ANNE J. HILL

KANE WIPED DOWN the counter with a bit of alcohol mixed in water. He scrubbed the same spot over and over, trying to get the red stain to fade. The tavern had been closed for an hour, with some guests asleep upstairs. The sign that read *Spirits & Skulls* was crooked, but he'd fix that later. Kane brushed his graying blond hair behind his ear and put his elbow into his work. The glass from the bottle of red wine was still shattered on the bar top, but the stain had his focus.

Red like blood. This time it was just wine, but the sight instantly transported him back to when he lived off of making men bleed.

Kane swallowed and glared at the stubborn stain. He'd retired so he wouldn't have to clean up red anymore . . .

His wife was upstairs, already in bed. His daughter had grown and had her own kids. And Kane had the life he always wanted—a chaotic type of peace. Cleaning up after these slobs and hearing their tragic tales was child's play to the adventures he'd gone on as a young man.

Kane dumped more Hidden Hell, a strong clear alcohol, on the butcher block and scrubbed harder. He caught sight of the tricorne hat that hung above the entrance. Two cutlasses lay criss-crossed behind it. *Spirits & Skulls* was Kane's pride and joy, and he'd be damned if he let her get ruined by younger men storming in and telling him what to do.

Then why was he considering leaving it all behind? Of heading back out into the wide world? To risk never returning to his wife and the tavern he'd built with his own two hands?

Kane whipped the rag on the edge of the counter with a *crack.*

The world was supposed to be fixed. He'd already settled the scores years ago with his friends and family at his side. He'd paid his dues. Balanced his scales after years of wrongfully slaying the innocent. Took up the sails, and hunted tyranny, and freed slaves. Plundered his enemies. He'd fought in wars, both on land and in souls. Bandaged wounds with Hidden Hell and a rag. Scaled steam engines and faced a dragon. Tilled the land until his body grew weak. Kane had served his time on this earth, for country, for king, for gods.

So why the bloody hell was the duke, his nephew, knocking at his peaceful tavern and demanding he leave his quiet corner of the world to join in one last fight?

Kane picked up a shard of the broken bottle. Flickering candlelight from behind him danced on the amber glass as Kane ran his thumb over the soft side.

His nephew wasn't one for violence, but he'd broken this bottle. Breaking bottles was *Kane's* forte. The duke meant business.

Damn the boy. Kane's kingdom needed him. Their enemies were closing in to take their lands. And Kane had looked enough dragons, emperors, and demons in the eye and survived, each time uncertain that he would. And now, as settled as he might be, he knew he could not rest until he brought down the kingdom's enemies or died trying. The sea was calling his name once again.

Kane tossed the rag aside, loaded his flintlock, took down the cutlasses from their display, and went to kiss his wife goodbye.

HOPE

AUDRAKATE GONZALEZ

When everyone thought hope couldn't be found,
Hope said, "Be still, don't make a sound."
When everyone fell to their knees and wept,
Hope said, "My promises shall be kept."
When sorrow turned to anger,
Hope said, "Let me be your anchor."
When anger became fear,
Hope said, "Fear not, I am still here."
When Hope was left alone on the cross,
Hope said, "This will be worth the cost."
When it appeared death had won,
Hope said, "It is done."
When one day turned to two, then three,
Hope said, "I have come to set you free."
When Hope came rising like the sun,
Hope said, "Eternity has begun."
When no one could believe it was true,
Hope said, "Believe it has been done for you."

THE WRONG MONSTER

MARY E. DIPPLE

MAGIC RAGED THROUGH the square, sucking life from every man and woman left in town. They'd evacuated the children and those unwilling or unable to give their life force to the seal. More had stayed than Emma thought would. She fought to rein in the magic. To make it take her life force instead. These people had suffered enough at her father's hands. As an immortal, she had more than enough power to create the seal, but every time she tried to direct the spell toward her own life force it would ricochet off her. It was almost like her curse of immortality was creating a barrier the spell couldn't penetrate.

Emma wept as the magic spread through her body, out her fingertips and over the cobblestones, sealing away the monster who'd terrorized the citizens of this world—her life—for the past century. But at what cost? "I can't. It's too much. The magic won't take the energy from me. I have to sto—"

"No." Jacob knelt next to her and took her tear-sodden face in his hands. His dark eyes were so full of life. So full of the love she'd always longed for. "You can't stop. We knew the price when we started this, Emma. We knew the cost to seal him away would be high, but it's worth it if it rids the world of his evil."

Emma gasped a sob. "I can't. This was supposed to free you. Sealing him away was supposed to give you peace."

Jacob placed his forehead to hers. "You warned us the spell could cost us our lives and we'll gladly give them if it means our children will live theirs in peace." Jacob's lips quirked in that half smile she loved as the magic snaked around his torso and neck. "We chose this, Emma. Remember that. We chose to pay the spell's price."

She shook her head, words of protest clogging her throat as the light faded from his eyes and he slipped to the cobblestones.

Emma screamed as her spell tore away the life of every man, woman, plant, and animal left in the city. The silvery strands of the spell turned gold as the life force was drawn from each one and pulled into the ground, strengthening and shaping the seal. She closed her eyes, but the spell etched each death on her heart.

When it was done, silence filled the square. Her hands trembled as she lifted them from the stone and dared to look upon what she'd done. Bodies littered the streets. So many of them were people she'd only just come to know. Her sobs echoed off the buildings as the last sparks of golden life settled into the cobblestones and faded from sight.

She cried out as her hands reached for Jacob's lifeless body. All her hopes. All the dreams she'd dared let herself imagine with him were gone. The years they would have had together now powered the seal she'd created. She'd killed him. She'd killed all of them.

She should have known her curse would get in the way. Her ignorance had cost thousands of lives. A cost that left her alone. Alone with more blood on her hands than that tyrant ever had.

CHILD UNBORN

ANNE J. HILL

"YOUR MAJESTY, IF you do this, you *will* die." The physician dabbed her head with a cloth. "There are things that can be done—to save you. I won't tell anyone."

Mira closed her eyes tight. Sitting on the bed that was once comfortable was now searing agony. Her unborn child threatened to be the death of her if she didn't allow the physician to *take care of it*. She was utterly lost. In her womb, she held the future of the kingdom. The next king to protect and guide her people. If only Fredrick could hold her hand and tell her what to do. But the king was away at war, and Mira was alone.

They'd tried so hard to have this baby. Years of miscarriages and seeing physicians and guilt for not producing an heir. And now that it was finally happening, she might die.

She gripped the bedsheets with trembling hands. She slumped her head between her knees, exhausted after endless pushing and screaming that seemed to get her nowhere. Mira was not strong enough for this. Not by herself. The kingdom needed the bloodline that ran through her unborn son's veins. Otherwise, the throne would pass down to Fredrick's younger cousin, a tyrant who wanted to enslave the lower class. But . . . Mira needed to *live*. She needed to see Fredrick again, to kiss him, and hold him . . .

Sweat mingled with tears and dripped down her lips. She muttered, "Do it."

She sunk into the bed as relief flooded her. Mira had made a choice, and she would be okay. They'd bury the body, and Mira would bury her guilt. And the kingdom would someday fall into pain and tyranny.

But Mira would live.

The physician nodded and gathered his instruments. "This will hurt, but you'll be all right in the end. Maybe in time, you can even try again and—"

"Just do it." She couldn't bear to think of the future, or to hear his false hope.

"Of course," the physician said. With well-trained hands, he began his work.

And something inside Mira cracked. Her fingers curled tighter around the bedsheets. This was the right choice, wasn't it? If she let this baby end her, Frederick would lose his wife, and she would lose him.

But if Mira let the physician continue, then her baby would perish, and a whole kingdom would crumble after Fredrick passed on.

Panic rushed through her. Her baby was dying. And she wasn't strong enough to stop it. To save her baby from death or her people from tyranny. She was just one person trying to survive, and was that so very wrong?

Yes, the word pounded in her head, unwelcome. Sobs erupted from her throat. She knew what she had to do even though every self-preserving instinct in her was shouting.

"Stop," she mumbled through trembling lips.

The physician froze, his brow furrowing. "Your Majesty?"

With a shuddering breath, she said more firmly, "Stop. I'm having the baby."

He blinked a few times and set his tools down. "But, Your Majesty . . . you'll—"

"I know." Tears trickled down her lips and plopped onto her throat. "I know." She turned her face into her pillow and wept. If there was even a hope of saving her people from tyranny, she *had* to do this.

Mira took a deep, slow breath, then turned her face back to the physician. "I'm ready."

Confusion still on his face, he nodded.

She pushed and screamed, and bled more than she ever knew a human could bleed. Sharp pains sliced through her body. Words she'd never dared utter were shouted across the room. Her body broke and tore, and she was dying. But with the help of the physician and one last guttural push, it was all over.

As Mira blinked through spotted vision, she heard the cries of hope. A warm weight lay on her chest, and she placed a shaking hand on her child's back. As Mira breathed her last, her son breathed his first.

EXOSKIN

VANESSA E. HOWARD

CHELLI DOUSED THE knife with decontamination spray before sliding the sharp tip into her skin beneath the sensor. Blood welled around the site where the tiny metal disk was embedded in her thigh. She hissed in pain and dug the knife deeper, using her other hand to hold a cloth to the trickle of blood. Finally, the sensor broke free with a tearing that made her yelp.

She worked in her bathroom, the only place in her Cube that didn't have cameras. Her dad's diary lay open on her right while a handful of tools made a semi-circle on her left. Her Exoskin, blue for her status as a factory worker, hung from a magnet on the back of the door. Just looking at it made her heart thump. She'd made the first cut. Too late to turn back now.

Placing the tiny disk in a tray, she went to work on the next site. The Exoskin snapped into place at fourteen sensor sites on her body. Seven on either side. Ankle, calf, thigh, hip, waist, shoulder, neck. It was going to be a long, painful night.

Chelli sliced through her skin again, after a glance at the diary. It had arrived via messenger while she was walking home from work. The messenger had slipped it into her hands without a glance, a word, or a pause.

She wanted to stop and cradle the diary, imagining her dad's beefy hand against it as he wrote, but she didn't have time. She had to finish before morning. The Association didn't patrol at night. There was no need, with everyone locked in their Cubes.

By the time the fourteenth sensor had been extracted, a pile of bloody cloth sat next to her. Lines of throbbing pain went up and down her sides. Groaning with every movement, she disconnected the motion-activated light fixture from the shower stall and added it to the pile of sensors and tools.

Consulting the instructions in the diary, she alternated between the micro torch and the circuit chisel, taking apart the controls and activators in the light, and manipulating the sensors. She hunched over the project for three hours, her fourteen wounds aching beneath their bandages.

Her dad had disappeared two years ago, branded an anarchist. The Association had told her he died attempting to escape the city. But hope burned like a bonfire in Chelli's heart. He'd made it to the Refuge.

Who else would have sent his diary?

At last, she stretched her back. With the sensors from her skin now connected to a loop made from bare wire, motion activators, circuit boards, and hacked timers, she had a stand-in for the Exoskin. A string of sensors set to 0500 in the morning would unlock the door. At least, that was what the diary said.

If this worked and she got out of her Cube before patrols began, she was supposed to sneak to the autorail and hide in the farming pod. Without her Exoskin alerting the Association to her whereabouts, she should be able to exit the city along with the automated farm equipment.

The only problem was, Chelli had one last errand. And her window of opportunity was miniscule.

She slicked back her dark hair into its customary tight bun. The Exoskin swung on its magnet, and she needed a deep breath before she lifted it off. Telling her fingers to stop shaking, she stepped into her Exoskin, pulling it up her body, sliding her arms in, and wincing as it rubbed against the sensor sites. A strange mix of joy and horror bubbled in her stomach when the suit *didn't* click into place against her body as it had every morning for twenty of her twenty-four years. She was unmoored, untethered, and it both delighted and terrified her.

The Exoskins kept people safe. The suit acted as armor, prevented most illnesses, and alerted the wearer to danger. They also kept everyone prisoner. Nothing could be done without the Exoskin, which meant the Association monitored and controlled everyone in this city. The suits were cleaned nightly in their sanitization bags and no other clothing was permitted outside of the Cubes.

Ripping two pages from the diary, she folded them into a tiny square and slid them up the tight sleeve of her suit. At the door of her Cube, she stopped.

This was it. She pushed the string of hacked sensors into the detector frame that usually read her Exoskin. For a moment, nothing happened. Chelli's muscles tightened.

Then the frame turned on with its familiar orange glow. The door slid open as it did every morning. But this time, it was at Chelli's bidding, not the Association's. She hurried out into the dark, her pulse pounding, her lips dry. All was quiet at this illegal hour.

Beauson's music shop was three blocks away. On the surface, it sold Association-approved audio and followed all the rules. But its proprietor was more than he appeared. The soft-spoken, balding man sold illegal music and audio files, and ran a secret communication network through those files. There was a drop point just outside his shop. If she was fast—and lucky—she could pass on this intel and still get to the autorail in time.

Her stomach plummeted to her toes when she turned onto Beauson's street. A man in an orange Exoskin paced under the light at the corner. The guard who manned that intersection was already there and it wasn't even dawn. Why was he early? She couldn't even turn around; he'd already spotted her.

"Chelli? What are you doing out here?"

Her heart gave a nervous lurch, but she tried to sound airy. "Good morning, Luther. I have a pass for a delivery. No rest for the weary, right? Hey, are you growing a beard?"

The guard ran a hand over his scruff and grinned. "Trying something new. What do you think?"

Chelli walked past him without slowing. "Looks good. Suits you."

"I still want to take you out to dinner." He walked a few steps with her. "I can apply for an evening pass for you. We could probably be approved by the weekend."

Regret twisted through her. She would have liked dinner with him, but that would never happen. Not now.

"No time. They're working me full hours. You know how it is." Every nerve clanging, she picked up her pace. Luther went back to his post, with his chin lower than it had been.

Next to Beauson's was a little brick alcove hidden from the cameras. She stepped in, found the fourth brick from the bottom, and pulled it out. Inside was a small plastic container. She shoved the pages in and leaned her forehead against the bricks, nearly sobbing.

She'd done it. Now she just had to get to the autorail and get out of this city. Keeping to the shadows and heading the opposite direction from Luther's post, she checked over her shoulder for any sign of him.

She ran into a solid chest. "Luther! I'm sorry. I should watch where I'm—"

His voice was low. "Your Cube just registered an unauthorized exit. What's going on, Chelli?"

"Really? That's weird." She tried to say it casually, but her voice came out shaky.

He glanced at the screen on his wrist. "Your Exoskin's not reading either."

She met his gaze. He knew.

"I have to detain you." Luther pulled restraints from his toolbelt. "I'm sorry about this. Maybe there's been a mistake," he murmured as he snapped the rubberized restraints on her forearms.

Chelli pressed her hands against the clear reinforced polycarbonate that made up the walls of her cell. Her fingers left smudges on the pristine plastic. The wardens would send a cleaning cloth through the food slot later and order her to wipe the walls down. They didn't like fingerprints on the polycarbonate.

In the weeks following her arrest, the word "trial" had been tossed about, but it was just lip service. There would be no trial. This cell was her new life.

She started to turn away from the clear wall when a door opened and a burly man in an orange Exoskin entered. Luther. He visited every Friday, as dependable as a timepiece.

And every Friday, he whispered news through the plastic.

"Eighty-four more this week," he said. "The most we've had so far."

Three months after her arrest, Luther had discovered other members of the resistance. But instead of arresting them, he'd become part of their network. She worried for him; he walked a dangerous line.

Eighty-four more escapes. Eighty-four people with a chance to leave the control of the Association. Eighty-four people making their own choices. For good or ill, their own choices. Chelli had to wipe a tear off her cheek. She only cried on Fridays.

She tugged at her uniform, adjusting the fabric. It was stiff and uncomfortable, but it wasn't an Exoskin. She put her temple against the plastic to grin up at her fellow rebel. She would have plenty of smudges to scrub later.

"I like you with a beard," Chelli said.

EUCALYPTUS & POMEGRANATES

ANNE J. HILL

I'M THE KING of the damned, but tonight, I'm just a father.

Fire devours outside my door. The screams of my kingdom claw at the walls, fingers splintering wood. And before me, on our bed, sits my wife with her arms wrapped around her stomach. Tears of cautious joy well in her eyes.

I cup her chin and brush her cheek. "You're sure?" I whisper. When she nods, I press my forehead against hers and breathe out. I nudge her arms free of her stomach. Dropping to my knees, I hold her waist and press a kiss to her middle. A smile flickers on my lips. "I'm a father?"

Her fingers tangle in my hair. "You're happy?"

I frown up at her. Why would she think I'd be anything but? "Of course I am, my love." I stand and catch her up in my arms. Kissing her jaw, her cheek, her nose, then finally, her lips. "Very happy." I smile.

Penella sinks against me. She buries her face into my neck and shudders. "The timing . . ."

I wince and tighten my grip on her. "I know. I know." I pick her up gently, her legs around me. I sit on the edge of the bed and rock her, watching the fire burn outside the window. War has come to the world above. With every death on Earth, fire sparks below. If the humans keep this up, my kingdom will burn to the ground. My wife and unborn child with it. I kiss her forehead. "But I must go . . ."

King of the damned—those shunned from the light above for reasons we're not to blame. King over the waiting ground for Hell. And the more the fire burns, the closer my name starts to sound like Hades. But I refuse to become that man. To let my kingdom fall into that eternal abyss.

I am Ulixes. And no human war will destroy my kingdom. Not while I still wear a broken crown.

Penella sniffs against my neck. "You'll be back . . . yes?"

I sink my fingers into her red hair and rest my lips on her head. "I'll always come back for you, Penella." I close my eyes. We fall back onto the bed, her lying on top of me. I smooth my hand down her back, and cold metal tickles my bare chest. Her necklace—a single jeweled pomegranate seed. The gift I gave her on our wedding day to match the pomegranate that adorns my neck. I lift her necklace and run it between my thumb and finger. "What does this mean, love?"

She looks up at me, her chin on my chest. "Our bond will never break."

I push her hair out of her eyes. "No Earth nor sea will divide us."

"Life and rebirth will hold us."

"And the fires of Hell will not consume us." I tuck the necklace into her dress and roll her onto her back. Tracing her stomach, I say softly, "The little one needs a name."

Penella reaches up and strokes my scruffy chin. "Telema for a girl; Machus for a boy?"

I kiss her fingers. "Perfect."

There's banging at the door. "Your Majesty?" Eury, my second in command, calls.

A sigh makes Penella's hair quiver on my lips. I lean my head away from her ears. "What?"

"We need to be going. The ship is ready."

My eyes squeeze shut. "Five more minutes. I'll be there." I hear his feet shuffle away. And tears glisten Penella's eyes. I sit us up, her on my lap, and cup her chin. "I love you." I give her all of my heart in a lingering kiss.

"I love you, too," she whispers when we part. "Eucalyptus?" She nods to the vase beside our bed.

I grab the leaves, hold them between us, and breathe in their honey-mint sweetness. They grow hot in my palm until they burst into flame. Penella cups her hands under mine, and together we whisper, "Strength, protection, abundance be with you. Strength for your spirit. Protection for your bones. And abundance for your health." The leaves turn to ash in my hands. I gently slide them into her palms, dip two fingers into the ash, and smear it across her forehead. She does the same to me. I discard the ashes into the vase and wrap her in my arms.

Hell, I'm going to miss her. I want to cry into her collarbone and let her comfort me before I go, but she needs me to be strong. I have to be. For her. For the baby. For the world. I tip her face up to mine and kiss her one more time. "I'll be back as soon as I can, my love. Burn the eucalyptus every night for us and keep the seed close. I'll be back . . ."

My legs are weighted to the bed. I hold her in my gaze and wish I could stay entwined with her here forever instead of rushing off to stop a war. I curl my fingers around her wrist and my eyes sting. I swear hours that are too short pass before there's another knock at the door. But I ignore it. They can wait. My wife is all that matters now.

Penella rubs my back. "It's time, X."

I take a deep breath, nod, sit up. Swallow. Run my fingers through my hair and dab my eyes. Turn to Penella. "I'll be home soon." And with that, I'm closing the door behind me, sealing my fate with a *click.*

THE FIFTH PRISONER

CLAIRE TUCKER

AFTER THREE YEARS, I finally smell freedom. It's in the salty tang of the air, the damp mustiness of the wooden crates, and the rank odor of fish. It's glorious.

Dock workers stand in a line by the administration buildings while soldiers search the harbor. Dogs trot eagerly by their handlers' sides, sniffing anything they walk past. One dog shows interest in a crate and soldiers hurry toward it. The handler moves a small box of fish. Then they start working on prying the lid off.

I fidget my stolen uniform and glance at the Gestapo officer. He's quizzing the dock workers and hasn't seen the commotion, which leaves the "honor" of joining the investigation to me.

My heart slams against my ribs and my hands sweat. Every interaction with the Third Reich's soldiers increases my risk of discovery. But right now, not interacting will definitely attract attention and lead to questions.

I draw a breath, adjust my black leather gloves, and stride toward the now-tight huddle.

"Anything?" I demand in fluent German.

One of the soldiers jumps.

"Nothing yet." He looks anywhere but at me and shifts away. Which, I've found, happens when you're supposed to be a Gestapo.

"Get that open," I snarl, pushing some soldiers aside for good measure.

The ones working on the lid redouble their efforts. The dog wags his tail slowly, ears perked, focused on the crate. Unease settles in the back of my mind and tightens my stomach.

What if there is someone, a fellow prisoner of war, in the crate? There could be a flash of recognition in his eyes as our gazes meet. I would be forced to continue my act while he's interrogated. And as that continues, my lack of knowledge about the inner workings of the Gestapo would become painfully apparent. Once discovered, I would be labeled a spy and shot.

The crate opens. I step forward, hoping my fears aren't plastered over my face.

Boxes of ammunition stare back at me. The chances of anyone hiding in there are very small. My heart doesn't calm, but I still have a part to play. I raise my gaze and glower at the handler.

"Your dog broken?"

He swallows. The dog whines and steps to the crate. He sniffs it over, then turns away, nose twitching, and walks straight to the box of fish. He barks and looks at his handler, tail wagging.

I clutch the crate, keeping myself upright as relief weakens my knees. The dog hasn't found an escaping prisoner. Hasn't somehow smelled the POW camp on me.

But if I don't do something, react somehow, someone might notice my inaction and get suspicious.

I slam the crate closed. "Search the rest of the docks."

The soldiers shift, glancing at each other. One, a grizzled man with tired eyes, dares to meet my gaze.

"We have. There's nothing."

I force a growl, hoping it comes out right, and turn my back on the group. My gaze settles on the nondescript, small fishing vessel at the end of the pier. The *Goede Hoop*. Resistance vessel, if my contact is correct. My ticket out of German-occupied territory.

I just have to get rid of the soldiers first.

"Search the town, set a watch on the harbor. Move out."

I'm sure I hear suppressed groans as I stride away. The usual places in Scheveningen, Holland, have been searched. Twice. The men are tired and ready to go to the nearest pub.

But when five POWs escape the same camp over a course of three days, the hunt won't be called off quickly. And the search will include places escapees don't normally go, such as a harbor in an out-of-the-way Dutch town.

The three who escaped through the tunnel were heading for Switzerland. Like everyone else usually does. Which was why I steered my course for Holland.

From the corner of my eye, I see the dog's handler take a fish from the box.

The fifth escapee must have used the chaos around my disappearance to slip from the confines of the wire. Not knowing his intended destination irritates me, mostly because no one knew mine. Moving in different directions is one of the best ways to keep more enemy troops searching for us than are needed. But to pull that off means we have to talk to each other and coordinate our escapes. And when I walked out of the camp dressed and accepted as a member of the Gestapo, I didn't know another one was being planned.

I roll my shoulders. It doesn't matter anymore. Once I am stowed on the *Goede Hoop*, my greatest concern will be seasickness. And just as soon as I am given a plane, I'll return and wreak havoc on the German army from the sky.

Approaching footsteps warn me to return to my act. My "fellow" Gestapo thumps toward me, scowling.

"You ordered the town searched. Again."

"I did."

He mutters a curse. "Do you like the stench of this place? The cold?"

"The smell . . ." I inhale, hold the air in my lungs, then exhale in his direction. "It reminds me of home. The cold is nothing a beer won't fix."

He shakes his head. "I'm calling it off. I can understand placing a watch on the docks for a few days, but I'm not marching around the town freezing my butt off just because you like the stench of rotting fish." He turns and stomps away, then looks back. "Coming?"

I almost glance at the *Goede Hoop*. Almost show signs of my taut nerves. But I manage to catch myself and shake my head instead. "I want to watch the water a bit."

He laughs, a harsh, bitter sound. "Don't stay too long. Wouldn't want to have to come looking for you."

I wave and turn eastward. The ocean sparkles where the setting sun touches her waves. Fishing vessels make their way toward the harbor. Ships bob at anchor just outside. Some have their bows turned for wherever it is they are heading. The horizon pulls my gaze toward itself. Toward freedom. Toward England and home.

Shouts draw my attention back to the soldiers. They're filing from the harbor, pushing dock workers around as they go. Some cast quizzical glances my way. The dog's handler gives the stolen fish to the dog.

And then they're gone, leaving the dock workers to their business.

And me to my escape.

I stroll along the pier toward the *Goede Hoop*, my shadow stretching toward the sea. Soon, I'll be heading home.

The hairs on the back of my neck prickle. I tense, gaze roving over the crates and boxes and fishing equipment lining the edge of the pier, unpleasant memories surfacing. Being shot up and flying wounded birds home. Having to land after taking a bullet in my arm. My plane plummeting to the earth, me bailing out. Getting captured.

Before each of those moments, those same hairs on the back of my neck prickled the same way as now.

I slow by the *Goede Hoop*, studying her, wondering if her name—"good hope"—conceals something sinister. But this vessel is just large enough for her three crewmembers. If my guess is right, the "passenger" goes where the catch is normally stored until they meet the next vessel and pass them on. And judging by the size of the hold, only one would fit.

Room for three crew and one passenger. If there's anything sinister about the *Goede Hoop*, then it's like a grenade—small and destructive.

A muffled wheeze slithers from the stacks of dank boxes behind me. I close my eyes, heart sinking. After years of listening to it, I'd know that sound anywhere.

Squadron Leader William "Wheezy" Barton. How the asthmatic got into the RAF was a favored subject of debate in the camp.

How he escaped is nothing short of miraculous. If it's him.

A sailor, a grizzled old man with one drooping eye, shuffles past and boards the *Goede Hoop*. I step back, half turning, and glance over the boxes.

Shadows wrap between them, creating a tiny hole a little bigger than the tunnels my fellow prisoners were obsessed with.

I blink, and a portion of shadows coalesce into a huddled figure with a bowed head.

Footsteps sound behind me and I look away from the man hunched between boxes of ammunition and crates of fish on an out-of-the-way Dutch dock. A second sailor boards the *Goede Hoop*, casting a long, mistrustful look my way.

The man among the crates could be anyone. A communist, a Jew on the run, or someone who simply got on the wrong side of the wrong person in Hitler's regime. It's my nerves that supplied Wheezy's name.

Another wheeze mixes with the splash of waves against the pier, drawing my gaze back to the man in hiding.

A ray from the setting sun has stabbed through a gap in the stacked boxes and highlighted the side of his face.

I take two steps toward the end of the pier, fists clenched.

It wasn't much, but it was enough for me to see the missing top of his ear and the scars wrapped around the back of his neck.

It is Wheezy. The man who somehow got into the RAF despite his medical history and somehow survived the crash that left him with half an ear and scars around his neck.

And now he's somehow managed to escape. And evade soldiers and dogs searching for him. He's the fifth prisoner.

As fate or chance or providence dictated, we're here together, both hoping to get onto a vessel that can take only one of us.

Another wheeze, softer than the last one, floats through the air. I clench my hand. Chivalry demands that, as a noncommissioned officer, I step aside for him—an officer with rank. Put Wheezy on the vessel and stay.

But the longer I remain in occupied Holland, the greater my chances of recapture. And I know how that ends.

My back against a wall, cloth tied over my eyes, while someone shouts "ready, aim, fire" in German. All because I've successfully played the part of a Gestapo and look remarkably like a spy.

My teeth ache. I roll my jaw, staring at the *Goede Hoop*, at my hope of freedom, of returning to rain down vengeance on the entire bloody German army. Now at risk because bloody British chivalry demands I step aside for someone who has bars on his uniform.

I blink, my fingers uncurling. This isn't about chivalry. It isn't even about rank.

A ray of dying sunlight strikes the side of my face, forcing me to squint. I turn to the ocean, to the vessels riding the waves. My shadow stretches for the horizon, for freedom, for home. Home, where they need all the help they can get to win the war.

Another memory surfaces. Sitting on a hospital bed with a bandaged arm while being presented with some or other medal I shoved in a drawer. One of the officers staying behind, asking for a few moments. Revealing that somehow, British Intelligence discovered my skill with languages, especially German. The request that I consider a transfer. One I refused.

I study my shadow. No one's asking me this time. Wheezy doesn't know NCO Ewan Locke is standing a pace or two from him. What he would see is a Gestapo, someone who's hunting him. I can board the *Goede Hoop* and sail for home and vengeance.

Or I can stay and put my skills to use. Get more escapees out. Send them with messages. Help win the war from here. Become the type of spy the Nazis would kill to find. Who knows? Maybe I'll survive, get home once it's over.

The ray of sunlight dies and my shadow pulls back from the ocean, returning to Dutch soil. A fisherman brushes past me with a sidelong glance. He boards the *Goede Hoop* and joins the others preparing her for departure. I shift back, closer to the crates and boxes concealing the fifth prisoner.

"Wheezy."

A hiss, the sharp intake of breath indicating surprise. I keep my gaze on the fisherman and the dock workers now milling around.

"If you can, find Lieutenant John Cavendish in Intelligence. Tell him I accept."

Silence. It's broken by muffled creaks and thumps from equipment being moved around the *Goede Hoop*.

Then a long sigh from the boxes behind me. "Watch your six, Locke."

My throat tightens even as a grin tugs at my mouth. "Copy that." I clasp my hands behind me, turn, and stroll toward the sunset.

THE BOOK OF JUDE

AUDRAKATE GONZALEZ

Clipped wings that fall from above
To follow a new order of flesh and blood
Rampant, they run to cause destruction
Ruining our hope while wearing masks of seduction
Whispering beautiful lies in our ear
Insisting there is nothing to fear
Lust, pride, greed, wrath, and envy
All deceptively wielded by the enemy

But we were placed with purpose in mind
To be shepherds leading the blind
Put up our arms, defend our faith
Scream into the void like a holy wraith
In the trenches we'll have His protection
As we point others in Heaven's direction

To Him be the glory, dominion, and majesty
Forever and ever, Amen

HAIL MOTHER EARTH

LARA E. MADDEN AND ANNE J. HILL

September 10, 2029
Chicago, USA

THE TV SCREEN flickered with static. Lines scrawled across the news anchor's face, sorrow cracking through his professional facade. "The price of paper has risen by eight dollars per ream over the last year alone."

Anika stood in her living room, watching the TV with nervous attention, eyes wide—fixed. She was biting her nails again.

First, it had been gas and oil that were taxed so highly that driving any farther than a few miles became a luxury. Plastics were next. Prices of most single-use products skyrocketed overnight, so they quickly lost their place in the market. At that point, though, the public was on board with the changes. Sure, people weren't traveling so much and a few old conveniences had to be done away with. Life goes on. *It's for the environment. We're making our sacrifices for the sake of the world.* But the leash continued to tighten. No non-emergency flights. Road trips over one hundred miles required prior approval by local city governments. Allotted amounts of fossil fuel usage were granted to each business and individual monthly. Local farmers often couldn't bear the strain of these new regulations, so most food was produced by government-owned farms.

But now paper?

The news anchor continued. "This will, of course, bring some changes to the daily lives of our viewers." His voice fell into a heavy monotone. "The last of the print newspapers will now be converting to online news sites. Reports say it is unlikely that more than a few of the larger printing and publishing companies will be able to keep their doors open. Within the next few months, consumers can expect nearly all books, magazines, and other paper media to be found exclusively online." He looked at the camera and paused, glanced down at his notes, and worried his brow over some internal struggle. "Of course . . . as we have all come to understand in our age of Artificial Intelligence, the things that we read, write, and watch online are highly prone to tampering. No one can know for sure whether—"

The news cut sharply to a commercial by Environ-Aid, a government-funded organization, ". . . Bringing you your daily reminder that *every* sacrifice *you* make in service of Mother Earth is a worthy one."

Anika turned the television off. The red light at the top of the monitor continued to glow next to a built-in lens. She stared at it for a long moment with a sudden ringing in her ears. The quiet settled heavily on her shoulders and neck, filling the space inside her skull with thick fog.

Lately, the cameras bothered her more. They made her feel claustrophobic. She should be used to the constant monitoring by now. Like everyone else, she didn't read the consent forms that came with each electronic product on the market, including the TV she'd bought nearly two years ago. Consent to "collect user data" was a given. To watch and study her. She hadn't cared much then.

But she was starting to care now.

Anika scrutinized the lens as if there were some insect-sized spy watching her from inside it. Abruptly, she left the living room and grabbed her coat off its hook beside the door.

Two envelopes were stuffed in her front door's mail slot. She picked them up and looked at the addresses. Physical mail had begun to fall out of favor several years ago, but now . . .

At least junk mail will be a thing of the past.

Anika glanced at the envelopes. One was a bill. Her mechanic was old-fashioned and had yet to catch up to the era of digital invoices. He'd been kind enough last month to pass her car's inspection even though it emitted more than her personal allowance of fossil fuels. She wasn't able to pay him in full at the time, so he'd offered to send the bill instead.

The other envelope was addressed from the state capitol building. Without opening it, she could feel that it was too light. Anika's heart sank. Her application to continue her photography business had been rejected. The law was new, meant to enforce fossil fuel limitations. Anika had been running this business since she graduated college over a decade ago, but once the law rolled out, she'd needed to apply for a license to legally continue operating. It was certainly her out-of-date car that had been the sticking point, thanks to the number of miles she traveled for photo shoots and events. She would have to see what she could change, and reapply again after the requisite two months had passed. Besides the car, her record was clean. She followed the rules, kept her head down. She didn't complain about the restrictions. If she played her cards right—only took jobs within the driving limit, maybe shared a vehicle with a neighbor—it might be possible to get her business approved. Until then . . .

Anika looked around at her small apartment, which suddenly felt very expensive. She wasn't sure what she was going to do.

Tossing the mail down on her kitchen counter, she left the apartment, slamming the door behind her. Her cell phone was intentionally left behind. She needed to get away, if only for a few moments, from the GPS trackers, and cameras, and recording devices that kept her chained down. And anyway, the only calls she worried about missing were from clients looking to book her photography services. A business that was now *officially* illegitimate from the moment she received that notice.

Down the steps. Past the overdosed homeless man in the hall. Was he alive today? She'd stopped checking. In any case, ambulances didn't come out for overdoses. It was determined to be an irresponsible fuel and emissions burden. The city council had recently announced—using more bureaucratic language of course—that it *wasn't their problem if someone wanted to off themselves.* Once, Anika would have believed that overlooking him made her a callous person, but she bought more into the dog-eat-dog philosophy these days. Every man for himself. No one else was looking out for her, after all, and the "right thing to do" was becoming less obvious every day.

She paused at the bottom of the staircase as a realization hit her in the chest. She was only one missed rent payment away from living in her car. And if she couldn't keep the car—only a few months from a bench, an alleyway, or a stairwell. So many people had become homeless when they couldn't afford to change with the new fossil fuel regulations. What made her so different? Anika glanced back up at the man. Who was he before this? Would she become him if she couldn't get her business license back?

A security camera blinked above Anika's head. She reigned in her thoughts and shoved through the front door. He wasn't her problem. Just like she wasn't anyone else's.

Walking three blocks east of her building, she passed two new government housing projects and an animal shelter the size of a small hospital. The projects were meant to cut back on the homeless crisis, but they weren't nearly enough to cover the extensive needs. The Environ-Aid shelter was to keep city streets clear of pets that had been owned by the people who no longer had homes. And it was luxurious compared with the shoddy, slap-dash construction of the new overpopulated housing.

Anika wrinkled her nose and side-stepped a pile of human excrement in the middle of the sidewalk. She'd move if she could. To somewhere with less people. Somewhere that still had trees.

Turning North, Anika continued another block and a half. At one corner of an intersection, there was a five-square-foot space that was completely out of view of any cameras. She'd discovered it several weeks ago. It must have been an error in the city-wide surveillance program set up last year. In this one small space, even though she was technically in public, she felt more privacy than anywhere else.

She sat down on the sidewalk, leaned her head against a lamp post, and watched the scant cars and pedestrians as they passed.

So much had changed in a few short years, somehow without her notice. Exchanging seemingly arbitrary freedoms for comfort and progress. Slowly. Insidiously. And now, there was hardly any freedom left. Don't drive your car. Don't send mail. Don't run your own business. Don't read or write anything that isn't online. And don't dare to complain about it, or you could lose the little you have.

Anika was the frog in boiling water. She had always told herself that she would see something like this coming. That she wouldn't be led along complacently.

The street and sidewalks were nearly empty. The sky was low and gray. Anika dropped her head into her hands and let out a long, slow exhale. She pulled herself back onto her feet, feeling unsteady and uncertain about what to do next. But she needed to do *something*. Too many lines had been crossed now; too many pieces of her life had been commandeered by faceless organizations.

If she said something or took any kind of stand, all chances of getting approved—for business, travel, *anything*—would be lost.

And yet . . .

An Environ-Aid sign was attached to the lamp post: "We sacrifice so that Mother Earth doesn't have to."

Anika stared at the sign a full minute before making her decision. With her gaze set in a determined grimace, she went home. On the way up to her apartment, she noticed that the homeless man in the hallway was stirring. So he was alive, then.

When she came through her door, Anika first grabbed a permanent marker and shoved it in her pocket. Next, she made a sandwich and wrapped it like a gift in a sheet of newspaper. Plastic bags were a thing of the past, and soon pages would be too.

Anika went back out, locked her door, and set the sandwich next to the homeless man, who was attempting to regain consciousness.

Without hesitating or slowing, she returned to the blind spot and the Environ-Aid sign.

It was such a small act. It wasn't going to change anything, most likely. And if she was found out, she could kiss her business license goodbye. Permanently.

Anika took out the marker and wrote on the sign.

Because she had to do *something.*

She stood back from the sign, recapped the marker, and walked away, feeling more like herself than she had in a while. Bold, black, handwritten words stood out over the Environ-Aid ad.

Five years ago, you would have called this evil.

EYE TO EYE

MASEEHA SEEDAT

DROP THE ANCHOR!" I ordered as I clenched the ship's helm with trembling hands. A chain of voices carried my message to the deck hands. They hurled the roughly-hewn stone anchor over the bulwark, and it crashed into the frigid waters below, spewing sea foam across the algae and barnacles along the hull. I inhaled sharply, the chilled air sharp against my cracked lips. We had left Nenzara a month ago in one final attempt to free the land of its famine. We were the kingdom's last hope to escape death, and I felt the weight of its despair even now, this far from home. I felt the weight of my own longing to return to my daughter, far braver than I could have ever hoped for in the face of disaster, of her mother's death, as I twisted the ancient wedding ring on my finger. I stared out across the horizon to the island of sloping hills I prayed would save us all.

"Are you ready?" Clay's bony hands closed over my shoulders. "Shall we have one final adventure, my King?"

His deathly grip ripped me out of my spiraling thoughts. I pulled myself free, loping my arm over his shoulders as we descended to the main deck. "You only call me that when you're in trouble."

"Do I look like I'm in trouble?" He met my gaze, and his playful grin dropped. "Fine, but I'm not the only one in trouble." Clay lowered his voice as we neared the crew. "Our food reserves are gone. Even if we survive the island and make it back to the ship intact, we won't make it back to Nenzara alive."

His words added another crushing load to my burden. "Then we'll hunt something on the island."

"But the Elder said—"

"Not to touch the sheep." I stopped beneath the main mast, raising my hand for silence as Clay straightened at my side. "As long as we don't go after those, we'll be fine. I promise."

The crew, a dozen volunteers from the royal guard, formed a circle around us, and I forced all apprehension out of my voice. I was their leader. From this moment forward, they couldn't know I feared death. I couldn't show any weakness.

"Brave warriors of Nenzara," I began, the same way my father had always addressed his men before he succumbed to his starvation, "hidden on that island is the Cyclops' Hoard of legend, a cave of shimmering treasures guarded by a fearsome shepherd who strayed from his flock, enamored by the glitter of metal, and who wields the power to control one by their name." At least, that was the island's secret according to the Elder. Even if the legends had festered into fantastical lies over the centuries, I would not take any risks. My men had families waiting for their arrival. I had a daughter waiting for me, ruling as stewardess in my place until I returned.

This would not be our final sunset.

Clay elbowed me in my protruding ribs, grounding me yet again. "The stories also tell of a secret tunnel along the coves leading to the Cyclops' cave," he continued. "That's our destination. We sneak in when the moon is at its highest, and we're out again by dawn. We'll hunt enough to last us the return journey, not going *near* the sheep, then we'll make sure this dies away in the kingdom's history as a dark splotch." His determination roared out as he closed his hand over my fist, hoisting my arm over my head. "For Nenzara!"

The men took up Clay's chant, and I allowed their hope to infect my hunger-fogged mind. Clay always had the ability to charm a crowd, no matter how dire the situation. He had even charmed my wild-spirited heart into believing I could rule as soon as my father passed away. I allowed myself a small smile. Many things were uncertain on the road ahead, but I was sure of one thing. With Clay by my side, we would make it home.

The secret passage was far less glamorous than the legends made it out to be. Cobwebs clung to the craggy walls, and our threadbare clothes turned to rags as we scraped our way across the narrow passage to the other side. I reached out in the darkness every few paces until I collided with a metal plate.

"Clay," I whispered, my throat dry from the dust and dehydration. I blinked back a swirl of sudden dizziness, licking my lips. He knelt beside my own hunched over body. Torchlight seeped through the crack between the shield and the ground as we heaved it out of our path.

The entrance revealed alcoves buried into the walls high above the wide rocky ledge we had discovered, and a pile of small rocks sat clustered near the edge of the platform. Twisting shadows danced across the earth, churning and writhing in my hunger-ridden vision. I opened my mouth to ask for a torch as the cry of a sheep's bleat echoed out in the half-light, the creature itself hidden in the shadows.

Not a soul moved among us, and I felt my body tense, eagerly awaiting another sound. It suddenly didn't matter that the Elder had warned against the sheep of the Cyclops; all I could think about was how long it'd been since we heard the noise of livestock. Instantly, my mouth watered, my stomach ached, and I couldn't remember what we'd come to this forsaken cavern for. Except for the savory, warm taste of roasted lamb.

"My King!" Clay hissed in my ear.

I blinked, turning my head, attempting to reorientate myself. "Are you in trouble?"

"No, but it looked like you were," he muttered. "I thought you were going to launch yourself at the sheep."

He was right. I may have suffered the same agonies as my people, but I was still their king. I reigned in my desire with an iron fist, forcing myself to look beyond the ledge of swirling darkness. The enormous torches of the treasure hoard were positioned just below the ledge, beyond which shadows plunged into mountains of gold, wrought and unwrought, resolute beneath the cavern ceiling. Their peaks vanished in the shadows above the reach of the alcoves as jewels twinkled in the golden shimmer. Smaller hills of fallen weapons scattered beside them, aged and rusted in this graveyard of fortune-seekers. I staggered to my feet, breath hissing through my teeth. Our answer lay right in front of us, ready for the taking.

"Torch," I ordered, and its pungent sulfur burned my nostrils as a soldier named Devlin brought one forward. A primitive staircase bordered the right side of the ledge, leading down to the treasure trove, but the torchlight didn't illuminate the rest of the space before us, leaving us to stand in suffocating darkness.

Devlin lit the torch before handing it to me, and my breath caught in my throat. In the firelight, the rock pile I had seen earlier morphed into a flock of enormous sheep, clumped together near the edge. Their small faces turned instantly at the new light, and they bleated at the intruders.

"Don't touch the sheep," I commanded as I felt my men cluster around me, hoping the authority of my voice would subdue my own rebellious desires. It was a simple instruction, but who would remember such an order when your bones poke through your rags, when translucent skin outlines your ribs, when red-rimmed sockets frame your wide, terrified eyes?

I raised a fist, signalling for the crew to be still, then pointed to the right where a series of rocky shelves formed a path down to our real target of this mission. "Single file," I instructed, tearing my gaze away from the flock as a gnawing hollow filled my stomach. "Let's get what we came here for."

My men obeyed, with Clay right behind me and Devlin taking the rear of our formation. My feet had just landed on the dusty floor below when the sheep's frantic bleating echoed off the walls. I spun around, tripping over my own feet, and I would have fallen if Clay hadn't caught me. In an instant, the flock thundered down the staircase, the click of their hooves rattling in my mind like a roll of a dice, a gamble.

A gentle dripping filled the silence as the sheep vanished in the maze of splendor. I paced towards the sound, torch held high, until red droplets splattered against my worn sandals. My heart thundered in my ears, and I bent to study the dark liquid. I had seen it enough times in my life to recognise it, and the sight made my stomach seize.

Blood.

"Who did this?" I demanded, my whole body trembling. Before anyone could answer, a thunderous howling consumed my senses.

"You killed my sheep," a voice boomed across the cavern, rattling the towers of jewels until they crashed down in a roaring wave of shimmering wealth. My men ducked for cover among the treasures as an enormous foot lumbered into our torchlight. Knotted vines of hair tangled over the splotched skin. Dirt clustered beneath the yellowing toenails. Another giant foot followed and set the ground quaking, riches clattering in a twinkling cascade. The commotion even set the rocky shelves trembling until something round and woolen fell to the ground. "That was my favorite sheep!" the voice howled in mourning.

"Take cover!" I yelled. We stumbled back, foolishly away from the staircase yet away from the giant footsteps. The uneven earth snagged against my sandals and prodded my feet, nearly tripping me and my men, until we were cornered against a column of fallen spears and swords of raiders before us.

My blurred gaze dropped to the sheep, which had landed not far from where we now stood. Blood splattered the poor creature's pristine coat; its golden eyes stared lifelessly into the darkness beyond our torches, and my thoughts scrambled as my stomach twisted itself into knots.

Devlin stooped to the crimson ground, blood-stained sword hanging loose around his protruding hips. He stretched out for just a taste of meat, a little morsel to satiate the gnawing turmoil in the pit of his stomach. He cast a wide, frantic look back at me. "I'm sorry, Your Highness," he whispered. Spittle flecked from his lips with each word. "I couldn't help myself—"

I slapped a hand over his mouth and made to drag the starving man back as the cyclops' thundering footsteps stopped, blocking off a clear route to the staircase. It was one instruction. One simple order. If only I hadn't been so lost in my own starvation, maybe I would have noticed Devlin's struggles and helped him to resist the temptation. Clay crouched beside me, and we used what little strength we had to pull Devlin up together. It was no use dying now if we could bargain a way out of this alive.

The cyclops bent to pick up the carcass, naked except for a scraggly cloth around his bulging stomach. His sickly, dirt-caked body almost glowed in the firelight. A breeze reeking of decay wafted over my men as the burly hand lifted the sheep out of our light, the creature a thimble in the cracked palm. A disheveled beard and an unruly head of soot-gray hair framed the cyclops' globular face. One massive, smoldering, flickering eye—an orb of fire shrouded in darkness—stared at us. Water drenched through our tattered clothes as our host's tears plummeted to the floor, exploding on impact.

I caught my crew opening their mouths to quench their thirst.

"Who are you?" the cyclops demanded. "Who do you think you are to deal death so freely?"

My men's anguished groans seeped into my bones as I stepped forward.

A hand gripped my shoulder. "What are you doing?" Clay hissed as he moved forward with me, panic clear in his eyes as he nodded to the staircase obscured behind the cyclops.

"I'm getting us out of here alive," I whispered, raising my torch so our host could better see the despair of my men, the desperation that drove us forward. He may have been a wayward shepherd, but the flock was still under his care. Leaving now would only turn his grief to vengeance.

I steadied my voice as I stood between the cyclops and my men. "To you, my liege, I am Nobody." I refused to fall to his command if he discovered my name. "We are mere travelers seeking a remedy for our kingdom."

"Which kingdom, Nobody?"

"Nenzara, Master . . ."

"Sarkis." The creature crouched before us, his heaving belly thudding against the beaten earth, and it took all my fading energy not to cower back. "Nenzara . . . the land of the righteous king. I hear he treats himself as one of his own subjects, starving along with the rest of them," he mused, disgust in his gaze as he glanced over my famine-ridden crew. "So tell me, Nobody, if the king himself deems fit to live the life of a peasant, what gives you the right to act with such greed and attack my flock?"

"Exactly what you said, my liege Sarkis. Starvation." I took a deep breath, brushing my grimy hair out of my face. We had already killed something dear to him. There was no use in informing him we intended to rob him too. "We meant no offense in harming your sheep. We only came seeking out the Hoard of legends, hoping our fame as explorers would save our people from destruction. The minstrels of the outside world would faint if they discover the wonders of your treasures."

"Enough riddles, Master Nobody. What legends do you speak of?"

I cleared my throat, ignoring the questioning look from Clay. I had to find a way to distract Sarkis so my men could sneak around him and escape back up the staircase. "The legends, my liege! They speak of a cave of . . . glittering towers with diamonds and opals for bricks and liquid silver as mortar to hold them together—"

"And the floors!" Clay interrupted, his hand steady on my shoulders as he stepped up beside me. It seemed he had finally caught on to my plan. "Golden coins cover the dirt like pebbles on a riverbank, and the epitome of all this royalty is the pristine, enormous flo—."

I elbowed him in his ribs. He didn't have to take the story *that* far. I could tell that, in his enthusiasm, he'd forgotten we didn't want to remind Sarkis of our offense against him. "All we wanted, my liege, was to glimpse this paradise, to steal a moment to become legends ourselves, but all we've stolen is a life precious to you. Please, grant my men safe passage back to our homeland, and we will never return. You have my word."

My breath caught in my throat as the torchlight flickered over Sarkis' bulbous nose and dark, beady eye. He stared out at my men and their frail, aching bodies, and a heavy weight sank in my stomach.

"Master Nobody," Sarkis heaved after an echoing silence, lowering the hand with the dead sheep, "what will you offer in exchange for their freedom?"

I swallowed my surprise. We had nothing to trade except the clothes on our backs and the weapons at our waists. Part of me wondered what I could even possibly trade to a cyclops who seemed to own every relic in his collection beneath the hills. No, whatever I had to offer him, it had to mean more than its glimmering value.

Clay squeezed my shoulder as I slipped my wedding ring off my finger, an heirloom passed down ten generations. Long ago, the golden band had been embellished with silver ivy twisting around it and emerald dahlias embedded in the silver. All that remained was a marital ring with the imprint of the foliage of prosperity past. It was the one treasure of mine I couldn't bring myself to give up for Nenzara, a reminder of my forefather's sacrifices and the potential future my daughter would have when we ended the famine. Right now, it was a bargaining chip, and I made a silent wish to the heavens that its value in my eyes would be clear to his.

"Master Sarkis," I began, "I know this ring is little more than a speck of sea foam in the vast oceans of your wealth, but to me this is worth more than the oceans and lands of this world combined. It is the last worthy possession I own, the rest of my treasures given to fight Nenzara's famine." I reluctantly placed the ring in his palm, my hand feeling naked without its weight. "Please, accept it as a symbol of our deal."

Sarkis raised the ring to his enormous eye, running the tip of his nail over the engravings as he crouched beneath the stalactites hanging from the cavern ceiling. The golden band was a fragment of a pebble between his thick fingers.

My throat closed in on itself when he threw it over his shoulders, his stomach quaking with laughter, but only for a moment as my despair broke free.

"*No!*" I screamed as my ring disappeared into the mountains of gold. Clay's grip tightened on my arm, stopping me from crumpling to the ground. "That ring was *all* I have." I knew it was a risky gamble, I *knew* it could've ended like this, yet that didn't stop the wave of grief swallowing me whole, filling my lungs until I had to choke for a steady breath. "Is all I own not enough for you? For you to see how *desperate* I am? Please . . ."

"Enough?" Sarkis scoffed. He leaned in close, his hot, rancid breath blowing across my face. "Look around you, little Nobody. I sleep beneath spires of gold. I recline against emeralds and rubies. The finest weapons of your world are mere toothpicks in my hands. Your little frame of metalwork without its jewels is worthless in comparison. All these trinkets will lose their shine one day. They will all rust and rot within this cave. Why would I need more?" The treasures rattled like thunder as he straightened. "Now, you will run, I will chase, and you will die. Are you ready, Master Nobody?"

"You didn't ask the rest of us if we were ready," Clay huffed.

As the cyclops let out an exasperated sigh, I turned to my men. "Split up. We loop around the maze, then head straight for the staircase, understood?"

"We can't outrun him," one of them replied.

I knew that, but this was our only chance of escape. "Trust me." I raised my hand, curling it into a fist. "Now!"

My footsteps pounded against the earth, a steady drumbeat alongside my men's footfalls as we broke off into smaller groups, racing around spires of glowing iron and darting through valleys of silver. Sarkis rose to his full height, chunks of rock falling when his head scraped against the roof of the cavern. A howling bellow resounded off the cave as big, galumphing footsteps gave chase.

I glanced over my shoulder at every turn, Clay keeping pace as I searched for my men among the treasure. The gaps between them soon widened, some of them stumbling around the corners, others' groaning in effort echoing as we skidded through Sarkis' hoard. Fatigue had festered in our bones, a sickness that would surely lead to our deaths. At this rate, it would take a miracle for us to outrun Sarkis. A miracle. That's what I had to be.

I had to stop Sarkis' chase.

I breathed a silent farewell to my daughter, wishing she had a better kingdom to inherit. With Clay by her side, she would build it into something better, I was certain.

I skidded to a stop.

"Head to the staircase!" I ordered before turning in the other direction, back to the pile of weapons we'd started at.

Clay ran alongside me as the rest of our men dashed past us. I didn't have time to convince him to follow the others. "What are you doing?" he asked.

I grabbed a rusting spear from a tower of fallen armor. "Making sure our host sees us eye to eye. Now go!"

Clay didn't move from my side as I cried out—throat dry and voice hoarse from starvation— but loud enough to draw Sarkis towards us.

"You fool," the cyclops sneered. "Do you really believe a little Nobody like you can overpower me?"

I ignored his taunts, instead pulling my arm back and launching the spear with every last ounce of strength I had. My knees buckled as it arched across the cavern's ceiling, skewering Sarkis' eye with a nauseating squelch that resounded off the walls.

The beast howled as black ooze dribbled down his face and dripped to the ground; his whimpering roar set the cave trembling. An avalanche of rock tumbled at the far end of the cave.

The end of the cave. The staircase. My men.

What have I done?

"My King, we have to go." Clay hoisted me up from under my arms, but my legs quivered as I tried to steady myself. The staircase—our *only* hope of escape—was going to be destroyed. I winced as Clay tugged me away from Sarkis' manic footsteps, away from my men's harrowing shrieks as they pierced through my pounding heart.

They were trapped. I couldn't bring myself to look over my shoulder to glimpse them and the fate I had caused.

"My King, this way! We need to hide!"

"You will die, Nobody!" Sarkis screamed, his voice a faint whisper in my mind as he gave chase yet again.

My eyes were wide open and unblinking as Clay dragged me along, but my vision swam. Whether from delirious hunger or blinding tears, I couldn't tell. Whatever it was, all I saw was Clay's head snap around. My gaze followed, but all I caught was a blur as the cyclops raised his foot.

"Watch out!" Clay yelled.

He released my arms in an instant, the ghost of his hands still clenched over my skin. The world teetered drunkenly as he shoved me aside, and I hit the dirt in a plume of dust that obscured my vision, filling my breathless lungs as I choked for air. I tried to blink the dark spots out of my eyes—only to catch a tattered fragment of Clay stumbling to his knees. His eyes were on mine, unblinking in the firelight, then he was gone as Sarkis' foot crashed down where he knelt.

A chilling numbness crept through my bones where I lay. I attempted a single breath to fill my lungs, but it came out trembling, until the shudders overpowered my whole body. I clenched my fists, pushing myself off the ground. Dust swirled through the piles of glittering metal, glimmering specks that made the world seem as if it were spinning backwards. I closed my eyes, allowing rivulets of tears to drip off my chin, and forced myself to take one look at Sarkis' foot a few feet away.

Fragments of wood from Clay's torch scattered the earth around the monster's toes, but Clay was nowhere in sight, and I didn't know whether it was a blessing or a curse not to see his mangled body. He was beneath Sarkis. Crushed to death. My sobs grew louder, consuming every ounce of air in my lungs until I was choking. I felt my shoulders shaking, my knees sagging, the thundering pounding of my heart against my frail ribs. The world spiraled as I gasped for air, but I couldn't let myself fall, not here, not after everything we'd endured.

Clay had always been the one to keep my thoughts steady. Now that he was gone, only one remained.

His sacrifice would not be in vain. No one else would perish today.

I dashed to the remains of the staircase as Sarkis fell to his knees, his howls reverberating off every crevice of the cavern. My men still stood at the bottom of the steps.

"You were supposed to leave," I muttered, the only words I could muster with Clay's final cries rebounding off the dark crevices of my mind.

"It looked like it would collapse," Devlin said, and I couldn't resist glaring at him just for a moment. If only he hadn't killed that sheep, maybe Clay wouldn't have—

But as much as I wanted to, I couldn't focus on my own anger, my own grief right then. Because I was their King. It was my duty to protect them.

I forced myself to survey the damage. It was not as life-ending as I imagined, but most of the rocky slabs were dislodged and shattered into smaller fragments. The first step was entirely destroyed; all that remained were chunks on the ground that wobbled when I placed my weight on them. It would be a treacherous climb back to the top.

“Follow my footsteps, and don’t stray from the path,” I ordered, and I don’t know what they heard in my voice or saw on my face, but every man was deathly silent. Not a single one questioned Clay’s absence.

I led the way back to the top, carefully testing each step with as much timeto slow down as I could allow. Sarkis’ roaring had softened in my mind to the distant sound of waves on the shore. I didn’t bother looking back. He could crash through his greed and destroy the palace he had built for himself. He could wander his cavern blindly for all eternity. That was punishment enough for me.

Once we reached the top, I ran for the tunnel without hesitation, scrabbling on my hands and knees until we reached the end. I collapsed on the grassy knoll, chest heaving, tears mixed with sweat trickling down my face. Around me, my men did the same.

We were alive. We would find another way to save Nenzara, but at that moment, all I could think about was Clay. How he’d shoved me out of harm’s way and perished to save me. I couldn’t get the *crunch* out of my head. I keeled over and threw up my empty insides—bile. Clay was gone. I’d failed him in life, but I wouldn’t fail him in death. I wiped my mouth and looked out at the horizon to where home lay beyond the sea. I couldn’t save Clay, but I could keep fighting for what he died for. We would not rest until we saved my kingdom. I vowed to take his legacy home with me and honor his name. I would be the king he’d always believed I could be—even if I died trying.

THE BIRD OF THE NIGHT

ANNE J. HILL

Blood drips from the fangs of hedonism
Seeping with a vampiric thirst for pleasure

Beauty that enchants the man
To wed the bird of the night
Who cries, "Give, give, give!"
Sipping on the ignorance of a nation
Spilling their blood on graves they built
In the name of Self-Comfort

The ground wails, for it loathes to be torn
By tiny coffins nailed in the name of Choice

The bird of the night is well-pleased

She sinks her teeth into intimacy
And severs the bloodline at the throat

Desire with no cause, pleasure that bleeds
Intoxication of the man, gripping her flesh
Pleading to drown in denial; drunk on *happiness*
That wears a facade over gnashing of teeth

The life is in the blood she slowly drains
Until he is nothing but a husk
With veins looking for a new host
Death follows where life is dried out

To his knees, he falls, bowing in his chains
A puppet for the bird to sing her song into
To fill the spaces in his empty veins
His head droops, eyes glazed in slavery

He can now name the fangs piercing his flesh:
Pleasure without meaning, self above all else
He shouts into the void, "Meaningless! Meaningless!"
All hope has been sucked away

Until new blood spills out
Dousing the lies in red for what they are

The bird shrivels in the light of day
Choking on the life of her victims
She wars against the new Spirit in his veins

"Lift your head, oh you of little faith"
A whisper so violent it tears the veil
Between the husk of a man and
The God he drove into the grave

A slaughtering meant for destruction
Turned to build an army for the war already won
The husk of flesh is filled with a new battle cry
"Take heart, for the life is in *His* blood!"

Find a dramatic reading by Ben Garrett,
on Haunted Cosmos' Dusty Tome, episode 47

A response to Haunted Cosmos, episode 6 -
"Vampires: The Life Is In The Blood"

Recommended to read at least once while listening to
"This My Soul" by The Gray Havens

ACKNOWLEDGMENTS

I can't believe this is the end of our *Black and Gold Anthologies.* What a *wild* ride it's been. Thank you so much to everyone who's stuck with us through this crazy journey. Before we get into thanking people specifically for *Though We Bleed*, I'd like to take a minute and shout out to several people who have been here since day one. None of these books would have bloomed so beautifully without all of you.

Andrew Winch: I don't think you know this, but meeting you at Realm Makers my first year and getting your feedback and encouragement on my writing has been the single event I can point back to and say, there: that's what sparked Twenty Hills. All I needed was someone more experienced in this field to say I could successfully self publish, and boom, Twenty Hills was born, for better or worse. If this all fails, I can blame you, right? Even though you had no idea one simple sentence you said set off a blaze of books. Not to mention, you've edited a good handful of Lara and my stories for most if not all of the anthologies in this series. We always get excited when your edits come back. So thank you, and here's to more edits to come!

And then the rest in no particular order: Beka Gremikova: who's written for most of our anthologies, and pitched in with edits. Hannah Carter: who's been published in every single one of our anthologies, and is always willing to jump in with extra editing, and keeps me from closing down Twenty Hills after every meltdown and burnout (though you technically came along after *What Darkness Fears,* but who's counting?). Maseeha Seedat: who's in *almost* every Twenty Hills anthology to date (*Briars & Blood* and *Tales of Many Book One* ruined your streak). L.A. Thornhill: who I met a few months before Twenty Hills took off and was one of my first editing clients, and has been in a handful of our books and an encouragement along the way. Savannah Jezowski: this blessed woman! She popped up in our *What Darkness Fears* era, and has formatted every book in this series, despite how difficult and picky I can be; *thank you.* AJ Skelly: We met before Twenty Hills began, I believe, and I've loved sharing publishing and writing tips along the way with you. Natalie Noel Truitt: you're one of my oldest writing friends, been in several of our books, and a dear friend. Elaine Wells: I've known you for years. You happen to be Lara's younger sister. Thank you for all your help with poetry through the years. All hail our Poetry Queen!

And before this gets crazy long, also thank you so much to the following authors I now consider friends who I met through *What Darkness Fears* or around the same time: Emily Barnett, Nathaniel Luscombe, Denica McCall, Crystal Grant, Effie Joe Stock, and I'm so sorry if I missed you!

And last but certainly not least, Lara E. Madden, my dearest friend, jump-on-board-with-my-crazy-ideas lady, my biggest cheerleader and tear-stories-apart-er, fellow anthology runner, platonic soul mate (it's a thing, right?), and right hand woman.

Now specifically for this book:

Our beta readers! Audra, Rynn, Ali, Brooke, Aisling, Kate, Natalie. Editors (goodness knows we need them): Beka, Ellaina, Ali, Sarah, and Andrew. JV Arts for the beautiful cover. Savannah for once again doing beautiful typesetting. To all the authors who dug deep and poured out their convictions onto the page. We honestly couldn't do this without you. You are the bread and butter here and it's been an honor working with you all on this book.

And as always, because He really is the reason for all of this, thank you God. You've brought all of us through so much, so many different quests in our lives to bring us to this point, and this is just another stop along the way, but it's been quite the adventure. Thank you for the gift of writing. Of giving us the desire to be like you with creativity. Thank you.

- Anne J. Hill

ABOUT THE AUTHORS

ANNE J. HILL

Anne J. Hill is an author who enjoys writing fantasy for all ages. Her love of words has led to her career as an editor and publisher. She runs Twenty Hills Publishing with the help of her circus performing best friend, Lara E. Madden. She spends her days dreaming up fantastical realms, researching ways to get away with murder...for her books, arguing over commas at the kitchen table, talking out loud to the characters in her head, promising her housemate that she isn't, in fact, crazy, and rearranging her personal library—affectionately dubbed the "Book Dungeon."

Instagram @anne.j.hill.editing
Twitter @AnneJHillAuthor
www.annejhill.com

LARA E. MADDEN

She might be crazy—the jury's still out—but Lara E. Madden would consider herself to be widely fascinated, with an affinity for wonder. She is madly in love with Jesus, with storytelling, and with the tribe of colorful characters that is her family and friends. When her feet are on the ground, she lives in Lancaster, PA with her housemate, Anne J. Hill, without whom she would likely never finish any project she starts. She is a novelist at heart but is currently focused on creating short fiction as she hones her writing craft.

Instagram @lara.e.madden
Facebook @Lara Madden
LaraTheWanderer.blogspot.com

YAKIRA GOLDSBERRY

Yakira Goldsberry started writing at the age of eight, when she first discovered the power of words. She has since then buried herself in the magical worlds of fiction--and has yet to return. She is the author of the *Tales of Faerie Land* series and has several short stories published in online magazines and anthologies. When not writing, she can be found feeding feral librarians, reading, or attempting to learn foreign languages. Her one mission in life--set the world afire with truth.

AUDRAKATE GONZALEZ

AudraKate Gonzalez started writing horror stories when she ran out of Goosebumps books to read as a child. Her love for horror grew and now she has a BA in Creative Writing and is working on her MFA. Her YA/Horror Series, *This is Noir*, is available now wherever you buy your books. She lives in Ohio with her handsome husband, and her adorable furry bad boys, Zero and Scrappy Doo. When AudraKate isn't writing, you can find her reading, watching scary movies or sleeping.

BEKA GREMIKOVA

Beka Gremikova writes folkloric fantasy from her little nook in the Ottawa Valley, Ontario, Canada. When she's not trekking across the globe, she plays video games, dabbles in art, or curls up in a cozy corner with a mystery novel. Her work can be found in various anthologies—including *Tales From the Tower*, *Equinox & Solstice*, *Fantasea*, and *Tide & Scale*—and her indie debut, *The Other Cinderella*, is now available in ebook and paperback from Amazon. Her first full-length book, a collection of fantasy and sci-fi tales entitled *Unexpected Encounters of a Draconic Kind and Other Stories*, is out now from SnowRidge Press.. To keep up with all her writing mayhem, you can sign up for her newsletter at bekagremikova.com, follow her on Instagram @beka.gremikova, or join her reader group, "Beka's Books," on Facebook.

MASEEHA SEEDAT

Born and raised in South Africa, Maseeha Seedat takes inspiration for her stories from the most memorable moments of her life. She's a full-time student and a part-time writer, with her first novel, *The Littlest Voices*, published a year after her publishing debut with Twenty Hills. Her writing ranges from the fun and whimsical to the dark and serious, most of the time settling somewhere in the middle. When she's not writing, Maseeha can be found surrounded by her family and friends, or clawing her way toward a degree in physiotherapy.

VANESSA E. HOWARD

Vanessa E. Howard writes primarily fantasy for young adult and middle grade. She has been a newspaper reporter, magazine writer, and college composition teacher. A member of American Christian Fiction Writers and the Flash Fiction Magic writing community, she is also a homeschool mom and co-op teacher. She has been published by Spark Flash Fiction, Havok Publishing, and Nightshade Publishing. Ms. Howard lives with her family on a couple of woodsy acres in Central Texas. She can be found at vanessaehoward.com and on Instagram @writervanessa.

ALI NOËL

Ali Noël lives in the greater Seattle area with her three young kids and rambunctious bulldog. If she's not writing or having a dance party, you can find her reading, baking or watching any take on a Jane Austen novel. Her work has been featured in *Z Publishing House, SobreMesa Zine* and *Wow! Women on Fiction.* You can find Ali and her poetry on Instagram @the.authoress.life

KELLY HELLMUTH

Kelly Hellmuth loves to tell compelling stories to kids of all ages. She originally began crafting worlds for her own children and is currently working on her first novel. More of Kelly's writing can be found on Instagram at @khelmetauthor, where she regularly writes flash fiction and poetry with a wonderful cottage full of creative souls. When Kelly isn't writing, she teaches Latin and Bible at a classical school and dabbles in a variety of artistic pursuits.

ELAINE WELLS

Elaine Wells is a crazy cat lady, and an aspiring author with a poet's heart. Her poetry portrays her truth-seeking attitude. Some of her favorite poets include Edgar Allen Poe and Emily Dickinson, while drawing inspiration from Olivia Gatwood. She has a passion for writing about mental health, and she also loves photography, good books, deep conversations, and soft blankets.

MIRIAM STUART

Miriam Stuart is a new author from Cedar Springs, Michigan. She lives on old, beautiful farmland with her husband and their two cats, JarJar and Piglet. When Miriam isn't working or helping renovate the house, you can find her writing her first novel, thrifting, or trying something new. Her passions are deeply rooted in her Christian faith, relationships with loved ones, and a desire to learn. You can find her on Instagram: @authormiriamstuart.

NATALIE NOEL TRUITT

Natalie Noel Truitt is an aspiring Christian author who spends her days working at the library and adding more books to her to-be- read list. She is often on her front porch drinking coffee, reading a good book, and hanging out with her cat.

CRYSTAL BAILEY

When not writing or homeschooling her son, Crystal Bailey enjoys reading and watching old movies and television shows (*The Golden Girls* and *I Love Lucy* are her all-time favorites). Perusing antique stores for unique vintage finds, hiking with her family, and Jesus round out some of her other loves. She's unapologetically obsessed with all things post-apocalyptic or dystopian. Though she's called both Idaho and California home in the past, she now lives with her husband and son in the beautiful Texas Hill Country.

LIZ KOETSIER

Liz Koetsier is a Christian fantasy author who writes stories about fearful characters becoming brave, and finding freedom in imaginative worlds. The weirder the world, the better. She lives with her cat and plants in Michigan and loves that feeling of invincibility you get from long, golden-hour summer evenings. Liz's debut short story was published in *Crowns: A Heartbooks Anthology* in December 2023.

CASSANDRA HAMM

Cassandra Hamm is an art collector, jigsaw puzzler, and cat lady who spends most of her time lost in another realm. Her award-winning work appears in various anthologies, including other collections from Twenty Hills such as *Wither and Bloom* and *Sharper Than Thorns.* She served as editor-in-chief for the charity anthology *The Sun Still Rises*. A mental health advocate with a passion for social justice, she writes about shattered girls finding their way in the world.

EMILY BARNETT

Emily seeks wonder in other worlds to remind readers of the wonder in ours. She is married to a bearded man, home schools their two young boys, and loves the slow process of sourdough and gardening. Her YA science fantasy, *Thread of Dreams*, is about a girl who steals dreams to save her sunless planet.

Instagram @embarnettauthor
Facebook @emilybarnettauthor
Twitter @embarnettauthor
www.emilybarnettauthor.com

B.R.R. CANNON

B.R.R. Cannon has always loved writing and storytelling. While fantasy and sci-fi are her staples, she also dabbles in other genres including poetry and nonfiction. She has previously published stories with Spark Flash Fiction, Havok, and Nightshade Publishing. Currently, she's working on her debut novel and an inspirational nonfiction work. When she's not creating imaginary worlds, she enjoys drinking Darjeeling, finding excuses to wear costumes, and spending time with her husband, children, and cat.

HANNAH CARTER

Hannah Carter is just a girl who wakes up every day hoping to figure out she's secretly a mermaid. She is the author of *The Atlantis Trilogy*, which includes THE DEPTHS OF ATLANTIS and A TWIST OF TIDES. Hannah's short stories and award-winning flash fiction pieces have been published in various anthologies, and in 2022, she won a Realm Award. In addition to fiction, she also has had over a dozen devotions published. In her spare time, she's either cuddling her cats, reading with a cup of tea, or listening to an absurd amount of Taylor Swift. Connect with her on Instagram at @mermaidhannahwrites.

DENICA MCCALL

Denica McCall is a young adult fantasy writer, poet, dreamer, and deep thinker who grew up in the Pacific Northwest and now resides in Kansas City where she enjoys working as a nanny, attending dance classes, drinking coffee, and planning her next travel adventure. She is currently working on her third YA novel which features fairies, a pegasus, and cave-stars. Find out more and sign up for her newsletter to receive a free short story at http://denicamccall.com/.

Instagram: @denicamcauthor

MARY E. DIPPLE

Mary E. Dipple- A lover of all things magical, Mary uses her talent of spinning stories, to shine a light into the darkness that so easily entangles our lives. She is currently writing her epic-fantasy series *The Lotus Chronicles*, due out between 2025-2027. When Mary isn't slaying the darkness with story, she enjoys spending her days tending her ever growing rose garden, playing with her lovable furry assistants, and writing flash fiction. You can find many of her flash fiction pieces on her website at www.marydipple.com.

CLAIRE TUCKER

Claire Tucker is a copyeditor, proofreader, science tutor, and violin teacher who lives in South Africa but frequently visits other worlds through books. She adores the world of fiction and loves to explore Christian themes through writing, particularly fantasy. Stories of hers have been published on Havok and in the anthology *Fool's Honor*. Claire also enjoys being in nature, especially if it involves hiking in the beautiful Drakensberg. You can connect with Claire via Instagram (@clairetucker_writer or @clairetucker_editor), LinkedIn (@claire-tucker-editor), and her website (EditWithClaire.com).

BROOKE J. KATZ

Brooke J. Katz is a stay at home/homeschooling mom by day and aspiring author by night. She loves Jesus, homemade lattes and Lyons tea. Her main passions are writing, painting and supporting others in their creative work. She always has a book on her and she's usually listening to 5sos.

JESS BRADY

Jess Brady is a wife and mom living with a rabble of four-legged critters. She is a home librarian, story creator, gardening enthusiast, and amateur theologian. Jess hopes to publish more works of speculative fiction in the future. Follow her at www.jessbrady.substack.com or on IG @jess.literarylife.

ANDREA RENAE

Andrea Renae is a lover of all things beautiful and rich in meaning. She believes in the power of a good story to bring hope and truth in the most unexpected ways. Her debut novel, *Where Darkness Dwells*, explores themes of depression, purpose, courage, and redemption in a fantastic world that feels strangely familiar. She hopes her words will point hungry hearts to deeper, soul-satisfying truths. You can find out more about her and her writing on her website: www.authorarenae.com.

Instagram @a.renae.author

RACHEL LAWRENCE

Rachel Lawrence writes from South Carolina, where she lives with her husband, four children, and no pets (despite the kids' constant campaign for one). She processes the world spinning around her and the thoughts swirling within her through stories and poetry. Her favorite poets range from King David to Elizabeth Barrett Browning to Taylor Swift. Her favorite Story is still being written.

Instagram @writehereallalong

MORGAN J. MANNS

Morgan J. Manns is a speculative fiction writer who enjoys crafting enchanting worlds and captivating magic systems, a skill she nurtures after tucking her children into bed. Her imagination is fueled by the works of Brandon Sanderson, Patrick Rothfuss, and Samantha Shannon, serving as constant inspiration. By day, Morgan works as an English teacher, seeking ways to ignite the writing potential in her students while helping them uncover the transformative power of the written word. When she's not writing, or teaching about writing, she can be found chasing after her two young children, delving into fantasy novels alongside her husband, or exploring the breathtaking Canadian vistas surrounding her home. One of her favourite pastimes is canoeing with her family on the glistening lake just behind her house.

Instagram @morgan.j.writes

HAILEY HUNTINGTON

Hailey Huntington is a speculative fiction author, penning tales of wonder, hope, and heroes, with a dash of wit. Her stories can be found online and in various print anthologies. When not writing or reading, Hailey can be found listening to her favorite film scores, making homemade ice cream, or spending time with her family. You can connect with her on Instagram and Facebook (@haileyhuntingtonauthor) or her website (https://haileyhuntington.com/).